Writing *In* and *Of* Color

Brody McVittie

A memoir

...and another one...

Forward (or things you really, really need to know before you read this book)

-*Writing in and of Color* is a novel about two very different writers (henceforth named *Red* and *Blue* and only) living in the same city, at the same time, and their respective struggles to have their novels finished and published.

Keeping this in mind, here is information you *don't* need to worry about:

-*Red* and *Blue's* real names—don't look for them; you're not going to find them.
-Setting—the name and location of the city don't matter (they could very well be living in yours, if in fact you live in a city.)
-Menial plot details—their day jobs, their parents, anything not relevant to the fact they have novels to finish, other than girls that get in the way (because *they're* relevant.)
-Sentence structure—yeah, they seem like run-on sentences, but, and really, do you think in any other diction?

And finally, a warning about *Red*:
-He means well, really. So ignore the language.

Enjoy *Writing in and of Color*.

Prologue

Two children are playing in a sandbox.

One of them will grow up and live their dream.

One of them will not grow up.

The cost to each is the same.

Act 1

The Book of Fucking Up

January

Red (and the importance of starting off *strong*, so *Chapter One*)

Fuck.

A good book, he knows, (--and not because he ever bothered to read anything thicker than instruction manuals or comics, but rather really and rationally because it makes sense--) should start off, and only, *strong*.

So,

Fuck.

It's the perfect first word for his perfect first chapter, an adjective and a verb and maybe a noun and maybe more; he knows he doesn't *give* one, because things like structure and grammar and convention matter as much to him as anything other than _____ing the girls he ignored the rest of English class in order *to*.

So here he is, years *north*, and his masterpiece, born not of post or secondary education, but rather hip-hop and pop culture, starts with his *favorite*-favorite word; the only word weaker than *cunt*, his *almost*-favorite and maybe too strong, *if there is such a thing*, word to start with.

When he sat down to write *this*, Chapter One and *fabulous*, and the first of many, he had no other concept or outline or plan other than to gingerly write the letter F, like that, in CAPITAL and proud and top left on his page, let everything after '*k*' and small case and the *period* that follows *follow*.

Maybe he'd introduce a character or a quest or some other 'in-quotations' *structurally-important* 'end quotations' plot point—maybe and probably and undoubtedly better than any who had done before, regardless of their concept or outline or plan—but really, the only thing that matters is offending the maximum amount of people who open to the first page and the first chapter and read that first word

Fuck

and, to follow and for effect, presenting his *second* most effective and therefore *second* word,

You.

Blue (and Chapter One)

Chapter One.
He wants to write
more

he kinda felt he was on a roll,
One
coming right after
Chapter
on the top of his page,

but his hand stops before his head does,
the clock on his kitchen wall starts ticking *ticks* until he writes again.

He comes close *twenty-eight* later;
pretty much gives up between tick *twenty-nine*, tick *thirty-two.*

He's a writer,
he tells himself,
over
and over
and.

This—
masterpiece—
all blank page and tiny blue pen,
is gonna get published,
gonna help some *real* writer realize

writing is something he really wants to do,

some kid who gets a little farther than the *One*

after *Chapter,*

some kid who saves the world

with the words under both.

That kid,

he remembers,

closing his writing book on day one

of writing his new masterpiece

—that kid was supposed to be him.

His name is_____,

and this

—*this*

--is the novel that is going to make him whole.

Red (and writing on Tuesday, and Chapter One)

Chapter One.

  She had a smile like—like that sundae on that Sunday when you were six; that day in the park somebody—maybe Ma—told you they loved you for the maybe not the first time, and for the first time, you really felt it.

  Yeah, she had a smile like that.

  Smile like that, but only when she smiled at Jim—which pretty much made him special, since she worked teller at the bank, and pretty much smiled at everybody.

  Yeah, she was Sunday anyway he spelled it, so when she—

Fuck.

LL Cool J raps something about 'Doin' it, and Doin' it, and Doin' it well' from the couch beside him, and suddenly fumbling for the cell phone, so *LL* can stop preaching his gospel-by-ringtone, is more important than a broken narrative about a sundae smile. More important, because *LL* is only 'Doin it' when it's a girl (*other than his bitch sister*) calling, a girl he *knows*, and, more importantly, a girl he *knows* he can have relations with.

  Relations, as in *fuck*, and since *fucking* is seventeen times the fun *writing* is, when the voice on the other end says

Hi!

the way the voice on the other end does, he's closed his writing book by the time he says

Well, hello there

back, already drawing breath to name the bar they're going to spend Tuesday night in, the Tuesday he set aside for writing.

  His name is_____, and this—*this*—is the novel that is going to make him famous.

Blue (and a Monday)

Monday,
and his baby sister calls
and he doesn't answer,
doesn't answer
because he's writing.

Red (and the difficulty of following *that* up)

The problem—and at first blush, it's hard to imagine there being one—with

Fuck You

right under Chapter One, is that *everything after* is nowhere near as evocative/effective, so coming up with something more than the *nothing* he has now, sitting under light far too close to *spot*, sweating and trying and failing, is as hard as *he* is thinking of how brilliant the rest of a manuscript that starts with

Fuck You

deserves to be.

So he's tempted to finish for the night, *Rome wasn't conquered in* and all that, satisfied and in need of further satisfaction and confident that the ninety-nine thousand, nine-hundred ninety-eight words he needs to follow the two he spent six hours hammering out will come the way he figures *he will* two hours from the seconds *same* it takes him to flip his cell phone, search for a name *feminine* enough to reinforce his need to

Fuck

and he lands under *D* in his contact list, so tonight it's…

…ah…

You.

Red (and what writing was like when he started writing)

He started writing *before*, before it was okay for poptarts to show pussy on the internet, before decency was only under 'D' somewhere on the internet, kids in schools closing web pages with words they have to look up and will never use and will never apply to them—words like decency-- in favor of pages with popups and poptarts and pussy.

He started writing when words like *fuck* and *fucking* and *cunt* were controversial, the kind of controversial he wanted to be, but years of *not* being published gave way to poptarts and albums with words like *fuck* and *fucking* and *cunt, fuck my fucking cunt* sung seductively to him in high C, with falsetto, by some fake singer with a fake ID on his radio, radio years before, left words like *fuck* and *fucking* and *cunt* banned and controversial and bad.

Obscene is passé in the way not obscene is incredibly and obscenely dated, leaving his writing too obscene, only for some red state somewhere south, too *not* obscene everywhere else.

This, he tries to remedy by being *real*, but real is as relevant and as real as Survivor on Thursday, so not really relevant, not really real.

Besides, the books that sell don't *really* sell, and the ones that buy are too old for his books, clinging to a feeling, (probably,) of security and familiarity, and too afraid of the technology the kids he targets, (his target audience,) run from, books and books like his, to embrace, *page* itself now something on a laptop with a picture of a poptart's *pussy*.

Blue (and the latest of best, at the time, ideas)

It's the best idea he's ever had.

Well, of the *two*,

anyways,

and the people who read the product of his first,

Pining For Someone Who May or May Not Know They're Being Pined For,

(so his first book,)

seemed to think

he was on to something,

so if he can't be published for that,

this

will surely earn him the respect

and career

and praise

he

craves/deserves.

It's been years

since he finished his first novel,

and,

sitting on the patio at his parent's place

he retreats to write

when he writes,

he gives himself a year,

a year to be published for idea *one*

or waiting to be published,

having finished *this*,

the best idea he's ever had

(and has yet to put on the paper,)

blank and in front of him.

He came here,

patio at his parent's,

forty-five from the city he lives

--and not really lives because it's not really living—

in,

because he wanted to recapture

the magic of the day,

six years ago,

he lived here and with them in the country and dreamed of being successful

and living in the big city

and wrote,

dreaming,

You

the first word of his first novel,

a novel he's given himself one year to be published,

one more year to dream,

like he did,

for maybe four years after;

the three

it took to get to the last word

You

of his first novel,

the two after

it took to build the courage to actually

have anyone even read it,

one in between he took off from writing

to take off from dreaming

and his parent's patio,

thinking

and

foolishly

that living poor in the big city was living his dream.

So now,

and six years between,

he's on to his second idea,

and it's the best one ever,

and he's given himself a year to promote his second best idea

Pining For Someone Who May or May Not Know They're Being Pined For,

 and finish writing *this*,

the best idea

and the best idea

he has yet to start.

So he has a plan,

and a patio,

and *again*,

so when he picks up his pen,

the second thing he writes,

to the right of

Best Idea Ever

is three-sixty-five,

in numbers,

(so 365,)

knowing that every page and every day is

one,

(so three-sixty-four tomorrow,)

closer to either living his dream,

or burying it beside the dog he buried six years ago

among the grass and weeds at the edge of the property line.

The property line visible from the patio he writes on,

the day he put down the shovel

and picked up the pen,

realizing that his innocence had gone the way of *Bear*,

his first and very best dog,

and the girl who inspired picking up the pen at all,

so

sadly,

and

inspirationally,

away.

Red (and the tedium of a Chapter Two)

It's the worst thing *ever*-ever.

Worse than the time that girl with the horse-lip took his comment about her horse-lip the way he only *kinda* intended, kicked like the word *before* lip (--so *horse*--) in an area he'd intended to keep her horse-lip around.

Chapter Two is a page with *Chapter Two*, and *only*, the pressure of repeating the magic of a chapter named *One* keeping him from coming up with anything remotely as magical as the words underneath; ones after *You* coming inspired and quickly and almost as quickly as his *usual* inspirations make him come.

Over, like one is about to, another night undoubtedly unforgettable for the things he'll do with and more, really, *to* her.

Undoubtedly unforgettable only to him, after he forgets her hair color the way he's already working on forgetting her name, only in that tonight, Tuesday, is a night like the *four* be_____ this one, so a night the page with *Chapter Two* and only *stayed* a page with *Chapter Two*, and *only*.

Red (and a Monday)

Monday, and his big sister calls and he doesn't answer, doesn't answer because he doesn't want to.

Blue (and the girl on TV)

He's in love with the Girl on TV.

Not like *that*,

fantasizing about something one dimension short;

the girl,

the one he's in love with,

wasn't always on TV.

She was,

once,

just another girl.

Not really, no,

never just another,

not at all,

not in her precious little life.

But she was there,

with him,

like the normal, real girls,

in the time

that time *since*

has proven the only

time,

really,

worth;

she was there, with him.

Now she's the Girl on TV.

Then,

when she just *should* be on TV,

she'd dream with him about the day

they

would make it;

 the day they would be on TV,

 together,

the sweetest of the sweetness she spoke when she spoke to him,

spoke about conquering the world, the dream worth dreaming before the

numbers after twenty began to *grey* him.

She conquered the world,

he did not.

That was six years ago.

He used to say he hadn't comma *yet*—

when the numbers closer to were closer to *zero* than *thirty,*

when the world on his shoulders was still growing, like his shoulders.

Yet—so he would go home,

surround himself with the hymns and promises of those who had made it,

and loved to sing about it,

guys with poetry and ambition and names cooler than his;

names like *Weezy* and *Jeezy* and *Shady* and, *for a moment, Puff,*

names like dwarves from fairy tales,

so ridiculous and ridiculously smooth off the tongue,

taken so seriously, because they were,
because of their writing and their words.

Guys who had come from *less*,
if possible,
than him.

Guys who, like him,
never thought they would or could.

So he would dream with them, syllables and sonnets driving his pen,
if he could finish the next word-line-sentence –paragraph-page-chapter-
novel—

Somewhere between paragraph,
 probably,
and page,
a year passed.

A year, and still he was *less* than,
conqueror of decidedly and absolutely nothing,
or less.

The boasts in his ear grew with the urgency,
the urgency in and around him,
around like stories of those who made it younger singing sweetly,
as if waiting for him to make it
too,
waiting in golden palaces,

like fairy tales.

Waiting for him,
like she was,
if he could be enough to *finish,*
to conquer the world,
to be worthy of the four letter word he ran from in their time together.

The year passed,
the first,
and she hadn't conquered the world
 yet
or
either,
and so he was content in his failure,
figuring the next
paragraph,
page,
would be enough to have his name kissed on lips decidedly farther, fame like
the fame in his ears, all the time.

Yeah, he told himself—*next year.*

And, when he rested his head,
content to wait,
the world on his shoulders grew.

No one ever read a word, ever.

They'd see him, sure,

and their curiosity always betrayed their courtesy,

but he knew that before he could let them see word or line or paragraph or

page *or*, he needed justification,

justification he had conquered the world.

So, no one ever read a word,

ever,

and a year past.

Still, she just *should* be on TV,

and the numbers after the *two* couldn't touch her,

though the times between the times he saw her grew,

her eyes burned as bright as the day they burned the day

they

burned

him,

and he rested his head, content.

Content,

and the world on his shoulders grew.

Somewhere between a page and a chapter,

she became a stranger.

The page could *keep* her,

keep the thought and the memory burned bright,

almost as bright as her bright eyes,

across his page and his memory,

but between the ink and the intent haphazardly strewn on the paper,

she fell away from him,

the girl who should be on TV started to do something about it.

Started to conquer the world,

and he rested his now weary head,

the content enough to *keep* him.

The world on his shoulders was heavy, after all.

Somewhere between a chapter and a novel,

he missed her,

and

missed her horribly.

The weight of the world was carrying him farther than it should,

and looking back over his shoulder had grown

and was growing infinitely harder.

A December

and a December

and a December

separated them now—

Decembers collectively farther than his dream and her dream.

TV was something he *watched* now,

his knowledge of the how and why dulled to the point he wondered if he had

ever known.

It was gone,

too many Decembers behind him now,

and his goal at the end of his burden seemed farther still.

He took a step,

and another,

and the world on his back grew heavier,

lines and paragraphs no longer worth the spaces in between,

spaces she was filling with new memories,

memories to replace the memories he raced to record,

raced with a whole world resting,

(if worlds ever rest,)

on his back.

A year passed,

and,

for the first time in his life,

he knew it would not be the last.

She asked him once,

without asking,

if he meant every word he never said.

Really meant it—

asked with her eyes,

the tilt of her head saved for mornings called Thursday,

asked with her smile and the space between.

Doctors,

experts,

and men far, far smarter than he would ever be,

men who may have just answered her instead,

called it

chemistry

or

connection

or something *important*,

and starting with *c*.

It starts with *c*,

but it's the thing she did

and does

with her *lips*,

and the space between the freckle adjacent to her beauty mark,

the one south of that dimple,

the dimple that won the war.

That's all it is,

and all it's called,

but it is

enough,

more than

(is and always was,)

to get him to do anything she asked

or would ever

ask,

at least *half* the stuff she does not.

She asked him,

only once,

and

without asking,

and he's been working on the answer,

a

word

line

paragraph

page

ever since.

Really, one little word,

right then,

would have done just fine.

Hindsight,

and all that.

One little word,

for six and something,

six

thousand

thousand

more.

Red (And how girls are like book titles and book titles are like girls)

One is easily the most important thing in his self-important little life; the other is book titles. Or maybe *one* is easily the most important thing in his self-important little life; and the other is *girls*.

They fight each other, kinda like *Ward* and *Gatti*, (so a *lot*,) on any given day for the championship title that has *priority-number-one* etched in little gold letters in the ring beside the brain cells he *hasn't* burned in his brain, and today they're fighting again and he's reasoning the reasons why.

Really, even to a writer, girls would-should be ever and always more important, and they *almost* are—the must-have accessory for *now*, (so winter,) the way they were the must-have accessory for last season and all the seasons since the must-have accessory of the season started to *matter*, the way *G.I Joe used* to, seasons before.

Honestly, though, to a writer and regardless of the girl at the table beside him, sitting beside her signing copies of his book at a book signing will be half the fun it should-will be if the book is called *Douchebag, the* _____ *story*.

So, see, the book title is important.

It's got to be *sex*, the girl in the dress at the department store, or at the very least the girl he takes to the department store to watch him hit on the girl at the department store.

It stays *longer* than, girls in department stores or to them; scrawled *north* of and forever connected to his name on the bottom of every hardcover he'll ever sit beside some girl at some table to sign.

And he knows they'll *equate* him to it; maybe not the girls ideally not intelligent enough to equate things other than the services necessarily rendered for the unnecessary heels he'll surprise them with to wear to the signing beside him, but *the fans*—the ones who will value him for his words (shockingly) more than his face, will forever and ever link the image of him to the vowels and consonants comprising and summing up the masterpiece under the covers he'll sign *for* and *to* them.

His worth and value surmised in maybe some synonym he'll think clever clearly won't be clever *enough*, leaving his legend in his mind and *only* and to the rest of the world *Douchebag* because he made a bad decision, one big enough to keep the world away from the three-hundred *good decisions* on the three-hundred pages underneath and beyond and really beyond whatever words he chooses for his cover.

Blue (and introducing Summer)

He almost fell in love again

after

and

once.

Really, the girl would have had

'dream'

be the adjective before,

to just about anybody else

--she was that beautiful.

Beautiful,

but they *all* are,

and still none as beautiful

in his mind

as the one *before*—

so this girl—

the beautiful one

with the soft curls

and

sky blue eyes

 and

adorable little horn rimmed glasses—

settled for

second,

from the

second

he told her

she came

first.

Her name was Summer

so, naturally,

he met her in fall.

He knew she looked *good*

smiling at him from behind the coffee shop counter,

but his heart wasn't in it,

the way it hadn't been

for the better part of three years.

Still,

his head told him he needed to fill

the space his heart knew too big

to fill,

so he smiled back,

asked for her number.

Not right away

--no,

he gave it two dozen

coffees,

two dozen

smiles

for her to grow tired of trying,

hoping the effort of pouring his black would outweigh

her curiosity.

She held on, though,

and his brooding artist façade

crumbled under the brilliance of her canines,

so some Tuesday or Wednesday

or Sunday

he broke,

and went home seven digits

and an extra large

richer.

He hated sugar,

but she was sweet,

sweet the way even the most jaded can find inspiration in,

so he called her on a Tuesday or Friday

or Saturday.

She wasn't a sports fan,

but she called the plays,

so the first time they went out,

it wasn't for coffee.

He might have kissed her then,

he might not have,

but her lips were fat like Oprah,

when Oprah was fat.

She told him
she loved him
by Christmas *One*;
by Christmas *Two*,
(judging by the amounts of presents under the tree,)
he believed her.

She laughed at his jokes,
rubbed his back when it was sore.

She moved into the house
he lied
when he said he bought for *them*,
took it on the chin when he wouldn't let her decorate.

He was picturing how perfect
he needed the house for *her*,
(the Girl on TV,)
dreaming of the day,
while Summer sat her winter
in the background.

She knew by Christmas *Three*,
having 'found' his manuscript on the coldest night of the year
--her heart probably broke on the *hottest*.

That night in July,
when she came home earlier than she should,

found the girl of his dreams

in the backyard of the house

of *hers*,

with the boy,

until moments before,

had been the boy of her dreams

since her dreams stopped starring ponies.

She chased the girl of his dreams

right over the back fence,

the back fence

connected

to the lawn,

the lawn

connected

 to the scene of the crime,

the deck

 connected

 to the house she couldn't

quite

call home anymore.

He couldn't understand

how one Friday could cost him

his favorite

and his

favorite

runner-up,

but *frantic-phone-call-Saturday*

did little to dull the pain of watching *two* chase *one* right out of his life,

so his home became a house,

and he was left

to his sense of interior decorating.

It took him about a year,

a year of no summer and less dreams,

 to realize he'd let something real slide through his hands chasing something

decidedly *not*,

and the ghosts haunting his half-sleep

doubled.

She called

every now and then,

though,

the way the other *wouldn't*,

because the season loved him,

maybe more than the *dream* did.

By the time he gave up on himself,

and let the memories bleed on the page in front of him,

that's all they had become

—words on a page,

chronicling some *other* bastard's bad luck.

So when he turned to the voice that stayed

on the other end of his phone line,

 it was beautifully too late,

and with his ghosts,

he had doubled his pain,

and it showed on his page.

Summer left

for a job on a cruise ship,

better to stay

somewhere

where summer was better suited.

Summer came back,

the way summer does,

some fall,

but it wasn't the fall

that she fell for him,

and so summer

was suddenly cold.

Blue (and Happy New Year!!!)

Happy New Year
—happy because Summer
is in bed beside him,
summer in winter,
the way it's been winter
since Summer.

Summer's here until spring
—or so she says,
but Summer's only *here*
—here on the cheap hotel bed beside him,
alone in the dark room while winter
and the party
rage outside the glass and wood
separating them from
what would have otherwise been
a *Happy* New Year
--until morning.

Happy,
because he spent the New Year,
and the hours before,
passed out *alone* on the bed,
too much vodka and weed
(and the things that come with too much vodka and weed,)
happy to spend the New Year
and everything *after*

asleep

and

alone.

Alone,

until the phone rang,

the way it only rings in summer.

And so the next *could* have been spent in winter,

looking for Summer

downtown,

because Summer called in winter

looking for a place to party

—could have,

and probably *did*,

but vodka and weed have a way of dancing with memory,

and it doesn't really matter anyway,

because Summer is in bed beside him.

Summer is drunk,

drunk and high the way he is,

the chemicals

betraying her smile

when she said

hello,

and her pupils said

party.

So now Summer's in bed,

drunk and high the way he is,

so he doesn't know why his hand

is moving up her leg,

but he bets it's because he's drunk and high.

So he doesn't ask why when his hand moves too high,

lets it go when Summer shows him

her *sunny* side,

takes the kiss in his mouth,

carried on lips fat like Oprah,

when Oprah was fat.

Happy New Year

—happy, until

he goes for the belt on the pants he passed out in,

and winter creeps in the dark room,

the wood on the door the only glimpse of sun,

because Summer is gone,

gone the way summer goes in winter.

Red (vs. Omar at the convenience store)

Hharh hyu hreadhhy?

He means "Are you ready," and, bless his little immigrant heart, his English isn't half bad.

Omar (—and, by the look on his face, he's not kidding about the nametag—) stares back at him with charcoal eyes, the kind of black-hole stare that makes his employee issue *Seven-Eleven* greens positively terrifying.

Yeah, it's daunting as all hell, and if he didn't need the bag of milk but *bad*, he'd contemplate leaving fast, leaving Omar and his sour little features to make the return trip to the cooler Aisle D.

It's nothing against people, cultures different than his own— employees here are *all* fucking pricks. Besides, here and now, eight twenty-something on *the dawn of the day after*, he's come to maybe the most important realization of his young life. Important enough that Omar (and, despite the snarl, *still* bless his little immigrant heart,) and the cat food fetish lady from C behind him are going to have to wait a goddamn minute.

And they've got Leonardo DiCaprio to thank for it.

Not really Leo, presence of, but the Leo staring at him, like *she* should, from the tabloid rack southeast of Omar and his disposition, staring at him with eyes and lips and a chin and that *thing* growing from it, staring at him with features heralded and renowned and universally deemed somehow *superior.*

Superior, and, strangely *not.*

So it hits him *here*, his moment of profound awakening, in the checkout line at *Seven Eleven*, eight-twenty *something-else* on the one after.

He is a pretty motherfucker.

Growing up, the seven to something else set, he never gave it much thought, the kisses from girls in kindergarten just part of playing along to what he saw on TV.

Now, something else—puberty and everything after—came a day late, and what he saw on TV left him behind, late at night comforting him in delicious insecurity, the box whispering in his ear, telling him his jaw should be a little more square, his adam's apple and ears a little more *less*, his muscles more than a little *more*.

The box lied brilliantly, passing beautiful twenty-something's with shampoo commercial hair as the same bewildered teenagers sharing the halls with him, teenagers, he assumed, a 'L'Oreal, Because We're Worth It' away from leaving him to join the pretty rich pretty things over in 9021 *something*.

His hair curled, more than it should, and the acne bit so bad that, really, he questioned the otherwise respectable list of high school girls he nailed had mistaken him for somebody *else*.

He was hard on them, too—Erin's nose bridged in a way Hollywood said it shouldn't, Nicole had shoulders like a linebacker, and, at ten years older, ten years older Val should have been a badge of honor, instead was something else.

He had excuses for Denae, Krista, Candice, Crompton, Blair, Danielle, Iwona, Kristy, and Ashleigh—standing in line with DiCaprio giving him that not-bad-player look he always gives on the covers of the magazines he covers, he begins to forget them all. Begins to forget, and, much to Omar's continued dismay, decides now is the perfect time to re-evaluate his feelings towards them all.

Really, Erin was hot in *that distinctly European* kind of way, all loose curls and tight shirts and drugstore makeup counter *never had a big sister teach me how to wear makeup* makeup. Nicole had those Scarlett Johanssen tits, the kind that, according to headline screaming at him southeast of that *thing* growing from it, DiCaprio and his goatee know all about. Val should count *twice*, ten years on, no matter how many pimples were on his face, and

Hmishter—

yeah, Denae tasted like Sunday, Krista's smile could power a reasonable sized apartment, Candice, Crompton, Blair and Danielle held his attention, if not his heart, which Iwona, his favorite, five by five-fire, the kind of strawberry blonde worth nights on the couch, tossed *back* when she left the night before *now*, the day after. Kristy could tie a knot in a cherry—

Hi'im ghoing toh have toh hask hyu toh lheavhe, hif hyu hwon't pay

He doesn't mean it, glowering there behind the counter—might maybe if he was ugly or dirty or lacking in one of those *other* qualities necessary to hold up a convenience store, basked in revelation's light.

So he smiles, smugly and sheepishly as only the *truly pretty* can, flicks his four fifty nine at Omar, exact change, gives DiCaprio a wink on the way out the door.

Blue (and home)

He lives on the East Side
—the side that the city *swears* has character,
in broche cures and maps and websites about the city.

If they mean
sunken eyes
and pale skin,
then,
yeah,
it has more character than it needs.

Really, the city
gave up
on the East Side
years ago;
all the construction in the opposite direction,
building as far West as they can,
North even more,
like the City itself runs from its mistake.

People just look *older* here,
walking
(when able)
down streets paved in cliché.

The sun doesn't hit the corner the way it *should,*

and nobody's smiling on Saturday.

Everybody stays in all night,

but they don't get the channels the pricks out West do,

and so *everybody else* goes out,

leaving *nobody*

to go to the bars, the dives, the back alley shops littering the cracks in the

pavement.

Nobody's the kind to stay away from anyway,

so the bars, the dives, the back alley shops stay busy

with just *nobody*,

and *everybody* is better off.

Naturally, *everybody* has some sad story,

(so naturally,)

here is the only place

he would-could be.

Could be,

really,

because the money doesn't come on days that end,

why or *any letter*,

so he spends the ones that *do*

staring at the holes in the linoleum floor,

 writing in fever,

and dreaming of being

anywhere else.

Dreaming,
but that is harder here too,
like the night sits a little lower,
just low enough to catch hope
in the atmosphere,
drown it black,
and let it fall
back to the concrete.

Looks almost always come sideways here—
in two and a half years,
he can't remember seeing
one smile worth keeping.

He thought the neighbor was joking the first time the cops came,
figured the glass breaking
on the other side of his living room wall
was an accident.

Really, little Suzie on the corner is the closest thing to cute
in the whole neighborhood;
the training wheels have come off her bike,
though,
and her missing baby teeth
don't look like they're growing back.

So he comes home,
waves to little Suzie
on the days

her abusive step-*something*
lets her outside,
and shuts the door
as tightly as he can.

He's got the music up by the time his pen comes out,
and,
headphones on or off,
the city still sneaks through.

It creeps in at the corners,

there

on the twenty-third line
on the page
of the book
he writes-in
when-he-writes
and *only when it hurts*,
in between the part about
missing the girl
and living the dream.

The despair hits
sometime before the candles go out,
leaving the day's writing
a little darker,

and by the time he hits the pillow,

the city is quiet,

like the East Side

just

has

nothing

left.

He closes his eyes,

and his neighborhood

dies another day.

Red (and home)

He's got his own place, and he doesn't give a shit what neighborhood it's in. His condo is hot, so if he's got to almost run down some dirty street kids on his way in, that's just what it is. His thoughts don't generally run deeper than wondering who's on the cover on next month's *Playboy,* so he hits the corners hard, announcing his arrival, letting the complex know the *King* is home.

He leaves his garage open, because, really, everybody knows to leave him well enough alone.

His city can burn, for all he cares, the ash decidedly *behind* him.

He writes alone, in the quiet, focusing on consonants and syllables and other things he has no names and no use for, but distractions come often—a phone call or a question from *Bam Bam* or a pot forgotten on the stove.

Bam Bam, Mohammed Bamhlahr, moved in two, three months ago, some sucker *in a line of* to help support the rent and women and the things that come with rent and women. He seemed nice enough in the interview, or as nice as one can be with a penis.

He'd wanted the 'looking for roommate' ad to read 'looking for hot female roommate, eighteen to twenty-five with little or no inhibitions and blonde, or black, *because-it's-the-new-blonde* hair,' but maybe that was the writer in him.

So he settled for Bam Bam, straight out of Pakistan, because buddy seemed quiet and nice and *nicely,* wasn't looking for receipts.

He showed up on a Sunday, soaked in rain, and those big Pakistan eyes were enough to earn him a room, and kill his *little-inhibitions* dreams—his eyes, or the eight hundred kept dry in and by his right hand.

Either way, he was in by Tuesday, and everything went well, until Friday and a half. The problem, he discovered, with half-drenched foreigners, is their inherit need to just sort of *be around*.

The 'room' in mate replaced horribly by 'house,' as in *wherever he was*.

Now, Bam Bam wasn't fresh off the plane—he came fully equipped with moderate and amusing English, and Farsi, and Hindu, and a couple other cool yet insignificant sounding tongues, tongues in a voice softer than it should be, given the stories of the place he'd lived for the first forty years, and he was easy as kindergarten, maybe twice as sensitive. He was called 'brother' the Thursday before the Friday and a half, and the first night he didn't come home, *thanks, Sandra*—he told him he missed him.

Yeah, Day Four was the first bump in the road.

And then he found the TV.

Red (and why)

He works out because he has to.

He's got *LL* to thank for that, *LL Cool J* and *50 Cent*, and all his favorites and their abs and arms, (which, in turn, are the girls he favors favorites,) so *LL* and *50* aren't only admired for their wordplay, or their money. The truth is he kinda loves it, the whole push-pull thing, the things it does for his *alpha*.

He knows not every guy walks into a party and spends the first few looking at the *guys*, seeing who's filling out their t-shirt, before looking at the *girls*, who's filling out *theirs*. Not every guy, but not every guy can fill out their t-shirt the way he can, meaning the girls, the ones who fill out theirs—are generally and almost always *open game*.

So the push-pull, on days named Monday and Tuesday and Wednesday and Thursday and Friday, means more on nights named Friday, before doing it again on <u>days</u> named Satur__, so *that* night can be spent without his t-shirt. Sunday—well, Sunday is for football, except the Sundays when it's not, and then Sunday isn't excluded.

LL and *Arnold* and every other superhero who's ever written a book (--*and he's read them all*, read them in a way he usually only reads the girl in the pictures' turnoffs—) warns him about something called *overtraining*, but overtraining is a word like *bathhouse*, as in a word for *fags*.

He's got Satur__ this week, like last week, in the next three, so to<u>day</u>, like every, is a workout day.

Blue (and the girl on TV, and, again, why he writes)

He's in love with the girl on TV

is, like was,

back when she wasn't on TV,

when he knew her

and she just should be on TV;

when she was

_____,

and_____

was,

like *it is*,

the sweetest of all the words he's heard.

He loved her more

than both girls and seasons,

and he knew he wanted to be a writer the Thursday she walked away,

a hundred hundred Thursdays

from the Thursday she walked the *other* way,

said

Hello

softly,

the way she only did on Thursday,

told him her name was _____ ,

the most beautiful word he's ever written.

So every time he wrote,

Thursday *after*,

if he wasn't writing *about* her,

he was writing *because* of her,

dreaming of the day she'd hold something real in her hands,

something like a published book,

something to show her that every<u>day</u>,

Thurs___ *and*,

had been spent working

to make himself enough for the love of her.

He thought it was

noble

and

romantic

and,

but really,

he did it for *himself* as much *as*,

the pen racing his head as good memories ran the other way,

ran to make the pain of holding good memories in the face of new memories,

memories decidedly *not*,

less

when he rested his head.

February

Red (and writing in February)

   Writing in February is about as effective as fucking with a condom on; judging by the *not-noise* this latest some-slut is making underneath him, Tuesday would have been *less* wasted staring at a blank page.

   As opposed to staring *into*, (like he *is*) and then out again, and then in again, fucking half-heartedly and staring into eyes that might be blue or might be brown or might be *neither*. Wearing a condom because she made him has left her eyes closed, and not out of bliss or agony or a bit of both, but the boredom that comes like he *won't*, trying to feel anything through the latex prison she's wrapped his February-something in.

   And all he can think about, putting effort better suited for anything *other* than the effort it takes putting it back in her—is anything other than the shape of her breasts, the curves her back should-would be taking if she could *feel* the <u>fuck</u> he's <u>ing</u> into her; all he can think about is the sentences he's *not* putting to paper tonight, February-something like February-everything-else, because and *really* fucking and writing and *anything* just isn't worth it for the *twenty-eight-plus-one-because-it's-a-fucking-leap-year* days it takes February to fuck off.

Red (and revelation, disguised as pornography)

He's watching this one dog fuck another, smaller dog, and he's having an epiphany.

This—as the aggressor fucks hard into the little dog (—and his little dog cock might be in, might not—from his vantage point on the couch across the room, it's hard to tell—) *this is all*, beautifully and totally—that *life is about*.

Really, and as the little dog breaks free, walks disinterestedly away, the bull (and *not* literally) dog follows, sniffing the sweet that must be coming out the little dog's ass, his profound discovery cements itself across his consciousness more.

It's like being on the balcony of some-any-sweet club, he muses, watching the dogs between clips of MTV on his buddy's sofa, the way she acts uninterested, lingering just enough to show him that ass; the way he *pursues*, nose carrying him *to* her, and then *on* her, and then *to* her again— they're just like the fools he spends his weekends with, or the fools he spends his weekends with are just like *them*.

The difference, he knows, is in the pretensions—people acting as if there's more to it than fucking or chasing fuck—champion and slut on the floor accepting it, rolling over for a well-deserved nap, and, right after the new *Beyonce* joint, chasing fuck again.

It's the kind of realization that is both freeing and damning to a serious artist—freeing in the sense that, in the grand scheme of things, writing about something as lewd as fucking doesn't matter, damning, because, really, writing, Shakespeare or, matters *less*.

Blue (and Summer in winter)

Chapter Thirteen and a half,

and Summer calls,

summer in winter,

so *Chapter Thirteen* ends

at *Chapter Thirteen and a half.*

Her voice shakes

softly

when she says

Hello

softly

the way she always *never* says it,

so by the time he says

What's wrong

instead of saying hello

softly

back,

she's halfway through telling him the problem,

and all the way through ruining his writing,

the writing he was writing

about the hero who saves the girl,

the girl who doesn't want to be saved.

He doesn't see the *parallels,*

because parallels

are for parking,

so he listens,

softly,

listens to Summer over the winter out the window,

the winter that whines with the wind,

whining and telling him to hang up the phone,

there in his kitchen,

leave Summer

until after spring.

Winter is like reason to him

when Summer shows him her sunny side,

and so reason is left outside his kitchen window

as he assesses the latest problem or crisis or tragedy,

still too weak to come up with anything after

What's wrong

memories of Happy New Year

anything *but*

as she runs the way

she runs away.

She'll *run now*,

he knows,

her words floating in and out and in

between his thoughts

as the cord from the phone,

there in his kitchen,

beams them into his brain

—just like she ran

then,

the other side of this winter,

when she rang in the New Year
with the important click of heels down hotel hallways,
hallways *away* from hotel rooms and Happy New Years.

Still,
he listens because he can't,
no matter how high winter whines outside the window,
there in the kitchen she used to claim,
cooking his dinner for him
only on days that ended in 'y'
and the seasons between.

The clock on his kitchen wall
laughs its mechanical laugh
in intervals;
sound coming into his consciousness before and after
Summer speaks sentences.

If it could speak,
sentences like Summer,
it might not wait until he hangs up the phone
to remind him *he* was the one who *never loved her,*
in the living room
next to the kitchen,
the kitchen where she cooked,
writing furiously,
and, later,
famously
—about somebody *else.*

Red (and the trouble with roommates)

Bam Bam is praying to his TV.

(Again) and it's as odd and oddly disconcerting as it was the first time and everytime since; the first time he came downstairs looking for hangover pills and found a shrine to *Allah* where his fifty-three inch plasma should be.

Bam Bam explained, sometime between praying to his TV (the way he is now and *often,*) that his spectacularly theatrical religion demands he face a certain direction and get down on his knees on a magic carpet and worship. And, *lucky for him*---prayer time is everytime Kelly Ripa and her suppleness should be beaming back at him in high definition.

Should be, but where Kelly Ripa needs to be, there is only Bam Bam and a magic carpet and odd and oddly disconcerting chanting.

So he goes for the coffee instead, caffeine desperately attempting to duplicate the surge he needs, in his loins and elsewhere, Kelly Ripa and her suppleness used to provide him each and every morning.

This—as Bam Bam hits an odd and oddly disconcerting crescendo in front of his TV—this is the trouble with roommates.

Red (and analyzing useless human practices again)

He doesn't get kissing.

It just looks stupid—pointless, really—like pretending intertwining tongues has any communication or reproductive purpose, really, seems as whimsical as pretending when people die they go anywhere other than *away* and *just*.

It's a polite way, and again, *just*, of signaling interest in devouring the insides of one's significant opposite, an awkward indication of a base and burning interest to stick a penis in a vagina, and really get to know somebody, in that special, *this-is-what-your-labia-feels-like-against-the-third-and-a-quarter-inch-of-my-real-favorite, no-matter-what-I-told-you-at-dinner-tonight, part-of-myself* way.

Blue (and feeling _____, because it's Saturday)

She pulls on her Saturday skirt,

there in front of him,

because February seven *is*,

and the February doesn't matter

the way the seven,

Saturday,

does.

He watches her,

from the bed called cold

they used to call solace,

back when Summer was more than a season,

and Saturday was more than sex.

Sex, but not the same sex as Saturday night,

the clubs away from a bed called cold,

wandering streets in Saturday's skirt,

February,

to her,

warmer than his bed.

She used to,

adjusting the two strings that pretend so hard to be her top,

be sweet like summer,

and Saturday, he remembers,

was just one and a half before hell,

hell and minimum wage,

so Saturday,

heaven to her *then*,

heaven to him *now*,

saved the clubs for the movies they watched in a bed called solace.

Same sheets he swims in now,

but the thread count feels *less*,

watching her hips wade waters decidedly warmer to his mirror,

adjusting makeup as unnecessary as his veneer when he smiles,

pretends he's okay with her leaving Saturday to the nameless boys,

and their nameless boy hands,

in the world outside their Saturday.

It's been years,

the voice whispers sweetly,

since,

but her curves curve

the way they used to,

when February wasn't far from.

Summer.

Smiles,

the smile that knows she won't spend a cent, tonight,

when the boys in the clubs are close enough to soak her scent,

hand her drinks to *dull* her,

maybe the memory of years,

when her curves curved the way they do,

and it still wasn't enough to keep him from having

_____ into their house,

making Saturday *since* as awkward as his smile.

When he smiles back,

and his eyes say *sorry*,

and maybe he made a mistake,

chasing words in a book he dreamed were a real girl,

a girl that,

TV or not,

couldn't measure to the colors he described in her eyes,

colors that bled from Summer's when she turned the pages he wrote and hid,

learned the love he said to her sweetly out of his mouth was forever promised

to someone *else*.

Colors she swallowed,

until the night she came home,

and found he'd breathed the girl of his dreams to life,

there in their backyard.

So now,

Saturday,

she smiles back,

he gets to watch Saturday and Saturday's skirt wade waters decidedly warmer,

the look in her eyes on the way out the door promising she hasn't bled colors

for him since.

She was,

from the pictures he used to see at her parent's house,

back when she was his,

and he was *welcome*,

the kind of little girl little girls should all get to be.

Summer's face,

there in the one in the cheap frame beside the phone,

all round and warm and pink,

smiling in summer,

the smile all little girls should get to smile.

It was his favorite,

then,

when he could see it—

his favorite of her as a little girl,

if not his *favorite* favorite—

now,

alone in a bed called cold,

it's just his favorite,

one of those

'*don't-know-what-you've-got*'

joints, and suddenly running his fingers across its glass

is at least a *lot* better

than running his fingers through thinning thread count.

Better because

that little girl

with her little girl smile

got to grow up to be *his* girl,

and her little girl smile

used to come close

to making him forget that part of the tortured writer act

involved torture.

Maybe her words tasted too soft on his tongue,

hers even more,

so when they kissed,

and she meant it,

and he wanted to *not* mean it

(so he could write about a girl he knew he'd never taste,)

he told himself

he *didn't* mean it,

so he could lie in the cold bed he'd spent thousands of words making.

Maybe,

or maybe new Summer,

with her cell phone calls

and her ecstasy pills

and her relatively random sexual partners she swears she knows,

and swears mean something,

(even when, for all her cell phone calls, they never call her cell phone,)

is just the Summer the Summer

in the summer picture,

smiling her little girl smile—

the smile all little girls should get to smile—

always wanted to grow up to be.

Red (and breaking up with Amber)

You're a fucking cunt.

This is Amber, and this is *how it goes.*

She's on about something again, parading around his living room in her underwear, his wife-beater, storming recklessly in the kind of tan tanning posters and anti-skin cancer clinics *wish* they could put on a poster. Part of it (and *really*), is the fight or the tan, could be her heritage, the way she said something about having a little Costa Rican under those underwear somewhere.

After five weeks together, this is the kind of thing she *could* be yelling about, the kind of thing she thinks he should know, but when she waves a cinnamon stick in front of his face, snapping two more together with a little Costa Rican *uumph*, he follows the tan, forgets the fingers.

We're fucking done!

This, apparently, is the wrong choice.

So he ducks the lamp that follows when it follows, calculating the *seventy-nine ninety-nine, plus tax, plus-gas-to-IKEA-for-a-new-one*, ignores the words after, too.

She's *tanorexic*, or whatever the new buzzword for the new disorder someone in the media decided was the new bulimia.

It's at least the sexiest thing about her.

The hair, waving as she finds more expensive designer shit to hurl his way, is a close second, raven kissed and straw straight, ethnicity and culture woven into thickness so thick he bet was a weave, sometime around the first fight, and the second lamp.

Yeah, she's *MAC* fresh, and he's tasting the lavender and rosemary of her moisturizer when she palms him, sting betrayed by sweet as she reaches back for another slap. He takes it too, takes it in and for the flavor and surge *south*, but despite her body language, he's just not *feeling* it.

So walking sex heads for the door and he's deeply inclined to let her fly through the lead based grey, *deeply*, but she's wearing his wife-beater, and Tuesday back-and-biceps at *Body Barn* won't be the same without it.

When he reaches for it, and her in it, he throws the switch, lets her think the electricity is for her, her and everything but underneath the fabric he clings to.

Pretending to be interested as she fumbles for the buttons on his *DKNY* shouldn't be difficult, but he's focused on a brunette *not* named Amber, and wondering if he can have her out the door by the time *Lost* starts.

Mmm…say you're sorry.

I'm sorry

-I'm not sorry.

I knew you would be.

Her 'sexy talk' comes in a fake voice, a kind of garbled baby talk and back road Spanish. He told her, sometime when he cared, that he liked it. *He lied.*

You're gonna tell me where you were all week.

No, I'm not.

She looks up from her position, down there on the floor, but he's sure she knows him enough to know this is as good as it's gonna get, and she's *trying*, and he can appreciate that, so he bites his lip just the way she likes, and she's back at it and him.

She's back at it, and all he can focus on is how well the *Paul Mitchell* is working out for her split ends.

Blue (and the thing about Thursday)

He wrote,

like he writes,

because of Thursday.

Thursday,

then,

when

she

stood in front of him,

waiting on the three little words that could've would've should've changed
Thursday

and everything *after.*

(I. Love. and You.)

He kind of blames his *lips,*

the way they don't part the way they should,

closed while she breathes

in and out and in,

breathes the moment away.

And so his *lips,*

while they taste honey *since*

the way they taste honey *before,*

don't taste the honey on *hers,*

and he and his

go home alone.

So he wrote,

Pining for Somebody who May or May Not Know They're Being Pined For,

Thursday.

Not the *whole* thing—

but the three little words,

and maybe a hundred-hundred more,

on the way to the *millions* it would take to explain why his hand could move

where his lips *couldn't.*

Red (and passing the time)

You're a writer?

A lie, and a smile, and this is how it goes.

Her name is *Denise* or *Danica* or *Samantha*, something that starts with D.

That he knows.

Still, she's got that sideways smile, the one that redheads—hot redheads—sometimes *always* have, and she seems interested, and whether it's genuine or not, after three and a half *Hypnotiq* mohitos, it's enough, and his smile communicates that, so it's gonna be another early night.

Beautifully hollow.

The rest of the mohito goes smooth, whispers in his ear on the way down, lets him know that, yeah, her thong is red, and yeah, it's enough to overlook the *overbite*. Not really, but Wednesday night is the one before Thursday, and Thursday is a *holy day*, so Denise or Danica or Samantha and her sexy little overbite will have to do.

She tastes like *Tropical Skittles*—good enough, but not like *red*, the kind she *should* taste like, the kind like her hair. *Blue* is good, (because it's *Skittles*,) but it doesn't knock his balls off the way *red* does; still, he tells himself, *Skittles* are *Skittles* are *Skittles*, *Tropical or*, so he bites deep, tastes the sugar, pretends that this—*this*—is all there is.

Tomorrow and tomorrow and tomorrow, he knows, it *is*.

Blue (and some of the tortured shit he writes when he writes—so an excerpt from *Pining For Someone Who May or May Not Know They're Being Pined For.*)

You say you wonder how I felt, all that time ago?

You're a math girl, try this:

You walked in on a Monday,

eight-thirty and change,

and maybe I felt you

before your hand touched the door.

It took *two and a half* seconds to see you,

all of you,

maybe another *five* to appreciate the sway in those hips.

You were closer by *eight*—

I think I realized what was happening to me by *ten*,

ten and a *quarter.*

I think it took all of *seventeen* before my heart skipped,

twenty-two and my soul jumped all the way into my mouth.

I needed air by *thirty*,

and you were only halfway across the room,

spent until at least *thirty-eight*

thinking about how to breathe without opening my mouth,

but at the time, *thirty* to *thirty-eight*

felt more like *thirty eight hundred.*

I knew I would lose

by the time your hand left the door,

eight-thirty and *change*,

but it took until *thirty-eight* and *one*,

after fighting to keep my soul in my mouth,

to really understand it.

Because at *eight-thirty* plus *forty* on Monday,
you looked at me for the first time,
and made *eight-thirty plus everything after*,
Monday to Monday,
pretty much insignificant.

Now, you sat down across from me *at eight-thirty* and *forty-four*,
and I spent at least forever
memorizing every detail on your flawless little face,
at least forever
because I knew right then I'd spend all of forever I'd ever have
remembering *eight-thirty* and *forty-four*.

I knew your name just before *eight-thirty one* on Monday,
and I know I'd have given anything just to stay there.

Eight-thirty two looked disappointing *one and fourteen* before,
and then you batted those eyes,
started the smile
I'd have to wait till *one* and *thirty-six* to really appreciate.
By *eight-thirty two* I'd decided I would spend the rest of whatever forever I'd
have
either promising forever
or spending it wishing I could go back,
eight-thirty and *change*,
Monday morning,
and find the courage to give you the smile,
eight-thirty one and *thirty-six*,
you spent *five* seconds too long waiting for.

Red (and angry all the time)

He is angry all the time.

And he knows *why* and really, and really why if he were to admit or acknowledge it, but admitting or acknowledging is close and *too* to resolving or steps in that general direction, and he prefers, when stepping, to step the *other* way.

So *away* and from issues that offer insight he doesn't want as to why he is and why he behaves and why he reacts the way he does; so *bad* and *badly* and *inappropriately*, which is and to him perfectly fine and acceptable and commendable, even.

A high-definition super-pixilated Polaroid of what a man *should* be, a physical champion and a mental savant and an emotionally-unavailable, *so pretty much perfect*, portrait of the *all* and *everything* everyone should admire-aspire to be.

Still, and for the all-everything he is, the anger stays below the surface and *just*, when it does at all, at times and often exploding out of every perfectly-pixilated pore and overtaking every thought and action and protecting him, really, from the hurt and the bother of the world when it reaches to hurt and bother him, withdrawn and warm in the warm blanket his temper provides.

So he hides, maybe, behind the screaming he screams when whispering the words to make the women go, *away* and before they can hurt him the way he reaches to hurt them; hides and behind the fists he throws fighting with the (any) men who deserve it the way they *always* do when he reaches to hurt them too.

And anger is *easier*, fighting fights with men and winning them and fighting fights with women and losing them and still fighting; easier than dealing with the any-every emotions of those less rational, so *everyone* else the way he doesn't and won't and can't—doesn't and won't and can't because he is angry all the time.

Blue (and a Tuesday)

Tuesday,

and his baby sister calls and he doesn't answer,

doesn't answer because the clock on the wall is laughing at him

and he's alone

and maybe he wants it that way.

Red (and a little on life and living with Bam Bam)

The cocksucking stove is filthy.

Again.

Fucking Bam Bam and his Muslim

we'll have the wife clean it oh wait the wife is all the way in fucking Pakistan so I guess I'll leave it for you

Muslim ways.

Writing time, on a *good* day, is from the time he comes home from work until the time he lays down for a well deserved and very much needed nap.

Nap time, *everyday*, is supposed to be from the time writing time is over until it's time to wake up and cook dinner, cook dinner on what is supposed to be a clean fucking stove.

Supposed to be, like *supposed* to be, is subjective, and wholly dependant on A) an uneventful forty minute rally, at at least forty over the limit, on the drive home, and B) the fucking stove and other stove-like shared appliances in said home being clean. Clean as in

no-forty-five-minutes-and-half-a-bottle-of-Fantastik,-don't-miss-writing-time-for-the fourth-in-a-row

clean. So today, like yesterday and yesterday and yesterday, goes down in the history of his life as another day he *didn't* make it, and another day he didn't do anything about making it, and he just puts his head on the pillow, and dreams of the day he *does*.

Dreams, but before, just before, in that sweet spot where tomorrow is just as bright as yesterday, he knows that, at least and for another, his cocksucking stove is clean.

Blue (and the thing with clocks)

He has this thing with clocks.

The one in the living room is his favorite—

Ma brought it home from an art show some birthday,

big iron custom thing,

all industrial and masculine.

It sits proudly above his fireplace,

so it's the first thing one sees walking in the front door,

(or,

hopefully,)

because the holes in the stained linoleum floor go a ways towards killing the

atmosphere.

Yeah, he's got another big one

on the wall opposite the stairs,

one right above the piece of shit mattress he rests on,

in the few and fitful moments

he rests.

Another one in the kitchen, one he's not so crazy about.

The one above the fireplace is best,

best because it talks to him,

talks to him when he sits on the couch beside the fire,

trying to make *something* from *less* than.

It tells him to *hurry,*

that every tick

he spends

stuck

or sad

or resting

or not writing

is a tick his dream is dying,

dying

or dead

or buried

or grown over;

reminds him gently when he needs it,

violently when he doesn't,

that every tick is a tick he remains absolutely *nothing*,

name not known,

just another fuck on his couch in his living room in his townhouse,

his townhouse of ten on the street,

ten across,

thirty-eight on the block,

thirty-eight blocks in the neighbourhood.

One, just another, another number not worth a name,

because names are for the faces of the numbers on the TV.

The clock in the kitchen just laughs at him.

Every time his good clock ticks,

ticks on the way to a new number,

it reminds him.

So he does all he can to spend the ticks between numbers writing,

but he has a mouth to feed,

and a house to keep,

and a joke to get ready to call *work* in the morning,

so the ticks come and go again,

and he's just some fuck on his couch in his living room in his townhouse,

watching the names attached to the faces of the numbers who made it on his

TV.

Sometimes the phone rings,

most times it doesn't,

sometimes his brain releases endorphins to fool him into believing he's living

the good life;

sometimes he takes weekends off,

sometimes he even comes home with somebody to kill the pain,

kill the pain,

but over the mess of blonde

or brunette

or red

or black

or a variation of the above,

the clock ticks,

ticks and reminds him the life he's living isn't really living at all.

And then the clock in the kitchen starts laughing again.

Red (and a Tuesday)

Tuesday, and his big sister calls and he doesn't answer, doesn't answer because fucking Bam Bam is praying to his TV and cooking on his stove and just kind of being around.

Red (and no mo)

It's 'moving' day, today, Sunday—another Sunday he should would be writing, but getting a new roommate—especially when the one 'leaving' is Mohammed Bahmlhar—is the *opposite* of.

He measures time in pages, three hundred until he's famous, but in the five months BamBam has been living with him, he's written forty, *tops*, meaning his dream has been delayed, significantly, because of his fucking roommate's inability to function independently.

This seemed simple enough—the new guy, name not yet worth remembering—showed up Saturday last, took *ten* to see the house, decided it was worth the *eight* up front, left a Cheque on his way out the door. In the meantime, Bam, in his infinite wisdom, decided he'd like to stick around a week *after* he got the keys to his shiny new house, something about

Enjoying my time here

and

Don't want to be alone.

His family is landing next week, next like not *this*, so this week—the week after the *last* week Mohammed paid for—he's sticking around, around as in moving all of his shit into the computer room.

Sunday, *day one*, and this has already been a problem at least six times.

Something about checking his email sitting on Bam's pillow, (pillow because his bed rests directly against the computer desk,) is slightly uncomfortable; logging on to find Pakistani television streaming in crystal clear audio/video, girls screaming Pakistani songs, is positively unsettling.

That, and closing said feed to find Pakistani programs installed on his hard drive—a hard drive reserved for pornography and music stealing software—is enough to make 'moving' day *hell*.

Hell, because this 'moving' day, instead of losing a roommate, he's keeping him, and adding another.

Hell, twice, because 'moving' day—today, Sunday—the only one he's had even part of a day to write in days—is *super.*

He's got at least a houseful coming over to watch Peyton fucking Manning and the Colts (—the same Colts who knocked his Patriots out of the playoffs *no-food-Sunday* past--) take on the Bears. Fine, but aside from the outside chance that Peyton is going to get a ring, a ring reserved for Brady, his friends are bringing friends, friends who aren't really friends, to make what is supposed to be a drunken orgy of man-ness into an awkward, uncomfortable evening of hosting awkward, uncomfortable-*looking* losers.

That, and today, after the nation of Islam declared his computer room temple to Allah, BamBam asked forty-seven questions about the Super Bowl, and, on the forty-seventh and a half, decided he was coming to the party.

An hour later, before, really, the storm clouds in his head had a chance to dissipate, *Cheque* called, said he'd be showing up to move his stuff—move, meaning *with his help*—at six—six, as in the same six the Super Bowl starts.

His name may not be worth remembering, and, aside from the fact that he has a sixteen year old daughter who *dances*, nothing is—nothing apart from the fact he's in the Army Reserves, which makes everything—*especially the part about the sixteen year old daughter who dances*—worth fucking remembering.

So suddenly Super Sunday is almost *anything* but, because first impressions, especially to Army Reservists, are important—so the coke and the weed, and all of the things that make Super Sunday super—are replaced by Coke and Diet Coke and Cheque and fucking BamBam. Coke and Diet Coke and Cheque and fucking BamBam and no writing.

Blue (and Happy Valentine's Day)

Happy Valentine's Day,

and she calls again,

less than she did when she loved him,

still more than she *should*,

a little Summer sun in a winter that won't-can't-end.

The half that was *chapter thirteen* when she called last

is *whole* now,

but she calls on Valentine's Day

and the chapter *after*—

the one he told himself he'd finish starting tonight,

a night like another,

alone save for the laughing of his clock—

is *Lost* like Wednesday on ABC.

She calls on holidays,

holidays and days ending in y,

y like the question he wants to ask her,

wants to but can't,

because she's carrying the conversation the way she never did,

and he's just along for the ride.

Along,

the way he *has* been,

when he should be writing,

her stories filling his head instead of his,

and so the writing takes the hit.

Her voice is sweet,

sweet like the honey on his toast tomorrow morning,

when he knows he'll regret not writing,

so tonight he listens,

because he can't do the other,

maybe because he's lonely.

Red (and a little more on moving day)

You're fucking insane

Bam Bam says on his way out the door and for good; and it's good and *better* that he peered himself away from the television long enough to leave and learn to swear on his way to where he goes and not a moment too soon, so *away*.

March

Blue (when he writes)

He only writes when it hurts.
Tonight,
and he holds the pen as tight as he can,
knowing the words that bleed on his paper need to come
faster
than the *fast* they've been coming,
faster because he's running out of time.

Coming out of college,
twenty-*nothing*,
the no-career '*I'm-an-artist*' thing was infinitely more feasible,
the way
now,
twenty and *everything* after,
all he has to show for it are the missed opportunities
and bad memories
stored in his head, and,
sporadically,
on the pages of the notebook he-writes-in-when-he-writes.

If he is to make something,
better <u>*any*</u>,
and then <u>*thing*</u>,
of himself,
the distance between his soul and fingers

needs to recede faster than his libido.

So tonight,

now,

he grabs his pen,

same pen,

four hundred pages on,

cranks up

'*Gotta Make It To Heaven*,'

--a song he assumed would still be on the radio--

the day he would do his first book signing,

five and everyday in it ago,

everyday in *five*

he's written

four,

maybe five

hundred pages

since.

He only writes when it hurts.

Red (and the modicum of a good man)

He doesn't like it when priests touch little boys.

Shit like that, he tells himself, makes him a *good* person—(because really, if he was the sociopath every girl for the past forever told him he was ten-seconds-before-the-last-time they-leave-him-*because-he-made-them-every-single-time*,) shit like some dirty Catholi-cally-inclined bastard grabbing up on some pre-pubescent therapy-inclined hairless balls *wouldn't* cause him concern *one*.

It does, though, and he sleeps soundly because of it.

On nights when he sleeps, so *never*, because sleep means *bed* and he's got no one but himself to lie to when he thinks of lying anyway but *Cuddle Position 5*, (because it's his favorite,) and around the latest some-slut he's spent the hour *before* every night fucking away on.

So he's a good person inside and every time including the time after the front door slams shut the way it just *did*, *ten* minutes after *Cuddle Position 5* grew tiresome, some *two* minutes after it started, *twelve* total since the first time she called him a sociopath, *five* south of the first *second* he decided it was *past* time for her to go.

And *away*, and *fuck her* for not being able to take the fuck he gave her and for getting vocal any other way than

Oh yeah

and

Oh God

and

Oh Fuck

when he did things to her that made her cuddle in *Cuddle Position 5*, for girls, (so *the fetal position and crying*,) some seconds before he decided it was past time for her to go, and curled around her to initiate the *end* of their whirlwind-six-hour-forty-seven, *but-who's-counting* minute romance.

She'll need therapy, maybe, and he doesn't care and he'll never hear from her again, but he doesn't like it when priests touch little boys, so the hours she'll spend showering and shaking the fuck off, *like she can*, don't make him a bad guy when he puts his head on his pillow, *pretends* to sleep.

Blue (and a little on his worldview)

A moment
—if the thoughts in his <u>mind</u> *don't*,
(*<u>mind</u>*)
for and for the moments
away from worrying
and
about writing
and
not
and *not* failing
and doing quite, quite well at it at that
—a moment,
in between lanes and changing them
and lights and running them,
a moment about his worldview.

We
—as in all and every,
and down to every last one of us—
--we're
Fucked.

It's a Tuesday or a Wednesday
or *maybe not*
and it's night, for sure,
and that's all that matters,
the way the days like the one it *might* be

don't

and

anymore.

The point he's getting to,

and in his mind and as concrete

as the concrete beneath his tires and beneath his feet,

too,

at the point he'll get to

at the end of *this*,

his *latest-in-a-series-of-lately-pointless-destination* evening drives,

is that *humanity*

--around him

and

behind him

and riding the ass of his *decidedly economic-and-therefore-indistinct-midsize-compact-import-money-trap*

--is nothing but a never ending series of selfish,

self-important,

pompous

and entirely unimportant

assholes.

And it's <u>not</u> and

____ just,

the bitch in the *decidedly-uneconomic-and-still-indistinct-minivan*

an inch and *closer-still* bite of the doughnut she's paying entirely too much

attention to

(instead of paying attention to the van she's an inch and *less* from ramming up his exhaust and ruining *comma* further *this*—his exhausting Tuesday or Wednesday evening--)

that has him hating *every other* member of humanity.

No *no,*

it's an entirely encompassing culmination

of years in both traffic and jams

and the city that houses them

and the fucking ignorant pigs like the one

___ing down behind

 and momentarily,

 on top of him

that has him wondering why he bothers to write anything

(as in *at all)*

when the street

and

the city

and

the world

around him is filled with *these*...

these people who don't/can't

care/feel...

these people

—every last one of them—

who probably *read* less.

Red (and drugs and a little about Spanish Jose)

He never ever liked *pennies*.

So *coppers*; all flashing loud lights and puffy chests and faster feet, feet chasing him down alleys not fit for marathons. They were are all assholes, every single one (—and there have been *many*, in numbers, many more than that—) he'd ever met, more crooked than the guys they chose/swore to oppress/protect.

So he's over his *good* shoulder tonight, often *more than*, looking back down back alleys while he waits to meet the sugar man he's waiting for.

Spanish Jose is French.

When you move as much blow as Spanish Jose moves, you get to be Spanish, or Venetian, or whatever-the-fuck-kind-of-Jose you want to be. He was Columbian Jose for a couple of years in the nineties, but he grew out of it; coming around the corner of eighty fifth, one would never know it.

He's over the shoulder one more time before drinking the sight of Spanish and the *I'm not suspicious* pea-coat he decided was a good idea for tonight's little transaction, the extra long model with hidden pockets might as well be a fake Louis off the shoulder bag, maybe the only thing in the fucking world more stereotypically inclined to contain pockets with packets of the sugar the sugar man looking sugar man has.

He's wearing it in that distinct *drug dealer chic* way, all popped collar as he walks his drug dealer walk scanning the alley with eyes moving too fast for anybody *but*, the glint in the left one, (the more open of the pair,) reminds him that Spanish Jose is a prick, but a prick who sells for seventy a g, and one who's generous with the eights.

So when he curls his lip to sneer

Hello

he stops chewing his mouth and looking over his good shoulder and offers a hand, thinking about the sweet he's about to score, how high he's about to get *her*, (Amber at his place,) and how then the

baby I had a bad day baby Ikea has a sale on that lamp I want baby do you think Janice has a fatter ass than me because last Tuesday she wore the same Parasuco as me you know the faded one with the butterfly pockets anyway she had such a fat ass

will be replaced by _____

and then maybe a little *uuunnnh.*

. . .

Later, and Amber draws *deep*, probably a little deeper than she should. She looks *good* tonight; couple of paragraphs worth, the promise of something more peeking from the top of the jeans Janice and her fat ass inspired so much doubt in.

She's not without her shortcomings, *sure*—sitting on the couch beside her, watching her take it all in, he's desperately trying to forget them, figuring she's got about two Tuesdays in her before the Tuesday he starts never seeing her again, for real this time.

The coke helps, burning away the acne on her face as it withers her pretty little nasal cavity, two pimples kind of dividing into one by the time he's done rubbing his nose, and that little scar on her chin is positively sexy by the time her tongue tastes his sugar side.

Blue (and a little history, and a little sister)

He was born blood *simple*,

on a farm on the small end,

smaller town.

Growing up, he had the dirt and the mud and sometimes the sky,

and not much of anything else.

He wasn't *Jesus*,

so the odds of him growing up to be *anything*, really,

were against him from the start,

but his mommy fooled him,

and his daddy promised him otherwise,

and it was enough.

They never let him feel *less*

when his baby sister was born,

and he wouldn't have minded anyway,

because he had someone to dream with,

someone to make more of the dirt and the mud and sometimes the sky,

someone to share Christmas gifts made and never bought.

She was the second girl he ever loved,

the last of the two he felt for because he was told to,

told to,

and would have anyways.

The years, he remembers,

years *on*,

were the best,

and even though she could throw a football

a little farther

and drive a go-cart

a little faster

and smile

a little prettier,

she always let him come *first*.

She gave him his sense of protection,

his first sense of social worth,

and his first audience.

She loved his stories about dinosaurs and superheroes and ninjas from outer

space,

even when they didn't have words like

faerie

and

pony

and

shortcake,

Strawberry *or.*

Red (and a big sister)

> *Bitch.*
>
> He hangs up the phone, calls her worse under his breath.
>
> In twenty six of the twenty six years he's been around, his older sister remains the only girl in the world who can get the better of him with a twist of her demon tongue.

It goes back, he knows, all the way back, past the first time he realized she was the favorite, past the time Pop gave her the keys on the day of his Superbowl party, all the way to the time he invited Hailey Brown over in the first grade, and lost her to the taller, better-looking sibling, and her taller, better-looking *Barbie*.

Leaving him to himself, himself and last year's *Joe*, an arm short of *G.I.*

Growing up, she was at least *every* adjective—taller, smarter, stronger, and *that one*, come pick-up football game behind the community center Sundays—*that one* really hurt. She was graceful on the days puberty bit, leaving him acne riddled and broken at the bottom of some stairs, or some hallway, or some level surface, the victim of feet far too big for legs far too *not*.

She drove before he did, passed her driver's test on try number one. His tries numbered somewhere *north* of four, before he told himself *no more*, and tried four more.

She knew more about football, always sat to the old man's right, picking apart nickel defenses and reading blitzes, while he sat on the left, reading her old nickel magazines about who movie stars were dating two weeks ago and picking zits.

She got into the *sweet* stuff way before he did, drinking with seniors when they weren't stuffing him in lockers, drinking sophisticated things with sophisticated names, names like *Hennessey* and *Pinot Grigio*, names significantly more significant than *Pabst Blue Ribbon* and *OV*.

She was grinding in clubs when the number after the one left at least *five* before legal, a number he spent grinding with his homeboy *Super Mario*, popping pimples and drinking *Fresca*.

She was half the size, finally, pressing twice the weight in her twenties, tanning darker on her way to Mexico or the Caribbean, or the Mardi Gras, seeing the world beyond the bench in the basement TV told him was out there.

He could go line for line Season Two of *The Fresh Prince*, and name every actor Michael Mann ever worked with, but he couldn't live half of her half life, and maybe jealousy rooted deeper than the goddamned acne.

Maybe, but he throws the phone in the backseat, downshifts to get to his date faster, because she called right before his exit, and she's as behind him as that homo in the minivan.

He takes the turn with a smile, because *he's* the pretty one now, *Ashlee* to her *Jessica*, and whatever she wanted to sit down and 'talk about' can wait for the night he *isn't* going to be sitting across
the dinner table from a set of breasts *not directly related*.

That, he knows, trying to remember this slut's name as he pulls in her laneway—that could *be awhile*.

Blue (and honesty, and the thought process)

He carries the burden of her on his shoulders,

burden

and

memory

and

nothing else,

though the weight of her would be far, far, far more bearable

if she was in fact astride him,

and

everywhere,

really,

but burned bright across at least *all* his even numbered memories.

The odd days he doesn't dream of her come as a relief and *not often*,

and they are the days he fools himself into thinking it's okay

not to write,

and to go on living

where and in the state he says he does,

but living is more *adjective* than *accurate*,

because the days he doesn't

are connected to nights he invariably and always *does*,

missing a memory until

mercifully,

his phone rings,

and,

when the hum connected to the '*on*' button is silenced by the '*off*' beside,

unmercifully

missing the voice on the other end,

knowing,

before drifting back into dream,

he's blown it with *both*.

All he remembers,

in the violence and static between dream,

eight years and a thousand-thousand bottles *on*,

is that his heart broke every time she blinked.

The other one,

the *real* one,

the one between the '*on*' and '*off*' button on his phone,

the one who calls him,

and looks at him,

and blinks a lot,

did the real things,

and maybe that's why she's the word *before* in <u>*other*</u> one.

Maybe she tasted like coffee between sips,

maybe she woke without makeup

and hair a hair left of perfect,

maybe,

probably,

she told him she loved him,

laid in the dirt right beside,

believed,

if only for a moment,

in his stupid dream.

Maybe she should have been on TV.

He can't remember why he let her go either,

like missing one *every-waking-and-in-between-moment*

not enough fuel for the career

he binds himself to,

the one to punish him,

knowing every verb forever will be,

at least and partly *always*,

connected to either of the faces that push his pen

—the one who pushed it *first*,

or the one who pushed him to push it *still*.

Everyday, he tells himself.

Everyday you don't

is a day

the one

you put the first word, and every word after down on paper

for,

could get sick

or

hurt

or

possessed by some notion to move away from

you

or

us,

move like she moved from the possibility of, probably years ago.

It's a weight on shoulders,

he knows,

no matter how *many* or how *often* he lifts,

he'll never be strong enough to carry,

or let go.

Red (and consumerism)

He has to have it.

He doesn't need it—he's kinda sure he doesn't even want it—but McDougall across the street has one, and *Access Hollywood* says they're the hottest thing this fall, so seven something on the seventeenth, and he's in line with the commoners, waiting for the new *Playstation*.

He doesn't even *play* videogames.

Anymore.

Still, he's fifth in line, two behind the fat monkey with the fat breakfast sandwich, one more from the *kind-of-cute-but-it's-early* brunette batting her *kind-of-cute* eyes at her *not-cute-at-all* boyfriend. He spends the next five, or maybe ten—time seems to move slower outside of the redneck big box store—studying, debating, judging whether or not *sugar-eyes* is worth the effort.

He figures he's close to making a decision when Crossan'wich one back drops at least half of his sandwich, the resounding

Fuck!

enough to turn her around, give him his first real good look, which, in turn, is enough to continue ruining his morning.

So he settles in, fifth in a line *teen* deep, waits for some toy, he knows, will make eating difficult for the next three or four or five months.

Mother, in her infinite wisdom, thought the six hundred fifty would be better served tackling that week long creative writing seminar, on him about the possibility of brown-nosing with agents and editors, but he knows *better*.

When he turns in his manuscript, when they see the marketing possibilities written across his finely chiseled features, they'll be falling over themselves to sign him, the way *kind-of-cute* is falling all over herself to get a better look.

So, he shifts his weight, blows her a kiss for the hell of it, sees no reason to deny himself the pleasure of *Madden* Mondays. He can't imagine something as mundane as holding his joystick could cut into his writing time anyways, so he settles down, content to wait the hour or *hour and more* until the doors open, reminds himself to go get a Crossan'wich.

Red (and going too far)

He sticks the needle in his shoulder, fights to keep his hand steady as he thumbs for the plunger.

He calls himself a pussy for the hesitation, alone there in the bathroom, reminds himself there's a two hundred ten pound *monster* waiting by the bench press on the other side of the door, waiting for him to draw for the first time.

Just a half needle, every other day

Spanish Jose promised when he promised at *least* fifteen more pounds, fifteen more pounds to make that ten pound swing from *gorgeous* to *God*.

He knows he doesn't *need* it need it—steroids--the way he can count six abs on his stomach, but six is *too* short of eight, and what is sticking out of his shoulder can take care of two plus *fifteen*, so he holds his breath, closes his eyes, takes the plunge.

He's brave enough to open his eyes, open his eyes and watch the dirty yellow disappear into his favorite shoulder, a shoulder he tells himself can soon be his *favorite* -favorite.

Sure, he could lose his gorgeous, flowing mane.

His muscles will get bigger.

Sure, he could become Italian, black body hair creeping through the Nair he cakes his body with.

His muscles will get bigger.

He's bleeding from his ass a little, *like he has been*—lately just a little bit more.

His muscles will get bigger.

And, yeah, the ten year war with *backne* could take a turn for the worse, goddamn pustules as resilient as the *Vietcong*.

His muscles—well, if he has to put up with fucking pimples—his muscles better get bigger. The other shit, he knows as he watches the last race into his body—the kidney trouble, the shrinking balls, the andro side effects—the other shit is science fiction, science fiction he can't *see, can't see so it doesn't matter.*

The needle burns, burns and tells him this was a *good* idea, still a good idea as it kisses him on the way out, leaving a trail of blood a little *darker* than it should. He listens to it as he gets off the toilet, hands shaking all the way to the garbage, the garbage holding the first needle, the first of many, should the hair stay rooted firmly on his head.

He knows he doesn't *need* it need it—he can think of sex symbols his size—but he hasn't had a date in two weeks, and the prospect list in his cell phone is shrinking, so maybe a 'brand-new-me' will get the girls he needs to get, girls who favor his favorites, favorites like *LL* and *50*, favorites with *zeroes* after the *two* on the tape measure wrapped around their arms.

So he reaches for the door with his *fourteen-and-a-half,* confident that he's on the way *up,* thinks nothing of the hair that falls out to fall fourteen and a half feet behind him.

. . .

Lift one, and on the way up, he blames his parents. While the other kids were watching *The Neverending Story,* his Mom was clueless enough to think *Rambo: First Blood Part II* was a kid's movie, so sixty six times between six and sixteen, Sylvester Stallone was what a man *looked* like.

He almost laughs on the way down, the bar a little lighter than he remembers. *Atreyu* would need more than his fucking *luck dragon* to bench *this.*

Lift two, and he's back at the movies, rolling his eyes while some skank next to him grabs his arm, probably wonders why it's not as big as McConaughey or Pitt or Norton, or whatever pretty boy put on *forty* and called it 'movie magic.' The way down, and it's the 'movie magic' running through his veins making thinking about the bar the last thing on his mind.

The last thing, so *three* could be *four* could be *five*, because he spends the next *couple* thinking about the blonde at the club last weekend, the blonde who was the best looking blonde at the club last weekend, the blonde who liked him enough to dance *beside* him for fifteen minutes, dance beside and smile and flirt with and at him without saying a word. The best looking blonde at the bar even *he* was scared to talk to, scared the way *one hundred sixty five* pound guys *get*; so lift *three* or *four* or *five* are spent angry, the way *six* and everything after are spent thinking *two hundred pound* guys don't *have* that problem.

Blue (and writing on Thursday)

Thursday is a holy day,
so no matter how hard
he presses the pen on the page,
the words don't sing back at him.

Don't
like they don't on Thursday,
but lately
Thursday
has been Monday
has been *Sunday*;
days with different names,
but the writing comes
like Thursday,
so not at all.

He tells himself
he's *tired*,
like he tells himself everyday,
his favorite in a line of excuses,
a line tough enough to stop the Patriots on Sunday,
another day
he hasn't been writing.

He knows that if he closes his eyes on Thursday,
there's no stopping Friday,
Friday and the weekend,

the weekend he pretends he has a life

by going out with people who *do*,

going out and *not* writing,

knowing Monday *and*

will be needed to recover from Sunday.

So he closes his eyes,

turns the radio up,

presses the pen hard enough to make the page bleed,

bleed like his dream bleeds,

bleed on the page,

hoping that when the blood dries,

what's left behind

is as great *as*,

if not greater *than*,

what's left behind.

Red (and Psychic Beth)

Psychic Beth is psychic.

Or so she says, and he believes her, because he *doesn't* believe her, but he believes in her *clients*.

They're blonde, mostly; young and *younger*, the kind worrying about boyfriends and pregnancies, and the kinds of things young and younger worry about; the kinds of things that make the salt on their skin sweeter, when they sit across the table from Psychic Beth.

She tells them they're 'Indigo children,' tells them like she's telling the young and younger blonde across the table *now*, thirteen feet in front of him, there in Psychic Beth's psychic sanctuary—thirteen feet out of earshot, yeah, but he's been *in* for a lot more than thirteen of these, and they're always the same.

Not the same to Stacey or Sherry or Cherry or whoever is attached to this sixty dollars on the table in front of *him*, thirteen from the table in front of *her*, eyes wide open as she buys every word Psychic Beth drops *here*, minute *seventeen* of Psychic *thirty*.

The sixty she's working so hard to earn could be his easily, he thinks, thinking that if Psychic Beth is psychic, she should know he's thinking of stealing it. Thinking, but instead he knows he's gonna wait, because thirteen minutes from now, Psychic Beth will have programmed Stacey or Sherry or Cherry into thinking he

That good looking guy, right over there—

--is an Indigo too,

    and

—wouldn't you know it—

--he's your soul mate.

He can't hear her say it, but as the salt shows on Stacey or Sherry or Cherry's skin, she looks his way with those big doe eyes, letting him know that the routine is right on schedule, and he's *thirteen* minutes from the *ten* minutes it will take to lick the sweet from her skin, sweet worth more than the *sixty* Psychic Beth knows he knows he won't take.

…

He met her (—Psychic Beth, not Stacey or Sherry or Cherry; he met *her* thirteen minutes from *now*, will be done with her *twenty* minutes after that—) because of writing.

She needed someone to ghostwrite a book on nutrition, and, being psychic, she knew he was the best. Best, and, he admits, least busy; not being a professional writer with a deadline, and all.

She was Crazy Beth the first, second, third and fourth times he met her, and not just because the first time he came over, time two, she answered her door naked and crying.

No, he called her crazy because he was convinced she was, all 'healing hands' and 'Indigo children;' he started coming around when she told him he was chilling with Jesus, at the Last Supper, in his last-*last* life, second from the left, in that painting, the one with the pretty hair.

By the time he saw her hustle, time five, he believed her, because he didn't believe her, but he believed her *client*.

See, *Shannon* was his soul mate, too.

Shannon was September, the September he spent recording Psychic Beth's psychic thoughts on healthy foods, quoting verbatim the facts, but not from sources as boring as books, or experts in fields decidedly *rational*.

No, Psychic Beth *channeled* all her information from a spirit named Elvis—not *the*, but the *Elvis-of-obscure-holistic-nutritional-wisdom*, just one of many, many like George, the *Elvis-of-believing-you're-actually-channeling-Elvis*, spirit *or*.

She paid cash money to have him sit there, and write the words in between the chanting and the crying, so, for all he cared, she could be channeling Elvis comma *the*.

She stopped being Crazy Beth the end of September and Shannon, even after telling him she was the only psychic in the world who could channel... *herself*.

Or, as the rest of the planet calls it, *thinking*.

She stopped being Crazy, *kinda*, the day she told him she knew a publisher at a real life publishing house out West—she started being Crazy when she told him Oprah wanted her to do her show once, and she declined.

Oprah.

Not like *Elvis* Elvis—Oprah.

She stopped being Crazy, for real for real, October one, when the one she put in his hand had *zeroes* after, the young and younger blonde coming through her door called herself Rebecca.

See, Rebecca was his soul mate.

His soul mate and October, the October he wrote thirty pages for Psychic Beth, October on the way to November and Callie-with-a-K, before December, thirty more to the thirty and the twenty-two, the *only* twenty-two because Callie-with-a-K had twelve inches on twenty-two, thirty-four of the biggest, realest, biggest arguments against real breasts he'd ever seen.

Four and a half girls later, right before the weather turned the way it turns, he had a book between, between seasons and psychics and spirits named.

He was pleased, pleased the way he was when he finished *anything*; Heidi, this month, included—pleased, and kinda sad the proverbial train, gravy *and*, was rolling to roll away from him. By now, he had seen Psychic Beth's hustle—how a gypsy from Quebec with a grade two education could have cheques for five thousand showing up at the door of her psychic sanctuary the *fifth* of every girl.

She hooked them easy, her 'Indigo children,' 'Indigo' 'cuz it's the color a body emits from the top of their head when they're enlightened, or on the way to, or some other shit.

April

Blue (and a note to himself)

Write.

C'mon, write the sentence that's going to save change your life,
the word that's going to make the last eight years,
and everything in everyone of those days

   okay;

write the clever little turn of phrase
   that's going to make your father do anything but smirk
   when you tell him it's what you really want to do for the rest of your life,
   and you're actually good at it,
and
yes,
you'll actually get somewhere doing it.

Yeah, write THAT sentence.

While you're at it,
   write the book that will make the season come back
and the girl on TV show up
for more than half an hour on Mondays;

maybe stay longer than two beers
before being chased out of your backyard

and your life

and your memories

and everything

and everywhere else

she runs away from.

Please, please, please write that.

Write the word,

because there has to be one,

if only and just,

to make the clock on your wall

and everyone you tell

when you tell them you're a writer,

and you're good at it,

and you're successful at it,

and you're not a complete and total fucking failure,

stop laughing in your face.

Red (and writing)

Write,

and he wants to, but Jessica Alba is on the cover of the new *GQ*, and she's wearing a white *Dolce & Gabanna* one-piece bathing suit-thing, and it doesn't look like the one-piece bathing-suits he's used to seeing, so, from his perch on the coffeeshop corner, the newsstand with the new *GQ* and Jessica Alba is a better place to be than the dingy table he bought a coffee to be able to write on.

The book he was writing in, part of a new technique to keep his writing organized and his new manuscript *progressing*, is closed before he leaves the dingy coffeeshop table and his dingy coffeeshop coffee, after the pang of excitement that takes him as he's vertical, sometime around the moment he realizes Jessica Alba's nipples are peeking at him from under the white Dolce & Gabanna bathing-suit thing.

Maybe the whole *writing-in-public-places* thing isn't for him anyway, the way he spent the better half of the half hour before Jessica Alba and her nipples and her white Dolce & Gabanna one-piece bathing-suit thing watching the brunette with the glasses do her homework on her term paper two tables over, deciding whether or not she'd be worth fucking.

Blue (and more of the shit he writes when he writes, so more from *Pining For Someone Who May or May Not Know They're Being Pined For*)

I put on a shirt today.

I thought about you.

It was blue—I tried, but I can't remember if that was a color you liked on me.

I started at the bottom, and I did up the first button.

I thought about you.

I tried—I want you to know that.

I closed my eyes, looked at the wall across from me.

I saw you, there in my head,

saw every day we ever had in the time it took me to open my eyes.

I tried to hold it,

tried to grab one memory to hold on to,

but they moved

so

fast.

So I opened my eyes, and the wall across from me stayed the same.

I did up the first button, and it hurt.

I started for the second button,

and I was sitting with you in the rain,

under the lattice work at that party.

You rested your head on my shoulder,

and your hair smelled like *jasmine*

and *juniper*
and other pretty things that start with *j*.

I think my shirt was blue that night,
but no matter how hard I try,
I can't remember.

So I fastened my second button,
thought about you.

By the third button,
I think I hated myself.

Because I remember the day I wanted my stuff back,
and you told me to look in your purse.
My fingers were shaking,
I lost the button;
I almost smiled.

No girl packs ten pairs of panties in their purse.

I assumed you forgot.

Couldn't get that button done up fast enough.

Button number four,
and I think I caught myself crying.

Back then,

I could tell you I was gonna grow up to be an astronaut,

and you'd smile

that

tiny

smile,

tell me you believe in me.

Back then,

I knew I'd do anything in the world to hold onto that,

and I knew I'd do anything in the world to hold onto you.

My fingers threaded the fabric,

the wall across stayed the same.

Fingers not strong enough to hold.

Red (and a minor accident, with little or no plot significance)

It bleeds and it's not right, red running importantly away from him, down the sink and gone, gone the way the *perfectness* of his writing hand is, the gash breathing at him as he fights to hold it closed.

He doesn't cry, not for the pain or the blood or the knowing that writing is going to take the hit; he cries, the tears that come, for mourning the perfectness of himself, the hand that, just the night before, so deftly unhooked some pretty thing's laced-covered inhibitions.

The blood takes his tan and testosterone, and all the other things he fills himself with, rivers of him down the drain, leaving the ugly hole, something less than what he started when he took the knife, opened the envelope and everything under in his writing hand.

Blue (and why, and maybe again)

If someone were to ask him why,

this is probably what he would say.

He'd mention the dirt,

again,

the dirt and the mud and the shit he was born into,

born into and told,

without really being told,

that the dirt is where he would *stay*.

And maybe some could be happy,

watching through the windows given the world

and those in it

born away from the nothing-everything of poverty,

and quietly accepting

the world through passing them by,

firmly and warmly rested in the nothing

they were handed and told to take.

He was never one of them.

And life was lonelier than it needed to be because of it,

the way he would look into the eyes

of those with whom

he shared his dreams

and realizing they didn't, really,

and wouldn't ever leave,

and,

crushingly,

would never really *want* to.

His first and bestest best friend,

playing with broken and handmade toys,

watching cartoons on the one channel clear enough to make out the castles

and alien planets they planned on conquering one day.

And lip service from seven year olds hurts

at least as bad as service attached to lips *fuller*,

and as soon as his finished co-plotting resistance to the Martian invasion,

or whatever the fuck they were planning the day he realized

life would be lonely;

the day his eyes told him twice as fast that

no,

the resistance would not be televised,

and

no,

Mars was too far away to travel to together,

he realized

and crushingly

that despite what little Matty mouthed,

he would be *married*

and *divorced*

and *settled*

by the time twenty hit *half.*

If someone were to ask him why,

he'd tell them Matty sells car insurance now,

and maybe that has a lot to do with it.

Maybe a breath later he'd mention Jenny

or Julie,

either of the early *J* girls,

girls whose breathes worded with words not *shopping*

had words like

forever

 in them,

words from lips *south*

of blue eyes

or blue-green eyes

that said

no,

not really.

And Jenny sells Mary-Kay,

ten years and ten times the weight she carried to the mall so well, then,

and Julie sells nothing,

but *buys* a lot,

the kind of things telling would make this story too tragic

to have weight like she the weight she buys and carries,

the weight he knew he'd have to carry *too*,

and much more,

if he was ever going to make it anywhere else.

The weight of the world

waiting to weigh

on his tiny shoulders,

shoulders as tired as the rest of him,

even then,

counting days until they had the weight

and the width

to carry what they would have to,

so *everything,*

if the dirt was to go the way of the girls who breathed *forever,*

so

away.

Blue (and Keri Lynn, or the first of three blown dates)

He's got this thing where he can't remember faces.
It's Friday,
as in three after Tuesday,
the Tuesday he spent across the table from Keri Lynn,
the pretty little thing that
Friday,
for the life of him,
he can't remember.

He's known her,
well,
seen her,
maybe thirty or forty or forty four times in the last ten years,
the little girl with the little girl eyes
used to run around his mother's art shows,
all grown up,
with little girl eyes.

Yeah, probably closer to forty four than thirty,
and still, she's a stranger at least every *other* time.

His stomach tells him she looked *good*, sitting across from him,
and he remembers she had a couple gin and tonics,
remembers her fashion sense was acceptable,
the shift from *left*
to *right*
to *left*

carrying the promise of *those* hips over the clatter of stiletto heels,
and all the other fun stuff worth remembering.

Today,
Friday,
he could tell you the color of the paint on her well-manicured fingernails,
the number following the Chanel on the label of her perfume,
the way her chest heaved when she breathed his name,
lower than the names of the other boys she breathed.

Her face,
not so much.

He's got the smell of her hair,
when she got too close in the hallway
of the bar he held the door;
the fresh memory of the curves
her neck took when she asked a question
she already knew the answer for;
the thing she did with her tiny little fingers
when he made her giggle
to assure him he's right to be anxious when his cell phone rings,
maybe a little more
when it *doesn't*.

Because the next time
or the time after
or the time after *that*,
could be her,

wanting to share more drinks and giggles,

more drinks and giggles

and maybe a little *more*.

She said she'd call,

and maybe it was the way he saw her believe him

when he said he was a writer,

maybe it was the way the little girl just missed

looking on him with those little girl eyes,

but he believed her,

enough to leave Wednesday and Thursday

and the one after

well enough alone,

waiting to not seem weak,

waiting because waiting is infinitely more comfortable,

at least twice as easy;

waiting,

because he knows deep,

deep

down,

that waiting is all he's really good at.

Better than the writing,

easily,

and the waiting

has a way of fueling

the *other* anyway,

after the waiting has turned too long,

and the opportunity has sat

in *his* seat,

across the table from the girl

who had grown tired

of waiting

for his waiting

to stop.

So he tells himself she'll call,

the comfort and the cold of knowing he's letting it pass him by

enough

to put his good side on the pillow,

tell him everything will stay nice and the same by the time his right closes,

left eye buried deep in the pillow that won't leave him.

Friday kisses him gently on the forehead as it leaves,

kisses him because Keri Lynn

probably won't,

because Friday leaves and

his cell phone doesn't ring,

won't like *he* won't pick it up,

kisses him and leaves,

but not before his pillow promises to be there in the morning.

Red (and more with Spanish Jose)

You take it in your hand, maybe you smile a little, maybe you don't; really, pretty much anything you do has been done before, done better.

Buying cocaine is nothing like, and oddly *just like* the way it is in the movies. He goes for the smile, Spanish Jose smiles back, and it's *that* smile, the

this isn't just because you think it's cool on TV anymore, now you're a mother fucking customer

smile—that *I've got you now, see you Thursday* smile.

So he nods a little, that

Thursday is a holy day, and this is still just because it's cool

nod, and Spanish Jose lets it go, because Spanish Jose knows the truth.

Still, he walks away thinking Spanish Jose looks ridiculous in that coat, thinking the danger of having eight on-the-way-to-an-ounce is kinda sexy, and thinking that, suddenly, he can relate to just about every rap song he's ever heard.

And that, that should help the writing, help contribute to making him a millionaire, help erase the picture of his mother and her *mother look* burned across his brain every single time he extends his left empty, and it comes back with a little white bag, a white bag filled with the *pretty snow.*

The thing about dealing, either with or *just*, is that it starts slow. He remembers smoking weed for the first time in years because the new guys did, remembers how the laughter and the *once-in-a-while* battled each other for control of his weekend, remembers how *the once-in-a-while* lost. Yeah, he remembers the first time somebody gave him four stalks to smoke for free, the first time he broke four stalks down and gave them to somebody and somebody, for profit.

Remembers the first time somebody and somebody asked for something a little *more*, remembers the first time he saw Spanish Jose in that stupid coat, the first time it *snowed* in September.

It has been snowing, that pretty, pretty snow, ever since.

Blue (and home, when not home)

He spends his favorite nights here.

Not *here*
here
—usually he's a little left,
but tonight Dad wants to lie down to watch the game,
so he settles for the armchair.
The TV room at Mom and Dad's, on game night,
is as close to happy
as a wannabe tortured artist can get,
so it's a bellyful of Hungarian goulash and a couple skunky *Papst Blue Ribbons*
instead of *Mansion* at midnight and a couple *liquid cocaines*.

It's better this way,
and the dreamer in him knows that if his book ever sells,
nights like this will be farther away,
replaced by
respect
and
adulation
and
other pretty shiny things,
pretty shiny things
replacing Patriots and *Pabst*
and the common dull things,
his favorite,
and things he knows

he can never ever take for granted.

The dreamer,

but the voice deepest in him

promises dreams like his don't come true,

so he settles into his armchair tonight,

because really,

tonight is just another.

Dad doesn't believe either,

but he's far too kind

to say it.

He just kind of smiles,

there to the right,

that

wouldn't-say-proud-but-quietly-satisfied

smile,

like its okay that the boy will never amount to *half*.

Really,

he knows Dad probably held him in the air,

some Thursday

or Friday

or Saturday,

held him up in Saturday's sun,

sun on Thursday

or Friday,

the way the sun seemed to shine

on at least every

and *all* those days,

and wondered…

Doctor? Lawyer? Pats quarterback? Fucking astronaut? Pats cornerback?

Sorry Dad,

he says

with every single smile he shoots back,

there to the left,

as some other son takes the snap on Sunday somewhere,

under Saturday's sun,

on Dad's TV,

which isn't a plasma,

 or an LCD,

or forty inches,

but it's Dad's TV,

and he had that *I'm-proud-of-you* smile

for *it,*

the first time it smiled back from the box,

so he's proud of it,

too.

It's not over forty,

but Dad's smile was so big that day,

that '*look-what-I-did*'

 enough

to make *Mansion* at midnight

and a couple of *liquid cocaines*

look decidedly *smaller.*

Besides,

he's seen *Rambo*

and *Rocky*

and *Superman*

and Terrell Owens

and Tom Brady

and *Batman,*

twice,

and *Stone Cold Steve Austin,*

and they can't amount to *half,*

either;

there on the armchair,

game night

right

right

of his hero.

Red (and his first writing workshop)

It didn't go well.

Well, but it *kinda* did, if going well is hearing how lyrical the writing is or how beautiful he looks reading it or how McConaughey or Pitt should play him in the eventual movie about his life.

Yeah, to *some* the writing workshop would be considered a success—maybe even before it ended, the first time the word *brilliant* got thrown his way, but the instructor—the instructor who is also the *editor* who is also the editor who knows the *agent* who got Shelley Saunders the international book deal—didn't take his manuscript home, said he couldn't until October and six-million months away, so the workshop was a complete fucking failure.

Waiting—like he's been waiting—isn't satiated by praise and admiration and awe thrown his way by homos and fellow writers and love struck would be fans. Besides, *McConaughey* and *Pitt* would be inspired choices, but he knows he's got a little *Depp* in him, probably a lot of *Beckham*.

Still, it's the only thing that kinda almost makes him happy on the way home, being compared to two of the '*Sexiest Men Alive*' ain't bad, even if the next '*Sexiest*' is headed home to spend his Saturday night about as far away from the paparazzi as possible.

Driving into his laneway, before the headlights burn out on another dream, he knows he'd give just about anything to have one of them hiding in his bushes.

Blue (and his first writing seminar)

That went well.

Well, *kinda*;

he didn't get his manuscript reviewed by the instructor

—the instructor who is also the editor

who knows the agent

who got Shelley Saunders the international book deal

—but he looked like he *meant* it

when he said he had promise,

and promised

to review his manuscript when his schedule allowed.

So

yeah,

he's gotta keep waiting

—like he's been waiting,

but he got to read some of his work aloud for the first time,

and everybody was *real* kind

—the cute girl in the corner said

fantastic

or

fabulous

or

some other word that started with '*f*'

and it was *enough.*

Enough

to get him to his house,

a house once a home,

a house on the East Side,

ten on the street,

ten across,

thirty-eight on the block,

thirty-eight blocks in the ghetto.

He knows that when he gets home,

his clock will be laughing at him

and

the phone won't be ringing

and

it won't be Summer,

but one more winter,

a winter with nothing

and no one else

—one

more

winter

worth the wait.

As the key turns

and his door opens

and his clock draws wind,

he knows that it will *have* to be.

May

Blue (and writing on Tuesday)

He's *stuck*,

somewhere between a sentence and a novel,

and the world on his shoulders

is digging somewhere between too,

so today,

Tuesday,

and stuck

is suddenly

done.

Done,

but not done writing,

just done writing

the novel

—the novel that will save his life,

because if it doesn't,

his life may as well be over,

and over

and done

--*now.*

He can tell himself the good stuff

—waiting for Summer to call,

telling himself the weekend is only tomorrow

and

tomorrow

and

tomorrow

away

—is coming around the corner,

tell himself the big stuff

—the career

and

the money

and

the self-respect

—can come after,

the next time good stuff needs coming.

Yeah,

that'll put his head on the pillow tonight,

numb,

while the good stuff comes,

cornering *hard*,

to the guy who *isn't* stuck,

sentence to novel.

So he writes,

to himself

—not just like he writes

when he writes

the novel,

writes with the intent to keep to himself

what he writes,

instead of the intent to share,

and, as he writes,

maybe the honesty

drives his pen harder

than the dream does.

I have never seen the sun bleed red off the shore of Somewhere, but I could fool you.

I have not, will not, win the Super Bowl or command a mission to that moon you see out your window; but with a turn of my wrist, you'd think I ran for one-fifty.

I'll never save a life in surgery, but the guy who does eats the same Corn Flakes I do—or at least, you'll believe he does.

It sucks,

or it doesn't,

but it's *something—*

something to make Tuesday,

like Monday before,

worth

something,

something to compete with Summer's

new summer job

and

his sister's new apartment

and

the Girl on TV

being on TV.

He tells himself it's a *step,*

a step to

a new summer job

and

a new apartment

and

either being *on* or *with*,

TV and the words before it,

but it's just a step,

a step

in a series of,

and still nowhere near enough

to keep Wednesday

from being Tuesday

being Monday,

Wednesday

and everything else,

always and ever the *same*.

Red (and motivation)

He thinks about fucking Kelly Ripa.

Other stuff, too, when he thinks about what it will be like to be published, and famous, and adored, and respected, and regarded as the first rock star author since Chaucer, but mainly, and always, it's fucking, and Kelly Ripa.

It plays in his head the same as a chapter before he writes it down—the interview on *Live*, the banter, the lunch, the part about Mark Conselous being a douche bag, the fucking.

He watched a movie (—and it wasn't easy—) about the secret to success, and in between stuff *not* blowing up, and Sylvester Stallone not starring, was some shit about the power of positive thinking, and visualizing all of one's dreams coming true. It kind of *stuck* with him, the way movies with Sylvester Stallone usually do, and so he's been visualizing being published, becoming a sensation, fucking—really, really fucking—Kelly Ripa, everyday since.

There's other stuff, too—that oversized royalty check, his first review in the paper, how good he'll look shirtless in the rain on the photo in the book jacket—but she's got *those* legs, and he kinda wants to suck on her toes in a way he's never really wanted to suck toes before, so being famous is all about being famous, when it's not about fucking, and Kelly Ripa.

Red (and being wonderfully creative)

The writing exercise at the writing seminar is *describe a doughnut* and it's at least as stupid as it sounds, so it's the stupidest fucking idea ever.

Ever –ever, but Bob the Editor is standing at the front of the raffia cream colored *twice-as-dull-as-it-sounds* library seminar room, and he's both dictating and impossible, so for now he'll take the dictation, advantage of the impossible *after*, when it's time to *share* and for Bob the Editor to stop dictating and listen, and to the most profound dissertation of pastry this tired man with his tired routine has heard, *ever*-ever.

The length of six long tables, in the-cream-family filled with uninspired and *less*-talented pretenders <u>away</u>—and *he is*, and *early*—Bob The Editor commands they have an hour and *begin*, and he knows he won't need it as he scrawls at at-least his fifth line, and not because he jumped the gun.

No, because *this*, hitting the turn of phrase at *sweetly slides*—this—is pathetic and beneath him and practically beneath him, like the sixth line, the line he starts with '*watch her.*'

. . .

She's hot out of the oven, sauntering into the room, just pretentious and classy enough to look like she's floating.

Everybody who sees her wants her, knows that underneath that sweaty golden skin she's full up with that cream; the stuff that stinks sweetly when it sweetly sticks to their lips, and they want it to when they watch her.

They follow her home, all of them, each and every one of them would too—but home for her cinnamon-skinned self is the VIP area with her name on it, and she rests there now, sexiest cinnamon skinned in a sea of.

Their eyes are on her, all of them, each and every one watching her so comfortable there in the VIP, with her name of it, and there's not a man, woman, or child, the fat bastards, who wouldn't want her full up with that cream inside of them.

So they line up for a taste of her, the fat bastards, and the fattest are always somewhat surprisingly the fastest, and it's not an error in spelling but a testament to their desire to devour the whole of her.

She's indifferent to all of this, the clamoring for her cinnamon and stuffing, perched and presented under the re-heating lights north of her and where her name sits, directly across from the fattest fat bastard, the first to throw his money on the counter for a taste of her.

And the cruelty of her existence is that she's just the latest in a series of many, many more, and she won't even go to the highest bidder, but the first, always the fattest.

Blue (and being, hopefully, at least a little creative)

It's interesting and challenging and far from the stupidest idea he's ever heard,

so when Bob The Editor

asks the writers' group

to *describe a doughnut,*

he sees it for what it could be,

is halfway down page one

before the unimaginative finish groaning unimaginatively.

…

It's disposable, like him.

Bad for him, he's bad for her.

Her and her and her, he guesses, so Billy and the donut are a perfect pair.

Until he burns through her, too, and she leaves a bad feeling in his stomach.

Like only girls and pastries do.

This one is double chocolate, very bad, but like Summer, its degrees, and cinnamon sugar or Girls on TV still hurt when they're gone.

He eats anyway, like he dates anyway, and Billy knows the end is bites or dates away, and fewer every time he indulges.

He knows its bad everytime he goes to the counter, or wherever he goes to meet girls, but he goes again.

And it's maybe the saddest part, as the last bite is somehow less satisfying than the feeling before, worse knowing the hunger will bring him back for more.

Blue (and settling)

He's at a job interview,
and it's the *second* saddest thing.

He's wearing one of Dad's ties, here at the factory job interview,
and Dad is happy somewhere,
because he's not dreaming
of being the writer
he *won't* be,
and his hair is down and subdued,
the down and subdued of his mood,
because if he gets the job,
the factory job,
he files his dream under *d*,
and not
dream,
dead.

He could file it in the cabinet there, to the left and closer,
the room and reality
crawling towards him,
and they're both beige,
like *dull*,
like this bland and dull and depressing waiting room,
and they're coming,
like Terri from human resources,
the dull and depressed receptionist he met on the way in,
coming to tell him he's *next*.

Terri from human resources

looks like a zombie from outer space,

one of the zombies from outer space

he would have written about in his *fourth* bestselling novel,

fourth because it would have taken three

to build the confidence

to write a novel about zombies from outer space,

confidence that comes from three bestselling novels,

almost *four* more

than he will ever have

if

and

after

he gets the factory job,

here.

Terri asks him if he's ready

and he's really-really not,

because if he was ready for the kind of reality

waiting for him on the other side of the door that crawls towards him

then he wouldn't have written the first word

You

he ever wrote, with the intention of the last word

You,

every one between

being read by at least *everybody* who reads

and half who don't

(--because maybe he'd be famous enough for a picture book or a picture show--)

miles in the millions

from Terri from human resources

and whoever is waiting for him on the other side of that door;

but he's not even famous enough to skip the interview at the factory,

not even famous enough to stop the walls crawling in.

…

So he's sitting across from Steve,

Steve the human resources manager

managing this interview,

which is going well,

because he plays this game,

and it *isn't* going well,

really

and

 really at all,

because this isn't really a game

and

it's real,

and

it's really not what he wants at all.

Steve asks a question,

and it's question number thousand-thousand,

and it's as ridiculous

as the thousand-thousand before

and he knows it

and

(-and but) before he knows *it*,

he's answering it,

because this interview is a reflex,

and he's going through the motions,

because this,

horribly,

is reality

and

probably the rest of his life.

Steve the human resources manager

looks like Terri from human resources,

so a zombie,

and from outer space,

the darker rings under his black little eyes

indicating his superiority in the human-resources-zombie-from-outer-space

hierarchy.

He's thinking less about the interview,

question thousand-thousand one,

and less about Steve the human resources manager,

and more about the walls closing in on him in this smaller beige room;

and the shade of beige,

(he knows because it's closer,)

is duller

than the shade in the waiting room,

and he can't even fathom what the factory room floor looks like,

and he knows he never ever

wants to know.

So as soon,

and maybe before,

(by the look on Steve the human resources manager zombie from outer space's face,)

as Steve sticks his left for the handshake,

he's up out of his seat

and

reaching

and

shaking

and

shaking with the enthusiasm of someone who's getting the fuck out of this trash-compacting hell-room and turning before the

We'll be in touch;

knowing that

no,

Steve,

we *won't,*

and if this is reality

then Steve

and Dad

and their factory floor

can count him out,

gone, like TuPac

before the *Thank you for coming.*

Red (and being very, very sick)

He fucking hates hospitals.

Loathes them, but 'loathes' is a gay word, so he sticks with 'hates' as he looks around the waiting room, but the waiting room is the same, the same since he's been waiting, so he tries to come up with a different word.

Tries, but 'hates', with 'fucking' before is really the only accurate way to describe having to sit in this waiting room for hour number two, two plus the twenty four he's gone without any food, waiting so some stranger can give him an enema, an enema and an x-ray.

Having something shot up his ass, he's told, is infinitely better than letting his potential cancer go undetected, and he knows the movie stars love them, so he sits.

Sits and waits.

He started bleeding—bleeding out of his ass—about three months ago. At first, it was kinda cool—something to show the boys, maybe testament to how hard he was putting up the weights. He figured it was the creatine—maybe the creatine or the argentine or the D-Bol or the juice he spent three months before shooting into his ass, but then the felt the *lump* for the first time a week ago, and suddenly the bleeding that came with it (—and the bleeding six or seven times a day—) stopped being cool, started being something else.

Something else, and suddenly hemorrhoid started being his favorite word, favorite because it wasn't cancer, and so now he sits, hour twenty six with an empty stomach, and fucking *hates* working it's way up his list of favorite words.

Twenty six, with twenty four being the agreement, twenty four with no food of any kind, so his system would be clean fro the enema and the x-ray, but twenty six is two over twenty four, and *too* many to go without a protein shake.

His abs thanked him this morning in the mirror, but sitting there, waiting in this waiting room, he can feel his stomach start to eat his biceps, start, so he knows it's time to *finish*, finish waiting in this fucking waiting room. He stands suddenly, suddenly standing on legs that feel suddenly *smaller.*

Delores is the name of the pig behind the desk, and, perfectly, Delores is devouring *Doritos*, so Delores must be on some kind of break, because there is no way a lady who touches as many potentially diseased people should be eating *Doritos* on the clock.

They look like *Cool Ranch*—no, coming closer, his stomach tells him it's that new *Jalapeño* jump-off, but it's hard to tell the way Delores is vacuuming them down her trough, beady little pig eyes calling his play before he crosses the line of scrimmage.

Her fat little pointer finger points to the little clock, the little hands showing him it's gonna be five before her fat little fingers move away from the *Doritos*, back to whatever it is she calls work.

Five, but by then it will be twenty six hours five minutes, at least one hundred twenty five more than both he, his stomach and his biceps bargained on. So Delores, her *Doritos*, and her fat little *Jalapeño* fingers are out of both time and luck.

Hey.

She kinda looks like a rodeo clown—or, more accurately, *two* rodeo clowns, the blush everywhere but between her pig eyes at least a half mile wide. The rouge on cheek left looks to be three shades less rouge than the rouge on cheek right; both threaten to swallow the beads of her beady little pig eyes when she begins to sneer an answer.

Mhnon bhreak.

(On *break.*)

.   Seriously, this bitch is talking to him with a mouthful of *Doritos*, a mouthful of Doritos he can't have like he hasn't had for hours, because of this bitch.

Break's over.

It's *not*, but it sounds like something Stallone would say, if Stallone had to go twenty six hours six minutes without food, and enough, apparently, to stop Delores from eating; he knows after she's done licking cheese from her fat little fingers, the rodeo will start.

. . .

Delores is shoving something up his ass.

Well, not *Delores*, but somebody just *like* her—as the nurse pushes the tube all the way in, he knows it's rodeo time.

Time, because Delores is shoving something up his ass.

He fucking *hates* hospitals.

He tries to think that this—*this*—will be good for him in the long run, but all he can think about—really think about, is the tube up his fucking ass.

Well, that, and remembering to ask his gay buddy how the fuck he does it.

Try to relax.

It's the other Delores, the other rodeo clown and what she's really saying is hold the fuck on.

Hold the fuck on, because Delores is shoving something up his ass.

...

Twenty six and something ago, he stopped eating. All he had, twenty six and something, was the prescribed laxative—so he spent twenty six and something, mostly, emptying his stomach onto the toilet, while on TV, his Patriots traded their most promising rookie to the fucking Colts.

Fucking fuck.

The point, he tells himself, as Delores Two finishes the insertion of the enema tube up his fucking ass (—and only finishes because the thing is poking him in the tonsils—) is that, after twenty six and *something*, he should not feel like he has to take a shit.

You're going to feel like you have to go to the bathroom—

He feels like he has to go to the bathroom.

Like, worse than ever. Right now.

--and I don't want you to push against the tube—

Push the fucking tube.

--I'm gonna need you to hold on. We're going to push some air into your stomach, and you're going to feel some cramping.

He hates that he is going to come out of this with an intimate understanding of both fags and rags.

Fucking fuck.

And then, we're going to secrete some barium into your stomach, so that we can take some pictures. When we introduce the barium, you're going to feel some discomfort.

Discomfort?

--no.

Do you have any questions before we get started?

(Before we—)

(--yes, I have a question.)

(Fuck you.)

Okay then, I'm going to get you to lay on your left side—

(There is a tube in my fucking ass, and you want me to roll over.)

--a little more—

.

--just a little more—all the way over—

(Fucking fuck.)

--put your knees together—

He's helpless, and alone, and afraid, and pretty sure the fucking guy who just walked in had a smirk on his face, seeing him all laid out on the cold table with a fucking tube in his ass, and his ass hanging out of his hospital gown, in the air and exposed and vulnerable and—

And, here we go—

(--fucking fuck) and he's on fire and he needs to shit now *right now* and he hates Delores and Delores Two and the fucking guy who just walked in and he's cold and kinda not hungry anymore but angry yeah angry and

--and relax.

(--relax yeah okay you try and)

And suddenly it doesn't hurt so bad. It still fucking hurts, and he is still about to let go all over the cold table he's laid out on, but Delores Two isn't shooting barium up his ass anymore, and—

And here we go with some air.

(--fucking fuck Peyton Manning and the Colts and Delores and)

Now, I need you to lie on your back so we can take an x-ray.

(There is something up my fucking ass. You come over here and fucking roll me.)

. . .

It goes on forever.

Forever and ever and ever, never-ending half-turns followed by full-turns, always twisting and turning so they can take their photos. It goes on forever, and about halfway through, he starts to think about how serious this is, is and could be.

Yeah, it could be hemmheroids, but it could be something *else*, something eating him from the inside, something that could mean more hospitals and more hospital gowns and more cold tables. He tells himself he's not scared, tells himself, but he knows he's lying, because he's lying on a cold table with a fucking tube up his ass and every other word he thinks is fucking or fuck, and suddenly the Patriots losing in the grand scheme of things isn't so bad, because there's always *next* season, next season unless there's *not*.

He closes his eyes and Delores Two asks him to lie on his stomach and he doesn't swear at her, not even in his thoughts, as he begins the quarter turn.

. . .

He sits in the bathroom, in the bathroom on the toilet, for another minute. One more will make thirty-three, but Delores Two said it would take time before the barium drained and the cramps stopped, and all of the thirty-two had both barium and cramps, so for thirty-three, he sits.

His hand almost stopped shaking at *seventeen*, (--almost, because it did, from *seventeen seven* to *seventeen thirteen*--) but now, *thirty-three something*, it's shaking as bad as when the tube came out, *thirty-three* something ago. He hit the bathroom *three* before they let him go and of him, locked them out, locked them and the world and the worry behind the hospital-white of the hospital-white door.

Locked them out, but *thirty-three something* and no matter how hard he pushes, the lump still stays, alone there with him in the bathroom, and the bathroom is cold, and the hand towel by the sink is kind of strewn there, like it's been touched a hundred hundred times by a hundred hundred hands, a hundred hundred diseases, and—

Fuck it.

He stands up, flushes the sickness and the barium down the toilet and washes his hands in the sink and dries them on the towel, a hundred hundred hands or not. He gets to his locker in the locker room and the hospital gown is gone before he locks the door.

His clothes are in the locker, and then *not*, and his jeans fit the same and his shirt is the shirt he picked up the last *three* girls in, so he puts it on and thinks of the rare day his sister smiled at him when she gave him the Prada wallet last Christmas, so he smiles as he fits it in his back pocket.

He's still smiling when he ignores the *Please-dispose-of-the-gown-in-the-hamper* sign; well, not really, because he *sees* the *Please-dispose-of-the-gown* just fine, throws it in the garbage on his way out.

They said something about waiting a week for the x-ray results, but they can go fuck themselves, themselves and the results because he already knows he's fine.

He'll get the hemmheroid off when its time to, spend the rest asking the next pretty little thing if he can stick a tube up *her* ass.

Blue (and Sabrina)

Sabrina standing in front of him is a *sight*,
sore eyes and all that.

He was in the bar *five* seconds
before he saw her serving drinks on the other side,
gave it two
before she saw him right back,
smiled a smile he hadn't seen her smile
since he'd seen her,
seven years ago.

She was one of those 'got-away' clichés,
the girl from art school
in high school
with the too-white teeth
and
the porcelain cheekbones
and
the art school *lazy-artist-put together-naturally-and-never-ever-work-at-or-for-it* body.

They always played on Friday;
seeing her
seeing him right back,
he bets memories of him
chasing her around the classroom,
laughing the laugh that comes with that smile
are dancing on the sweet spot of *her* brain, too.

So he heads right for her,

swimming through the army of cologne-bombed fresh pretty things

striving for her attention,

attention focused on,

the way he suddenly remembers,

suddenly and not so subtly, based on that damning smile

—him

and

 again, only him.

He's nervous,

he tells himself,

dodging the Hilton-esque seven-out-of-ten on his way to her,

nervous because it's been seven

and she's *ten,*

and maybe she's changed

and maybe he's changed

but more than maybe

he wants to sit across a table somewhere,

work on making the seven between something *smaller.*

To do that, he knows,

he's going to have to ask Sabrina out—

out out,

as in a date,

a date and a place

somewhere decidedly

else,

a date on an evening,

an evening connected to an afternoon

of worrying whether or not that's a zit,

(and it *is*,)

or a shaving bump

racing to the surface,

racing to ruin said evening.

He's going to have to ask her out—

something seven ago

and no matter how many smiles,

he could never do.

And she's shouting his name from across the bar,

pushing the consonants out

like she means it;

vowels hiding in his title come like honey,

honey

and

September

and

sweet,

as sweet as,

if not sweeter than,

the first time she tried it,

a September more than *seven* Septembers ago.

Suddenly, asking her out—

her and those hips

peeking at him from across the bar—

is still daunting,

but entirely necessary.

He knows he's overlooking things,

but the girl holds up

to the picture he's had in his head

when he's pictured her,

so he really can't blame himself

as he sucks breath,

tries to part the clouds in his head.

Okay,

he came here tonight,

Friday,

because a buddy needed to get out,

a buddy probably swimming the Hilton channel

somewhere behind him.

He didn't want to;

the way he's watching her cornea vibrate,

soaking seven years of change on his face,

he's

at least

overly glad he did.

Buddy and his emotional problems can *stay* behind him

for another minute,

or ten,

or however long it takes to soak his consciousness in her scent,

write   the   ten   digits

that will make this Friday,

the ensuing emotional-problem spill,

that much better.

The bar,

(since he's taking a step back,)

is one of the better in the city

—better by other's judgment,

because everybody pretends *harder* here,

every fresh pretty thing a lawyer or a doctor or well on their way to being,

thanks to the run-off from the University up the road.

It's about as far away from the East Side

—his side

—as a city can run,

and every fresh pretty laugh

competing with the thumping from fresh speakers

reminds

him.

The music just kind of *sounds* better around here;

better,

by other's judgment,

bar

better

by *his*

simply for their taste in bartenders.

Taking a step back isn't *half* the fun of the forward,

butterflies or not,

so he approaches the trendy mahogany of the bar,

almost catches her reflection

between polish and puddles of the pours she's had trouble pouring

since she saw him.

And she's talking again,

his name and other sweetness,

but it's not so much talking

as *lulling*,

like every precious word,

and the ones between,

stringing the precious ones together,

are floating

there above the bar,

weaving in

and

out

and

in

of the beat in the ether.

It's intoxicating,

intoxicating in the way

the vodka in the puddles *wants* to be,

pooling around his fingers as he grabs the mahogany,

leans into the sweetness,

tasting her words out of the ether

just as she sings them.

He's got this thing where he can't remember faces,

but he remembers hers,

now

the way,

beautifully,

it was just then,

no new wrinkle

or mark

or mar

to remember

when he will remember this,

nothing to hide the lie on her skin

that tells him its *okay*,

that time hasn't bled from him.

The line behind him

adds vodka-starved fresh pretty things

and emotion-spilling buddies,

all watching him take up her time,

her time

and

her hands

and

her smile,

and

he's smiling,

both because of her smile and because of the line growing behind him.

Sabrina's not counting the tip money she's losing

as she laughs her soft little laugh,

matching *Mariah's* highest high note on the fresh speakers

when she tells him

she still has the mark from where he stabbed her leg in art school.

It's sexier than it sounds

when she calls it the _____ leg,

and suddenly he's chasing her around the classroom,

seven something ago,

and

she's laughing *that* laugh

when he pins her to the table,

playfully stabs her precious little leg

a little harder than he should.

She's laughing about it

now,

seven and something,

the way she laughed about it

then;

but laughing

then

came between tears,

because play-<u>stabbing</u>

still has the word after *play* in it.

As far as reminders go, though, he'll take it;

seven something

has a lot of days in it,

days with things like showers,

toweling off that little leg

with that little mark,

that little mark

that says *hello*,

everyday

for seven something.

She looks like she tastes like butterscotch,

searching for a pen to write

the ten he's been hoping for,

butterscotch

because he doesn't know what's in it,

but he knows it tastes *good*,

and

write the ten,

with her name on top,

because she used to practice all over his art book,

Sabrina

and

SABRINA!

and

Sabrina.

Red (and a Wednesday)

Wednesday, and his big sister calls and he doesn't answer, doesn't answer because he is bleeding out of his ass.

Red (and a Wednesday night)

She says it hurts, in and around the usual *uunnhs* and *ooohhs*, and he doesn't care.

He met this girl at some bar the other night—*he thinks*, the alcohol and the sickness are making memory hard, hard like he's fucking this girl, in her ass.

He's growling, now; growling, or his stomach is, reminding him (as if he needed it) that he's sick and *still*, but he ignores it, because as bad as his stomach hurts, what's going on in *her* ass is at least and infinitely more exciting than what's going on in *his*.

She came over some hours ago, spent some hours trying to conversate about decidedly trivial and inconsequential things, things like

So what do you do for a living

and

Hey, do you remember

when all he really wanted to hear was

Let's fuck

the way they are, hours later,

now;

and

uuunnh, not so hard

when he fucks her harder, for making him wait for the hours that he's waited to.

And before he can come, she's sliding off the end of the only topic of conversation he remembers being even remotely interested in. And it's tragic and hardly amusing watching the ass he's waited hours (hours he spent <u>hard</u> in order to fuck her ___) in and he can't imagine why until he looks down and realizes there is something (so sickness) escaping from *his* ass, when the only liquids he planned on watching would be coming (so his come) from *hers*.

And maybe she vomits and maybe he vomits—he can't be sure, because he's suddenly violently embarrassed and violently nauseous—and then she's leaving and leaving him to the somewhat sickening notion that he might not be the man he thought he was, moments and asses ago.

Even worse, worse than the

You're fucking insane

she throws his way on her way (half naked and sore-assed) past roommate Cheque on her way down the stairs, is that all at once roommate Cheque is watching him be sick, and he knows his Wednesday night is going to end far, far worse than he planned.

And it does, because once the fever subsides, and the bleeding slows, he's spending the rest of Wednesday night on the couch beside roommate Cheque, and he's concerned, roommate Cheque is, and he's offering personal anecdotes and reassurances and hot soup.

And the soup he'll take, *thank-you-very-much*, but the personal anecdotes and reassurances can fuck right off

(--like that girl--) because getting closer to his roommate is dangerously close to personal growth.

So he's sick again, and at the thought of growing up, and at (as the bleeding comes roaring back) the thought of not getting the chance to.

Blue (and Sabrina, kinda; so the second of three blown dates)

He's writing

now,

Sunday,

and he's thinking about the phone call

he *hasn't* gotten yet,

the call he's been waiting on

since

Saturday

last,

the phone call from Sabrina.

Sitting alone,

concentrating on concentrating,

he tries to get a page worth,

but he's anxious,

anxious kinda like he hasn't been since school,

since he fell in love with the girl on TV.

Maybe it's because he's lonely,

lonely like he's been since summer left

seven seasons ago;

maybe it's because he's scared lonely

is becoming *comfortable*,

like lonely is the way it's gonna be,

seven seasons on.

It kind of starts small,

a rumble somewhere low,

lower than his stomach,

somewhere between adjectives,

and the writing becomes *less* about plot advancement

and more about self-loathing.

By the time he hits the seventeenth line,

about halfway down,

he can't remember where he was going with the sentence

—the one about the hero's third uncle and his alcoholic wife

—third,

or

second

uncle—*if he references chapter three*

—and it's gone,

the dreams of some Saturday,

some book signing with his name bright in lights

replaced by reality,

another Sunday alone on his couch.

So some second or third uncle and his alcoholic wife

are becoming less and less important

—and the way the phone sits there on his table,

just kind of *not* ringing

is taking up the space he reserves for characters.

Really, he waited until Monday to call her

—the three day thing, to not look desperate

—he was more than a little relieved when he got her answering machine, the way his heart was pounding,

Hey, I was wondering if you wanted to go for a drink, maybe Wednesday

comes out more like

Yeah, hi—it's uh—anyway, I-ah—was k-kind of wondering—

It put the ball in her court;

he figured she'd call the way Keri-Lynn wouldn't,

no way *two* get away

a month apart.

No way,

but maybe,

so until the phone rings,

alcoholics and third and second uncles and Sundays

and

writing

are all going to have to wait.

The book he writes in

when he writes

closes,

closes like his eyes

as he draws breath,

knowing no matter how hard he tries,

he can't get the clock on the wall

to stop laughing at him.

June

Blue (and the halfway _____s)

So he's sitting in his living room,

again,

and he's alone,

again,

and the clock on the wall

is reminding him

in familiar ticks

and

tocks

and

ticks

and

tocks

and

ticks

and

that he needs to write the sentence to save his life,

some

tick

before

next.

Because there's always

a,

next

in ticks

and

tocks

and

ticks

and

tocks

and

ticks

and

—a next breath between

tock

the clock on his living room wall draws

to laugh at him for failing,

and

again,

to be anywhere

other than alone

in his living room

and

again.

And there's a

next

before the hydro bill he can't afford,

and

though the thought

of not affording the batteries

or

the power

to power

the fucking clock on the wall

is momentarily,

admittedly,

placating,

the mechanical laugh reminds him he's a

next

from broke,

tock

from

too late

and

too old

to be chasing dreams.

Which are best enjoyed *sleeping* anyway,

and

he hasn't as well anymore,

terrified

though-no-longer-alone

between sheets

south of a respectable thread count

of *ending up that way*

and

old

and

nowhere farther than a flight of broken-down stairs

and

two left turns

from a living room

called lonely

and

a clock on the lonely living room wall

winding

and

waiting,

ticks

and

tocks

and

ticks

and

tocks

and

ticks

and

to laugh at him

again.

Blue (and more with Summer, and the Girl on TV)

He told himself,

the whole time,

ever and all,

that he never loved her,

but if she wanted something

—if she asked for something

—he would have her have it.

He thinks about it *now*,

Saturday,

when he shouldn't,

writing in the dark of the night,

Saturday,

Summer is somewhere else,

somewhere where tables are covered in vodka

and not paper,

paper he writes on

when he thinks

of her.

And *her*,

because the TV keeps him company,

and not the company

Summer keeps,

but the kind of company

he'd have given,

he thinks,

Summer,

season

and

to keep;

because

the Girl on TV

is on TV,

and maybe his writing suffers for it.

Maybe,

and does,

because every third word

is either

fucked by *her* blonde hair

or

her blonde hair,

and the chapter intended for comic relief

is suddenly,

Saturday night in summer,

alone

with his lovely ghosts,

comically tragic.

He needs Summer

like the Lakers need Kobe,

so a lot;

someone on the other end of the phone

when the phone rings,

rings like it won't tonight,

unless it rings

somewhere in the ungodly hour

when vodka has beat down inhibition,

and she's looking for someone *new* to fuck up.

He needs the Girl on TV

to stay there,

and

in his head

and

his dreams

and,

so that the pain he needs to write

when he writes

everything but the chapter

intended for comic relief,

has an air of authenticity,

like the word

hurt

really,

really

hurts

when he writes it,
context
and.

Sometimes,
and always on Saturday,
he wonders what it would be like
to just kind of be normal,
to be able to let go of *her* blonde hair
and
her blonde hair
and
leave his memories where just about everybody else does,
in his head
instead of his
page.

Sometimes,
and always;

but he looks at the phone
from the couch he writes on
when he writes,
and it doesn't ring,

no Keri Lynn
or

Sabrina

to chase the memories from his forethought,

so he sits on his couch,

Saturday,

and

his clock laughs when he writes,

leaving Saturday for Summer

and

——————————,

and

maybe,

probably,

Keri Lynn

or

Sabrina.

Blue (and a Wednesday)

Wednesday,

and his baby sister calls

and he doesn't answer,

doesn't answer

because she's a girl,

and

girls leave him.

Red (and sick)

It's hard to be a player from the toilet seat.

After three, three and a half weeks of explosive diarrhea, it's impossible—impossible, the way holding in all the perceptions and walls and lies about himself is. Yeah, impossible like holding *lunch* is, so when today's toast, with honey, runs like water when it runs into the bowl he now calls home, after three, three and a half weeks, his game is like his tan, so his game is *gone*.

Gone, and he's kinda questioning his priorities and what he places on them, how missing protein and steroids is hurting his arm size, when protein and steroids could be what got him here, one month from being raped by science, now sick, and x-rays and doctors unable to tell him why a twenty-six year old lady killer can't kill ladies wearing fucking *Depends*.

Depends, because he needs them, like he needs the phone calls from the girls from *last* week, but the girls from last week aren't calling, because last week he was two and a half weeks sick, and the kind of girls from last week aren't the kind of girls who like guys who haven't tanned in two and a half weeks.

So he sits, and his phone doesn't ring the way it *doesn't*, and, for half a second, he's just _____ , and nothing else. Sits, and for the ten minutes it takes a half second to pass, he thinks about being a little boy, when musclemen were in comic books and could *stay* there, and the only girl worth chasing was his big sister, in the mud around the farm far away from steroids and *Depends*.

His half second passes, ten minutes too soon, and his moment of weakness is flushed away with his toast, honey *and*.

Some weakness stays as he stands, struggles to pull up his *Depends*, *Depends* because he needs them, but only in everywhere *but* his mind. Because there, as he walks, left in front of right, the way he walks when he walks on days without *Depends*, he's already calculating the days and doses it will take the sixteen-and-a-half on his arms back to seventeen, seventeen on the way to twenty, *twenty* like the minutes per day he'll expose himself to radiation, so girls like last week will call the way they called two and a half ago.

Blue (and friends)

He's got friends,

he tells himself,

and

leaves it at that,

maybe just because the rest,

he's-got-friends, but-only-when-it's-convenient-for-them,

hurts

like it should

every now and then,

and

always when he's alone,

alone on the sunny days.

He's not depressed,

writing

alone

on his couch

some Sunday,

Sunday's sun

lighting his page

while the clock on his wall

laughs,

but when he thinks of Summer,

and not the one outside,

he thinks of her friends,
and
how summer days,
and
those ending in *why*
are spent with her sunny friends
and
he's left with the question at the end of his.

He'll go when they call,
and
they know that
every time
they punch his ten
he'll pick up
ring *three*,
be out the door *five* later,
ten away
from some adventure
of *their* design.

He calls,
never knowing
by punch ten on his touch pad
if the static following the ring
will be broken by

Hello

or

Hello,
I'm unavailable to pick up the phone

and
so maybe his finger shakes,
his day riding
on their decision
when his caller ID flashes.

Today,
some Sunday,

they *don't*,

the way

they don't

on Sundays,
and
so he's back on his couch,
dreaming of being somebody
and
coming up empty

when he dreams
of the friends
he'd take with him
to the better life.

Red (and a moment of insecurity, probably induced by sickness)

I will be published.

It's how he starts every page, every page because it's a reminder, and every page because it's true.

I will be fucking famous.

Fucking, because it adds a certain weight, *famous* because it's all he ever wanted, so it's the way he ends every single page from his pen, every single rep from his arm.

He's writing today, writing because girls aren't calling, aren't calling because he's whiter than his knuckles when he grips the pen, or the dumbbell, or the needle that makes gripping the dumbbell easier, makes gripping the pen easier too, since the needle and the dumbbell put him on the toilet, the toilet beside the pen.

He's writing, and it's *coming,* because he's *not,* so he's making progress, the kind of progress he hasn't made since he realized his kind of pretty was worth protecting. The good thing—(--and there is none, really—) about shitting himself everyday is that it kind of fucks with ego a little bit, a little bit like *enough,* enough to worry less about looks, and more about writing.

I will be published,

again, because he's starting a new page, the one after the last new page.

Blue (and Laura, and date number one)

The model
—and
model
for-real-for-real,

(not the kind of *had-glamour-shots-taken-in-a-strip-mall-once*
every girl
with even a hint of blonde
always seems to be)

—sitting across the table from him

is Laura,

and,
judging by her smile,
as first dates go,
this one is going well.

At least
a lot better
than the first date with Keri Lynn,
the one he thought
was going well
until she never ever called him again,
and
Sabrina,

the first date that kinda never really happened

because she didn't call,

at all.

He's here,

on a first date

for-real for-real,

and

the smile

on Laura's model,

for-real-for-real

face

has bled into a smile

as warm

and

as real

as the trail coming from the steak on his plate,

on the table in front of him

and

across from her

at their table,

there in the middle of the best

and

thereby

worst

priced restaurant in town.

He won't be able to eat for the next week or so,

the way the bill

will cut into his bank account

at least as easy

as this wonderful fucking knife

cuts his steak

—judging by the crease

he's already falling in love with

on her forehead when she howls,

he doesn't

and

isn't

going to mind,

five days

and

probably

five pounds

from now.

Right now,

the beautiful girl

(—the model, for Christ's sake--)

is still laughing

at some joke

he can't remember telling,

and

he's laughing,

because the money

this will bleed from him

can't take the memory of this

he'll carry with him

some winter,

when he's alone

and

writing

and

remembering

that for one night,

he left the *tortured*

before

off the

writer

after

on the business card

he's too embarrassed

to show her.

He knows, in between bites

(—and the steak is perfect, too--)

that he's supposed to be good at this,

and

it's supposed to be easy

and

natural,

and

maybe it was,

knowing when to tell her

he's having a good time

and

that she looks beautiful

and

when to ask

if she wants to see a movie

and

when to just grab her

and

press his lips slowly

and

softly

against hers

the way he always used to,

but used to

is like *was*,

as in a *long time ago*,

at least forever

and

well before he blew it

with the Girl on TV

and

the season

and

Keri Lynn

and

Sabrina,

so he's more than a little nervous,

the way he has been since she said

Hey

and

got into his car wearing *that* dress.

There has been

at least a thousand thousand words since,

and

smiles,

and

laughter

and

steak,

and

all the little indications that would tell a rational mind

to just relax

and

go with it,

but he wants to be a writer someday.

So,

every laugh

and

smile

and

bite of brilliant,

brilliant

meat

(—really, it is beyond--)

is another tiny victory

on the tightrope he walks,

halfway now

between bravado

and

praying

first *date*

loses the

first,

adds

's.'

And

it looks like he's got a shot,

though there's the matter of the date zit above his lip,

the way zits always pop up

on days with dates in them,

trying to fuck his date up

the way

this one surely is,

but she's not looking at him

like he's a greasy faced pig,

so he rocks it,

an accessory like his arm bracelet.

Really,

he needed something to worry about tonight anyway,

and

if it wasn't the date zit above his lip

it would be the creases in his button-down

or the piece of brilliant fucking meat lodged between his third

and

fourth

prettiest teeth

or whether or not she liked the hip-hop

he played on the way over.

Still,

she won't stop smiling,

save the times she's chewing softly

or softly staring

with those saucer eyes,

and

he's at least overly glad

he found the courage to ask her out,

not disheartened when his almost friends told him she was a dead ringer for

Kiera Knightey

or that she was a model,

or, the way he's usually scared,

that she was a *girl*.

So she finishes her chicken-*something*,

this model,

and

he asks if she wants to catch a movie

and

she says

yes

before he has a chance to be afraid

she'll say

no,

and

they're leaving,

and

she's smiling,

and

he's amazed he made it out of there

without making an ass of himself,

even once.

Red (and a Thursday)

Thursday, and his big sister calls and he doesn't answer, doesn't answer because he is violently ill.

Blue (and the agony of post date one)

He's looking at the phone,
and
it's not ringing,

so Laura's not calling,

and
no matter how hard he looks,
he can't make her,
and
he can't make *it*.

So he sits,
like he sat,
everyday
since the day
he thought was different;

waiting,
like he's waited,
wondering

what he did this time
to make his phone
not
ring.

Maybe it's the way he *killed* her in miniputt,

putting her down playfully with every stroke he gained,

forgetting that putting her down

playfully

still has the three before *playfully;*

maybe it's that they played miniputt,

at all.

He wanted her

to be *that* girl,

the one to fill the *whole*,

the one to leave the stars where they hang,

and

laugh at his jokes,

and

maybe even hang out with him

on days with datezits,

or zits without dates.

She called the night after,

after miniputt

and

ice cream

and

meeting her mom

and

walking her dog,

asked him if he wanted to come to the bar where she worked,

because she *wasn't*,

and

she was on the patio drinking with friends,

friends who heard all about him,

him

and

the night before.

He said no,

and

he doesn't know why and she hasn't called since.

She'd had a fashion show that evening,

because she's a fashion model,

and

he said *no*.

So she's gone away,

and

his phone hasn't rang

since he's thought of her,

so the thoughts of her,

and

the possibilities he put aside

for days in bed

and

pancakes

and

trips to places with sun in seasons other *than*,

goes the way of her thoughts of him,

so *gone.*

And

it's at least

as sad

as Keri Lynn

and

Sabrina,

not as epic as others

or as it could have been,

but it hurts a little,

with the number attached,

the thought of filing her face away

in a list of faces

with tragedies behind their smiles

when they smile at him,

only,

and

ever again,

in his memories.

Blue (Thursday)

The words come and go like Tuesday.

Today,
(Thursday,)
they're *going*
far more than *coming*,
a thousand-thousand things,
things decidedly not related
to sentence structure
and
paragraphs
keeping him
everywhere
but focused,
Thursday,
not even a holy day,
being the *most*
and
least
of reasons his pen leaves the page.

Today,
his reasons for writing
and
not
are a girl
and

the *latest*,

and

the latest to obsess/lament over in ways that both,

infuriatingly,

fuel

and

hinder the hand that moves the pen

and

not,

and

today,

not across his page.

Blue (and Laura calls!)

It's not the voice he's used to,

coming in

and

out

and

in

of the static

attached to the earpiece

of the phone

in his kitchen

—this one still has *color*,

like he

hasn't

and

maybe

won't,

(but would like to get the chance to,)

grey her.

How have you—

Small talk

and

other sweetness,

but he needs it,

knowing the voice on the other end

isn't connected to lips

intended to hurt him,

though,

eight days on,

he was beginning to wonder.

Good, I've been good

It's a half-lie,

and

he's rambling,

and

rambling makes him sound stupid

and

needy,

so stop rambling,

and—

Sorry I haven't called

Its okay

It's *not,*

not after Sabrina

and

Keri Lynn

and

everything that comes

with knowing you've presented

at least as best as you can,

and

you think it's going well,

and

then Thursday

and

then Friday

and

then Saturday

and

Sunday,

and

then,

god,

Monday.

I wanted to

(*Then, call.*)

But I've been really busy with work, and I had a shoot, and—what have you been doing?

(*Nothing.*)

Nothing.

(*Idiot.*)

(Awkward pause—quit breathing into the phone, and say something.)

So—

So—
--what are you doing this week?

Nothing.

(Again, you fucking idiot. Make something up, tell her you're headlining a community fundraiser or saving the rainforest—something, anything.)

Would you, I don't know, wanna go get something to eat one night?

And
then it's gone,
the tension
and
awkwardness of coming across like a complete asshole,
gone
and
faded
and
turning into something *else*,
something almost like confidence,
because Laura, the model
—and model
for-real,

for-real

is asking him out,

a date after first,

as in a date he hasn't been past

in at least

Septembers.

So he says

Yes

or

Yeah,

something to come across as not overly excited,

though excited

and

overly

he at least *definitely* is.

She says something,

and

then goodbye,

and

is gone before he has a chance to set a definite day,

or restaurant,

or more likely,

make a bigger ass of himself.

So the 'off' button leaves a better feeling than he's used to, something resembling a smile

as he turns the light,

leaves the clock on the kitchen wall less to laugh at.

Blue (and for real, date number two)

The model
—*for-real*,
for-real
—is sitting across from him,
again,
and
she's laughing,
the laugh he hasn't heard
since date, last.

Which makes *this*,
he notes between sips of a martini
he's nowhere near sophisticated enough to be drinking,
beautifully
and
really,
date number two,
number two
as in *one more* than he's had,
and
one more,
after her week of not calling,
than he figured he *would* be.

He brushes it off as the good stuff,
that pull *south* of his stomach
and

his reason

he hasn't felt in two forevers,

the angst agony

and

anticipation

of wondering if the pretty girl

liked his hair

and

his outfit

and

his datezit enough to give him another try.

The week,

he reasons,

was worth it;

lost now,

Friday night on the patio of the bar she works

when she's not modeling,

for real,

lost in the green-green of her eyes

and

the logo,

between stares,

of her tight little top

and

the pleasantries

and

alarming

and

alarmingly

warm symmetry of her face,

face

filled with features that glow softly

when he speaks of his dreams,

there on the patio.

It comes easy,

his confession,

three martinis

and

the strength three martinis bless,

and

he's on about how he'd love to be published

and

recognized

and

not the least embarrassed when he talks of writing in his underwear

somewhere

where the spoils of his words,

on paper,

have earned him the response his words,

on air,

seem to be earning him now.

He talks,

and

stops, politely,

and

then she races the silence,

keeping the pace of their moment admirably

and

instantly,

save for trips to the martini glass she swore was *last*

three glasses ago.

She talks,

and

he listens,

of how she wants it,

and

she'll take it,

this modeling career,

if the word

after

modeling,

key word,

she's blessed with;

but she doesn't believe in it,

jaded beautifully the way only intelligent

and

real

and

genuine models can be,

defeating

stereotypes

and

oxymorons

between bathing in the headlights of the city

that passes them by,

there on the patio of the bar she works at,

when she's not modeling.

And

he's watching

and

thinking

of her lips when she speaks,

softly speaking both words

and

questions worth thinking about to keep the magic

and

the moment flowing like the chocolate in his last martini,

chocolate

he would really, really like her to taste on *his*

when he presses lips for the first time,

wondering if that magic

and

that moment wait at the bottom of *this*,

the latest

and

nowhere near *last*,

of the glasses that pile proudly

on the table

unmercifully

between them.

She shifts like stick,

on now about leaving the city for a bigger,

better

city,

and he doesn't mind,

because they're sharing dreams,

and

that's all they are,

the way they only shared words on date the last,

and

she's not going anywhere

as

sure

as he's not getting published,

so

pretty,

like her,

at the table across from him,

his to lose,

and

tonight,

for sure,

not to a bigger,

better

city.

She blinks a third less than she should,

showing him,

without showing him

she's enamored about his history,

history he spills,

unlike the martini,

every drop fuel for the next,

faster than history should spill on dates numbered two.

He doesn't care,

and,

for her blinking,

she doesn't care,

so they share more than the comforts of awkward dates with numbers will

allow,

blowing through inhibition

with half-plus-more

the passion that blows her hair softly on the patio.

And

for the first time in two forevers,

he's not bound to the self-imposed misery

that guides his pen,

and

his writing will suffer for it,

and

maybe it's a good thing,

the way his life has spent two forevers suffering for his writing,

writing he would love to share with her,

this model,

for-real

for-real

smiling at him across the table.

He knows,

when she leans in to absorb the vowels he throws at her,

that she's *books* worth,

vowels

and

consonants

and

punctuation marks

like this !;

punctuation

he's not had the smile

and

sense to write

since writing

became more than cheques,

one day

for

cheques.

July

Red (and relief)

He's writing now, Sunday, and he's thinking about the phone call he got *then*, Thursday, the phone call that told him what he already knows now, and knew then—that he doesn't have cancer.

Sitting alone, concentrating on concentrating, he tries to get a page worth, but mortality keeps creeping in the corners; maybe the scare of hospital gowns and things shoved up his fucking ass are working to *grey* him, him and the hair he plucked this morning, the hair gone grey.

Still, Sunday is not the day for reflection, so he writes, because he's suddenly half done the manuscript *after* the manuscript that will make him the kind of famous he deserves to be, and he hurries, because he needs to be that kind of famous *now*, before the grey sneaks in.

Things like character and plot come easy, easy like they *always* have, because when it comes to writing, it's like he's looking at a rainbow, (*and not the gay one,*) and he's seeing *another* color. So he writes, and until the phone rings, or the TV starts, or the stomach rumbles, the writing is good and honest and pure and good—but then the phone rings, or the TV starts, *or—* and he's done writing, Sunday and maybe Monday more.

Still, writing on Sunday—any Sunday, and any writing day—is good, good because Sunday is the one after Saturday, and any Saturday was spent out, out at the clubs, with mortality and hospital gowns furthest from his mind.

So he's kind of happy that it's mortality, and not Michelle—Michelle with her strawberry-*esque* wavy blonde hair and her cute *just-a-little-too-close-together* eyes and her real-*esque* breasts distracting him from the big reveal in chapter nineteen, the big reveal he's half a sentence from compl—

And then there's a call on his cell.

Damn Michelle, and damn real-*esque*.

And writing on Sunday—Sunday and maybe Monday—is over, *over* like Michelle, Michelle and her *just-a-little-too-close-together* eyes, calling to tell him she's on her way over.

Blue (and a Thursday)

Thursday,
and
his baby sister calls
and
he doesn't answer,
doesn't answer
because he's writing.

Blue (and progress)

When the years run,

they could beat Marion Jones,

and

that bitch

is fast.

Progress, he names it *nicely*,

but

for one thousand eight hundred seventy five days,

he's got four,

five hundred pages,

so progress is just a polite word for pain.

Pain,

with the capital,

because the p doesn't stand for 'published,' *yet*,

and

'yet'

is coming close to leaving 'published' alone.

He doesn't give up,

because letting go of his dream is like letting go

of anything

to him,

and

not letting go,

next to writing,

(he hopes,) is all he's ever been good at.

Well, not all

—he could kiss, he was told,

and

more than once

—with lips softer than that ice cream he used to eat

when he was a kid,

and

that ice cream…

He was *good.*

The writing, too,

or so he's been told,

too,

but he never really believed,

the way he wanted to believe the kiss,

because maybe he figures writing is his dream,

and

being good at your dream is something like *living* it.

And

living his dream,

back when he dreamed about living it,

was maybe less about writing,

and

more about _____.

So when one dream died to birth another,

the act of dreaming kind of went the way

of the *years* since he dreamed first,

and

progress, with a *p*, wasn't far behind.

Blue (and another date with a number)

This,

thankfully,

is a date with a number,

and

the number is three,

and

tonight,

the datezit is directly between his eyes,

eyes,

he hopes,

shine brighter blue

than the red between.

Red,

really,

because he picked at it,

this datezit,

not wanting it to ruin *now*

like it threatens to,

across the court from the model,

for-real

for-real,

the model with the ball

and

the lane between,

between

like the datezit,

his eyes.

Playing one-on-one

on *three*

was her idea,

to him *three*

better suited for drinks

and

dinner

than basket

and

ball,

but she's more competitive

and

aggressive

than he gave her credit for,

right about now regretting telling her

he was shooting guard sophomore

and

star

senior,

when sophomore was spent riding benches

and

senior was spent being *stuffed*,

stuffed

like she did him,

the last time he had the rock,

and

the score was just *embarrassing*.

It's worse now,

and

she's everywhere in the lane,

and

he's admiring the sculpture of those legs

in those shorts

more than the fake she's making,

at least as good as the fake

when she told him she was dressed for dinner,

showed up outside her door with her buddy *Spaulding*

instead,

Spaulding raining on his night

and

his parade

and

his net,

and

not his rim,

because two baskets ago,

when she was up by a *lot*,

she said rims are for *pussies*.

She's kind,

though,

passing,

and

in passing,

assuming through lips far too precious to assume anything at all

that he's letting her win,

knowing,

dates ago

and

crushing defeat at miniputt,

that he's not the kind to let anybody win

anything at all.

So she earns it

when he tries the go-behind,

stealing the ball as effortlessly

as that laugh he learned to love *dates* ago,

maybe making it okay

when she checks,

drives,

and

ends,

mercifully,

the one-on-one

portion of *three*.

She's still laughing

and

holding the ball

and

suddenly the sun is setting somewhere behind her

and

it's of no consequence,

save for the shine the sun set

is shining on the *good* side,

so both sides, really,

of her face,

and

she's breathing hard

and

looking at him

and

he's looking at her

and

hardly breathing.

She moves a little,

and

it's his way

and

its close,

and

he's thinking about both

breathing

and

his breath,

hoping hard that his datezit

is the most unattractive thing

on

or

about him

when her left hip pops,

the way left hips on models pop

before they pout,

and

she does,

and

suddenly it's less about

sunsets

and

basketballs

and

all about lips,

and

hers.

So he's here,

and

two more steps

and

she's here,

and

he knows it's time

to close his eyes

and

move his lips

on

and

against

her lips,

and

put aside worrying about phone calls

and

datezits

and

not being a published or famous or even *remotely* successful writer,

because right now,

and

right here,

he's at least good enough for the beautiful girl, the model

for-real

for-real,

the one who closes her eyes,

moves her lips on

and

against his.

Her name is Laura,

and

she tastes like strawberries

and

Skittles

and

all the things that taste good

and

are bad for you,

but she's not,

not right now,

and

suddenly Laura is his favorite name

and

-and

because she's saving him from insecurity

and

sadness,

saving him with strawberries

and

Skittles

and

those lips.

These lips,

because he's still

and

slowly

searching them,

and

every ridge

and

every bump

and

every side, top to bottom,

are perfect

and

delicious

and

pure,

and

the longer he holds her there,

lingering

and

licking

and

all the things that come with kissing a beautiful girl for the first time,

the farther

and

smaller his problems

and

insecurities

and

failures

seem to be.

This, thankfully, is a date with a number,

and

the number is *three*,

but it might as well be *one*,

and

only,

as in all

and

only;

the *only* one that matters.

Red (and still sick, and not cancer, but...)

So he's here, and it's a month later, and it's not cancer, but it's still *wrong*, and now the blood they take when they take blood is for HIV, and it seems laughably appropriate, the way it's not really laughable at all.

He hates the acronym the most, hates it the way he hates weighing one hundred forty five pounds, pounds running from him almost as fast as friends, friends not waiting for test results to label him *less.*

In the month, the month he lost twenty somewhere between twenty tests, tests on blood and piss and shit, ultrasounds and x-rays and, he's almost thrown away his façade, his identity; the him that always said HIV was only in the movies, usually after fucking some pretty-dirty-pretty thing.

He can almost smile now, one month and twenty pounds less—he always wanted to be in movies anyway.

Red (and Bob the Editor takes his manuscript)

He sits across the table, trying to look *whole*, trying to look calm, trying to look like the kind of guy who's okay with the guy sitting across the table holding his life in his overly-manicured hands; like the bead of sweat tickling his *good* brow is for anything *but* the man holding his life.

Not his life in the *might-have-a-new-acronym-still-waiting-for-the-test-results* sense, life in the *this-is-all-I've-ever-kinda-wanted, don't-fuck-with-my-dream* sense.

Dream before, anyway, before dreams were all about not being one hundred forty five pounds, not having that *H* thing—when dreams were all steroids and beaches and Jenna and Jenna's tits.

Before, he knows, looking into the beady little beady eyes buried behind one and a quarter inch glass, he could have flexed a little, heaved in a way to suggest his *alpha*, suggest whatever he paid six hundred dollars *he doesn't have* to hear come out of Bob's mouth starts with *published*, as in gonna be, or *agent*, as in gonna get.

Suggest, like he can't, because dreaming he's not one hundred forty five pounds does little to change the reality that he *is*, so he sits, some bone in his ass digging into the chair, sits, across the table, hoping his dreams don't go the way of his weight.

. . .

He struggled to finish it, this stack of paper in front of him in front of *him*, perfectly placed in the middle of the table between them, struggled like he struggled to get off the toilet long enough to sit here instead, some bone in his ass letting him know he'd rather be home.

Home, though, isn't where his dream lives anymore—it's here, on the table across from Bob and his *have-to-be-into-books* fucking glasses and his seven hundred months of editorial seminars at thirty-eight dollars *per*, and his six hundred something more for an opinion—Bob's opinion, which pretty much gives his dream the go/no go, Tuesdays on signing books at *Barnes &* *Noble* or Tuesdays on signing condo fee cheques at two hundred more, *per*.

So when Bob takes the manuscript in his right, right after he takes the cheque and doesn't bother to check the title, which at this point oughta be

Fuck You And Your Ridiculous Glasses You Overbearing Effeminate Twat I'll Burn Your Life Down You Crush My Dream,

by _____, it's not without significance that the rumble in his tummy tells him that maybe dreams are better left in hands *other than*.

Or, maybe his tummy just tells him to get the fuck out of there.

Either way, Bob the Editor tells Tina the Agent if he likes what he reads, likes like he *has*, so Tina goes and gets un-solicited manuscripts everything but *un*, *un* like *she* has, some fuck whose name he can't remember, can't but should, because that fuck is from his hometown, *was* from his hometown, now living in Hollywood and in millions, millions of miles from here, because Bob the Editor told Tina the Agent he likes what he reads.

And if *someone*, (getting up from his chair earlier than his tummy tells him he should because Bob's decided their time together is *up*,) from his hometown can make anything starting with *m*, rising not from a chair but the mud and filth and shit hometowns always seem to be, (*his especially*,) then the grip he gives Bob the Editor's outstretched right, the right that took his manuscript, right after his check, is at least one hundred forty five pounds worth.

Blue (and Bob the Editor takes his manuscript)

He wrote

Pining for Somebody who May or May Not Know They're Being Pined For

for one person to read,

and

one person only,

and

that person,

sitting on the *Pined For* side

of the manuscript sitting in the middle of the table,

was *not* Bob the Editor.

From his vantage point,

there on the *Pining For* side

and six years removed,

the romanticism of handing the girl on TV

a published cornucopia of words

to replace three he never said,

three including

'*I*'

and

'*You*,'

is replaced by the reality that

'*Love*'

and

the emotion in,

need to be read by just about everyone *else*
first,
if the *published* part of his dream is to come true.

So he smiles when he hands over the Cheque
and,
six hundred something little smiles he hopes,
words within,

three especially,

are enough to sway Bob the Editor to smile back,
smile on his way to telling Tina the Agent
that

Pining for Somebody

needs
published by

on the title page,
somewhere under

Pined For.
The little smiles aren't really smiles, though,
they're dollars
—dollars he doesn't have,
dollars for dreams,
so he smiles *really* hard,

because though the
everyone *else*
who's read his manuscript loves it,

loves

like the word;
everyone else
's opinion doesn't matter
half as much
as Bob the Editor's.

The room (—because he doesn't step back to look at these kinds of things
enough—)
is at least seventeen shades *colder*
than a library conference room should be
—he knows because he's been coming to rooms just like this,
for what seems like seventeen months,
seventeen months of Bob's seminars on better writing,
and
the conference rooms are always warmer.

It could be a sign,
the blue-something
where beige paint should be,
the lack of comforting amenities,
not even a cheesy over-used *Starry Night* on the wall opposite

—it could be nothing,

probably nothing,

nothing

but the nerves,

making a library conference room seem more like a *prison*,

a prison

or

a courtroom,

a courtroom with Bob the Editor ruling

on what will be,

decidedly,

the rest of his life.

The rest of his life,

but Bob the Editor smiles back,

and

his smile says the ruling won't come down until after

he reads

You

three hundred pages away.

Red (and the phone call)

So the phone rings, and it's Tuesday, Tuesday *two* since the Tuesday they took blood, so the phone rings, and it's that *this-is-either-gonna-be-really-good-news-or-really-bad-news* ring.

Technically, it's supposed to be a *your-results-are-in-let's-make-an-appointment* call, but he made a deal with the nurse—the one who told him he had all the symptoms—and Tuesday two is long enough, so it's a good news/bad news call, medical malpractice be damned.

He thinks about the dirty pretty girls when he reaches for the receiver, the way he left condoms for the movies when he heard them say

I'm clean,

took their word for it, every time.

He's kinda sorta sure it's not the *HIV*, the way he's put eight pounds on in two Tuesdays, running as far away from one forty-five as chemically possible. Now the nurse—the one, he's sure, is about to tell him he's gonna live on the other end of the phone—also told him that working out wasn't an option, but, reaching for the news hanging from the cord on the kitchen wall, he's glad there's freshly injected testosterone in his fingertips.

Besides,

Ring

if—and this isn't really an option—

Ring

if he's gonna die, all *Tom Hanks in Philly,*

Ring

then he's gonna die ripped and pretty, and pretty ripped.

Ring

Hello?

Mr. _____ ?

Yeah,

I'm sorry,

He's picking up the receiver, fighting the tangle in the cord with testosterone induced rage, and the picture he's picturing when he pictures the conversation isn't pretty, because self-assurance and eight plus aside, there's still the / *bad news* option, no matter how *pretty* he's spent Tuesdays Two becoming.

So in the time it takes for the tangle, to the receiver whispering static hum soundtrack for what will be, *since cancer*, the most important call *ever*-ever, he thinks, briefly and for a moment, (because that's all he has,) about things and faces, as hard as it is, other than his.

His mother.

Mom, I have HIV.

His mother crying.

His father.

Daddy—

--for the first time since T-Ball—

--I love you, but—

Because really, they made him to be stronger than some virus that eats him from the inside-out. Stronger, and maybe not, because the phone is almost to his ear.

His sister.

I'm going to die soon.

Sunny days chasing her through some field some spring, when rat tails were *cool*, and her smile was as white as *now*, just a few teeth shy.

That old girlfriend, the one who got away, the one that still makes his tummy—

Shit, there were none.

And the phone, mercifully and not, whispers static hum soundtrack.

Hello?

His voice does not have the strength of his fingertips.

Hello, Mr._____?

The voice over the soundtrack does not sound happy. Is she unhappy because she's about to tell him, essentially, that his life is over, that his days as an emerging cocksman and promising author end at *promising*, that the hollow look in his left profile this morning was more than piss-poor lighting in his bathroom mirror, that that night that August in the hot tub really did act as an incubator for all the shit in the fluids they spent all that night in August exchanging, that—

It's nurse Sonya, from—

He knows who the fuck she is, and where the fuck she's calling from and why the fuck she's calling, so—

--your test results have come in.

And she's got *that* tone, like sorry is about *I'm* and *very* away, like he's about ten seconds from denial, a day from anger, some Thursday shy of bargaining, a month away from depression, maybe two from acceptance, unless of course the testosterone gives him the strength/weakness to wrap the phone cord around his neck, making the only *sure* time the time it takes for her to get that third word—the '*s*' one—in.

He feels sick.

I'm happy to tell you

He feels great.

He hopes it's the testosterone making his fingers shake as he fights the tangle, hangs up the phone before she gets to

test results negative.

It should be a moment, one like when the phone came the other way, filled with faces, and faces are there, but they're connected to the breasts of the girls he's picking up the phone to call.

It should be one of those *corners* he knows everyone wants him to turn, like he turned left in the bathroom mirror, his profile hollow from piss-poor lighting, and not HIV.

Red (and back to getting better)

As options go, the cherry-faced motherfucker sitting across from him, Dr. Sour, was decidedly *last*.

Dr. <u>Sour</u>, and really, because Dr. Sour is one of those names so ridiculous even a writer couldn't come up with it, Dr. *DuWayne Cavanaugh* or Dr. *Michael Weatherbottom*, or Dr. *Rush Fantastico* infinitely better, and less outrageous, and, astonishingly, less real, than the last man assigned to fix him, Dr. Terry, like *Berry* , like *very*, Sour.

Really—it's posted on at least three suspect-looking medical certificates hanging on the walls here in Dr. Terry, (as in,) Sour's office, the crown jewel of the dirty, curry-stenched strip-mall he's resigned and resorted to, six months of sickness and a hundred fucking forty-five pounds, two months and at least sixteen pounds from where he would *should* be.

See, Sour is a herbalist, oné of those '*medical-companies-bad-nature-is-the-answer-let-me-cook-you-a-cure-in-my-medicine-hat* peace-piping hippies, the kind new-age fascists and neo-soul half-gypsies like, god bless, his half-gypsy mom believe at least whole-heartedly in; after a half-life filled with artists and psychics, he's exposed and ready, if not sold, to 'resources' like Sour, hence the trip today, and meeting Mrs. Sour the receptionist and Candi *not-really-but-might-as-well-be* Sour the daughter slash *something*, and, finally, sitting in the chair, meeting the man.

The man so sweet he's _____ , with his *half-hippie limp-wristed hug-it-out-'cuz-love, baby-is-all-we-have* handshake, hand and his *can relate to you being a little pussy*, shoulders jutting alarmingly and everywhere from his two sizes too small *yes-it's-compensating* faux white faux medical jacket, Sour emblazoned as boldly as the lifestyle choices he questioned up to and even after meeting 'Mrs.,' the receptionist.

He's on guard, and justifiably, because Dr. Sour is the kind who isn't going to agree with his cure-by-injectable horse, *race* horse, medication, and the whirring gizmo he's rambling about hooking him up to right now looks like the kind that can detect a testosterone rate at least and *ideally* three times over serviceable human limit.

Still, he's been on the toilet times comma *many* today, and it's only two o'clock, blood and everything else running away just a little slower, but with equal deliberation as the girls who *used* to call and the friends who *used* to stop by and the will to get over a month and another of watching, in motion slower than the blood, himself deteriorate in front of his favorite mirror.

Medical science—not the veterinary kind he supplements in half-vain—still can't tell him what's wrong, just that it's not cancer and it's not the HIV, and it's not anything, obviously, they can fucking find, so, on guard *or*, Dr. Sour and his magical mystery machine and his herbs are the answer, at least, (and, why not,) two o'clock today.

Besides, as he instructs him to hold the copper conductor in one hand, the magical mystery machine humming to life somewhere in the cornucopia of wires and laptops—*high-tech hippies, who knew*—behind, revealing that *yes*, he takes steroids can't be near as embarrassing as revealing that *yes*, he's prone to shitting himself.

It's called the *endographic dichometer*—not really, the writer in him naming the gizmo Sour names before poking him in the wrist with a kind of dull pointed aluminum pen connected to a shiny red wire connected to something connected to a laptop; but he doesn't hear, or doesn't care, names not as important as dull pointed aluminum pens poking him at various pressure points on his wrist.

He's told he can watch, a mockup of his hand and all the nerve centers burning bright on a computer screen beside him, the gizmo checking his kidney function and his metabolism and his small intestine and his iron level in percentages, and, amazingly, all through his hand, results displayed in little red graphs like the one Dr. Sour is urging him to check out right now, but he's gone, daydreaming about being better and being bigger, and the things that come with both, things in thongs and thongs on beaches, walking on beaches he *belongs* on.

He's regulating the levels, as he says, making him whole by placing vials of important-sounding herbs on the endographic dichometer, the ·right concoction leveling him off, trial and error and tiny vials, vials that will go into the *no-doubt real-as-Sour's-name* expensive herbal soup he'll spend next *forever* drinking, drinking and hopefully healing so that beach time is north of one hundred forty-five, ideally south of *ninety*, especially on the volleyball courts.

How a vial of liquid *something* can be read through a machine and be read through a dull ball-point pen with a shiny bright red wire and read through his kidneys read through a pressure point on his index finger, now, he'll never know, never truly believe in, or never truly *care to*, as long as Sour's got the sweets, the sweets and the touch to make him blessedly regular once more.

So it's acupuncture, sort of, for an hour--every pressure-able pressure point on both hands (--and, strangely, both feet--) prodded and poked and tested, the end result an hour and *four-hundred something* on three vials of diced up liquid remedy he's to drop in his water, ten to fifteen per three times a day, 'till the vials are gone and the four hundred (hopefully) doesn't hurt, and the pounds, with the aid of veterinary science, racing back as fast as he races from the curry-stained strip-mall, a smile at 'Mrs.', maybe, even *less* now, the way Sour was into rubbing his feet, on the way out the door, feeling strangely optimistic, knowing he's tried everything but the rain-dance to make the misery go the way of his paycheck, as in *four hundred-something shy*, and now, gone.

Blue (and tired)

Maybe he's a little down
and
maybe it's Sunday,
but as of right now,
Sunday,
he's just about done with women.

Not like *that*,
and
though there's nothing,
like the dated sitcom on his TV says in front of him,

wrong with it,

he's done in the way he's done
until one throws it at him,
so done worrying about
and
chasing
and
analyzing
the actions of

easily

the most illogical creatures on earth.

So today,

Sunday,

he's done writing about the Girl on TV,

the girl he started writing about six years to the day

she left

and

two more to the day she smiled,

started fucking with his head,

the girl one book

and

four years

 can't touch;

two years of steady smiles,

two years of sporadic smiles,

since the smile

she smiled

the *last* time,

before jumping his fence

to get away from the relationship

she helped ruin,

the storm

and

the season.

Summer.

The last

and

latest

of the girls worth books

and

no sleep,

writing to figure out

how a girl with no right to

can call

and

come over

and

not be over

and

be

so

over him,

leaving him alone

and

not

until

Laura,

the source of the *down*, now,

and

the Sunday,

because it's Sunday

and

it's supposed to be date number four

and

it's *not*

because his phone isn't ringing

and

the clock on his wall is laughing,

and

it can shut the fuck up,

because today,

Sunday,

he's done worrying about why it's not ringing,

and

so,

sweetly

and

not,

for now,

Laura is out of luck.

Red (and the overwhelming joy of having some skank tattoo his writing on her body)

She says it hurts, above the hum of the needle, and he doesn't care.

He met this girl—this *model*—two times ago, and now, two times later, she's having his words tattooed into the skin on the back of her neck, and it's not his name, but after only two times, and to a writer, it's at least the *next* best thing, and maybe *better.*

No, she hasn't read word one, but she liked the way he could turn a phrase, so when she told him family was important, and asked *where,* *ever beholden, defying....*

and the back of her neck, and not even hours later, was his answer. And now she's hunched in the chair and slightly sweating, and, even if he's never with her after tonight, he's always, or '*ever,*' with her, forever.

Which is something the fuck she told him about last time, the loser she's 'seeing' who had the nerve to tell her he's a writer, too, is going to have to deal with for the rest of his life, also.

Yeah, she's 'seeing' some other guy, but she's *here*, seeing him seeing her getting his words on the back of her neck, here in the sleaziest tattoo parlor in his city.

And she's at least the cleanest thing in the place, hunched over with the ink running between wipes from Buzz, (like the noise!) the tattoo-of-a-machine-gun-on-the-side-of-his-head tattoo artist, ink running to pool on the brim of her bright white tank top, *Abercrombie and* on hers, and it would match Buzz's, save for the beer and *Doritos* stains and the *Hate* stitched on his.

Even her panties are pink, pink like her fingernails and her sandals and the back of her neck, and he's noticing and noticing that Buzz is noticing, too; probably because she's the sweetest, most innocent thing to come in here, the shop with the *Manson*, (and not *Marilyn*,) poster in the window, and the back door with the coke dealer he scored the gram from, the gram she said she's never, and would never, snort, like the tattoo she would never get two hours ago, and it's the sexiest thing about her, *panties aside*, like *they will be.*

She likes the wild she sees in him, the wild the other guy must *not* have, and she likes it enough to maybe throw her 'no-tattoos' modeling career away; and the look on the mother she lives with face, when he drops her off at home and her tanned long tanned model legs are shaking and she's sniffing and her strawberry blonde straw-straight-photo-shoot-on-Tuesday hair has the smell of his *fuck* in it will be worth the forty he threw in so her allowance money could cover the ink now almost done covering the back of her neck.

Yeah, sitting there in the chair, peeking at him between buzzes of Buzz's needle, she's as wholesome as Dorothy, and he's her wicked little witch, and those pink sandals aren't red, but after the blow she's two hours from doing and two hours from *giving*, she'll be clicking them together as fast as she can.

Blue (and date number four)

It should be a night with a date

and

a number,

and

the number *would* be four,

one

after the magic of three,

and

it is a night,

but

a night *without*,

because he blew it,

as he does,

the night before.

Laura hadn't called after she kissed,

and

the number of the *whys*

and

<u>day</u>s ending in

was growing,

like his like for her,

so by Satur___, one week from *Spaulding*

and

figuring seven was long enough, yesterday,

he decided that instead of calling,

like he hadn't either,

showing up at her work with his pretend

and

almost-friends, on *guys* night, would be a good idea.

Now,

Sunday,

sighing

and

reflecting on,

he knows it *wasn't.*

Maybe it's the way the guys on guys night heaved

and

sighed when it turned out she was working the shift he said

she said

she *wasn't,*

knowing full well she *was*

and

not being a good enough liar when they called him on it,

two drinks deep

and

deeply settled

on the patio of the pub she pretends to work hard at

when the only work anybody with that body should be working at or on

is some runway,

miles from here

and

him

like *now*, Sunday

and

reflecting on,

she is

and

will be.

Still, she tapped him on the shoulder

and

the

Hey

she pushed through the pout

and

purse of her lips

was shy of the hug

and

HEY

he was expecting,

and,

after a week of kissing, but not calling,

the way she walked her little model walk on the way somewhere *else*

was more than enough,

two drinks deep,

for him to indulge the doubt dancing on the tip of his tongue

before drowning it in alcohol nowhere near strong enough

when she disappears into the pub

and

he swears there's a tattoo on the back of her neck

where there wasn't one before.

She's working,

and

he was,

he tells himself he told himself then,

and,

reflecting the way he is,

it's not like she wasn't busy

or

even knew he was coming,

and,

after not calling the way he-she-they did, week on,

maybe she was *too*

and

already;

really model's

—*for-real, for-real*—

in waitressing

and

horn-rimmed glasses like she *was*

is

and

are

in high demand,

and

any number of the well-groomed university

(or at least *esque*)

boys could have wooed her in the time between,

taking her attention

and

time away

and

from him with a smile

or

a drink

or

a dinner,

days worth of between the last he had with her.

And

it hurts *now*,

the way it started *then*,

before

and

a little the closing of the pub door left the trace of her

and

whatever was attached to her neck,

knowing by the time

and

maybe before

the big oak with the brass handle rested against it's partner,

completing the *Wink's Pub* portion

that had been just *Pub* seconds before;

the name of the bar etched in the glass of the door she ran from should read

Lose Again, like he does

and

maybe did, the moment

Hey

stayed at a tap on the shoulder.

He could feel the hurt,

knowing Sunday would end up like it *has*,

sitting there on the patio of the pub she pretends to work at,

pretending to be interested in anything

his pretend

and

almost friends had to say

and

wishing the waitress taking drinks was the waitress he waited all week to sit there waiting for.

He hadn't blown it yet,

in retrospect,

but he was about to,

and,

the events playing over

and

over

and

he knows *now* he'd give anything to record over

in the disaster movie that is his love life

playing over

and

over

and,

always

and

only, there in his mind, the mind that made up,

sitting on the patio the night before,

the idea that making her jealous would be anything *but* a bad idea

when he spotted an ex-girlfriend spotting him from across the patio,

and

started smiling

and

coming his way

and

bringing her chair with her,

girl number two

and

again,

and

on *guy's* night.

Now,

and

he shudders a little, amazed at how two drinks

and

a little hurt pride can make a really, really bad idea sound anything but.

So he sat there, blowing it

and

not knowing it,

skipping scanning his pretend

and

almost friends' faces

and

their very real *lets-get-the-fuck-out-of-here* reactions

trying to scan a look of *another-girl-I'm-jealous-why-don't-you-get-the-fuck-out-of-here*

reaction on Laura's crushingly indifferent reaction less face.

So he sat, stubbornly,

and

played with his ex-girlfriend,

and

her name is Kristy

(and

unfortunately it doesn't matter,)

and

her emotions, telling her

You didn't call me

and

I really liked you

and

disagreeing when she answered, faster

and

with more breath

and

breast than she should

I called you

and

I really liked you

and

You really didn't like me

and

he *didn't*,

but she was sweet,

and

he was hung up on somebody decidedly *else*,

so when time passed

and

Laura didn't look

and

Kristy's boyfriend of a year *did*

and

started approaching the table, too

and

drunk

and

with too many drunk friends, he should have taken the *loss*

and

left the table, having blown it,

but not really

and

yet.

Red (and a Friday)

Friday, and his big sister calls and he doesn't answer, doesn't answer because Psychic Beth just finished telling some-skank she's his *soul mate*.

Blue (and blowing it, for-real-for-real; so the third of three blown dates)

It *should* be a night with a date

and

a number;

instead it's the *first* since *last* night,

the night he failed to make her jealous

and

stay,

like she *won't* now,

leaving the restaurant he invited her to with a look over her shoulder.

The conversation *before*,

before her turning the way she *is* to curse him

before the door she reaches for,

was all about *last* night,

and

the fight he *almost-kinda* caused

and

unnecessarily;

making some poor girl's poor boyfriend believe he wanted *anything* to do with

her

and

not the model,

for-real-for-real

really leaving him

and

the dinner he ordered

and

the dinner she ordered

but didn't touch.

And

she's reaching

and

turning fresh tattoo,

the *same* tattoo she looked at him like he was *wrong* to ask

who-the-hell-she-got-it-with

and

muttering something under her breath,

the latest in a <u>line</u> of her drawing the ____ because of his *jealousy*

and

his unwarranted *possessiveness,*

and,

if he hears her right, his

fucking insanity.

Blue (in da club)

He's not good in the clubs.

The dance thing was never his,

knowing where the left foot goes when his hips pop south,

staring dumb ahead,

pretending the convulsions in his neck anything close to the beat,

the beat he knows he doesn't have near enough *color* to see.

Tonight,

Sunday,

is always *never* a club night,

the twelve on the club clock *six* too close to Monday

and

Monday morning;

but his friends called,

his ten digits pressed the way they always never are on Sunday,

so now,

Sun night,

he tells himself to be thankful for the call at all,

shakes his ass to the poetry about shaking ass

and

selling rock

sold to him from the speakers.

He knows he should be home,

writing

or

sleeping,

or

sleeping so writing

(—the way he hasn't, either, in days,

days to nights he spends here,

pretending,

like all the other pretenders,

he knows how to shake his ass—)

can come, but its coming more like that girl across the bar,

so not at all.

He doesn't know how to shake his ass,

so he stops,

decides to be the guy posted up on the wall,

lost in a sea of kinda friends,

guys posted on walls, pretending,

all of them,

that they're there for anything other than the asses that shake.

The girls look *good* tonight,

almost good enough to forget seasons

and

girls on TV

and

writing about *either*,

failures named

Keri Lynn

and

Sabrina

and

Laura,

necessities as necessary as sleep.

…

So he's still here,

and

he's clubbing,

and

it's later

and

he's wondering how they can do it,

shaking ass like it's not *one-thirty something* Sunday night-Monday morning.

Watching them,

ass decidedly *still*,

he wonders if the drinks they drink are to *numb* them,

a way to slow the sun from coming up on a Monday their dreams don't come

true.

There has to be a logic for the sweet poison,

the things it will do to them when they wake,

and

they're on the wrong side of the TV,

the stars they were before they rested their heads

faded

like the denim on the designer jeans

whoever they stumbled home with left on their floor.

Then again,

maybe they're right,

and

he's the one confused—

looking out at the sea of them,

the line at the bar to his left,

the numbers would name *him* fool,

like maybe they've let go of their dreams,

left him hanging,

not letting go the way he *can't*,

one-thirty something

better for dreaming about being published

and

girls on TV

than shaking his ass.

It's Monday anyway,

black outside the club already thinking about fading to blue,

the kind of blue overhead that makes living *underneath*,

when Monday goes black

and

Bob the Editor doesn't call,

a little less *sad* than it *is* Sunday night,

just some guy posted up on the wall in a club full of people

who will never amount to anything at all.

Red (and in da club)

He's good in clubs, and clubs are good to him.

He reminds himself this, Sunday, is the best night of the week to be here, because the dirty pretty girls—the ones who loved him before *one forty-five pounds*—are the kind who don't work Monday morning, or don't care, at least not *one forty-five* Sunday night.

He hasn't been out since he ran away, *eight* in miles and pounds and counting since the sickness, the sickness that stayed, and stayed unexplained, rumbling his tummy as he heads for the door, content to drown its warnings in *Amaretto*, nature's perfect remedy.

He knows that not knowing is worth drinking to too, because two months on and not knowing was kind of scary, but not as scary as it *could have been*, knowing and HIV. So he takes his medicine, orders another round from the *kinda* dirty pretty, *but-not-dirty though-pretty-enough* waitress, matches her smile as the sour hits, but his smile is not for her—it's for the familiar face he sees in the mirror behind her and the bottles, the bottles like *Amaretto*, the bottle he might as well buy.

It's a face he hasn't seen in half forever, one he loves and has desperately, desperately missed, missed for going on two months, two months of missing that familiar smile reflected back on him from mirrors, mirrors lately beside toilets in the bathrooms he's lived.

Lived, like he might this morning, but not until the sour—(mixing in his stomach with medicine prescribed by a *Doctor* of the same name--) on the tip of his tongue has kissed away reason, the kind of reason that would-should stop him, two weeks from the scariest two weeks of his life, from taking home the qualifying bottle blonde, her and her bottle tan leaking on sheets he they will writhe on *naked*-naked—the kind of latex free naked he would-should know by now to know *better*.

Yeah, he *thinks*…and as the qualifying bottle blonde shows her bottle whites, does something with her lips, when sober, would be intended as a smile, (and just before the sour races past the tip, on it's way to fight the uncertainty in his tummy—) he thinks…and doesn't.

…

He's on her, and he's counting it like the weights; *one*, and up, *two*, and up, *three*, and up, while he's in her and out her and in her, he's thinking about the weights too, how the stomping he's giving her at one fifty-three and climbing (!) would really be that much better at one sixty and something.

Maybe *five*, and her breasts are great, bouncing away there underneath, but another D-Bol cycle and some suffering could be really great, great for his vascularity, which, looking past the stupid

I-can't-fucking-take-this-fucking

look on her face, could be a lot greater in the forearms connected to the hands he holds hers down with.

Blue (and a party)

So he's at this party,
and
it's not the club,
but it might as well be,
the way he's alone in a sea of people,
people who pretend real, real hard to be friends.

The guy to his left,
Beans,
pretends almost hardest,
and
he's laughing,
laughing at the joke in the ether,
the unfunny one he took a sip of his beer to avoid having to laugh at.

He sips deep,
has to,
the way the laughter is permeating the cramped apartment atmosphere,
tries not to snort up his drink when Beans punches him mock-lovingly on his
writing arm.

Beans is one of those South Asian hip-hop heads,
the kind two shades too light to pass for the shade
he *wants* to pass for,
the kind whose gospel comes from the words between the notes
that blast from speakers like the one behind them now,

Jeezy preaching something about never picking up the phone when friends
call,

Beans taking it in,

(--subliminally

or—)

and

he's the one paying for it when he picks up the phone.

He didn't want to be here,

like he *doesn't* want to be here,

but Beans called the way he only does when there's alcohol

or

girls involved,

and,

with *Jeezy* blaring in the background,

convinced him to come here,

Friday,

the way things (with not so much the alcohol,)

but the girls

—only always get him to.

It's as much a mistake *now*,

hours on,

as it was when he agreed to come,

and

not only because the ratio

of girls to

*horny-looking-to-score-but-won't-and-wouldn't-really-want-to-anyway-the-way-the-best-
looking-of-them-is-miles-from-good-looking*

guys

is killing the atmosphere,

the way Beans is killing the beer.

He knows like he knew, really, that Friday was better suited

for a dark table at some coffee shop on some corner,

writing furiously while making pretty eyes at intelligent artist-types,

all curly hair and mocha-latte triple-chinos—

the kind that look like they have something to say

when their thinner lips part,

miles away from the bottle yellow iron-straightened collagen-lipped

interchangeable whores,

their lips only parting in admiration of the lines they snort,

lines like Beans, in between beers.

He doesn't fuck with it,

no matter what it would do for his creativity,

and

tonight isn't about writing anyway,

unfortunately

(and

again,)

it's about people like Beans

and

Barbie,

and

trying to score, the highlight

and

habit of his social existence,

going home with some phone number so he can never call,

and

wonder why they never do either.

So he's at this party,

and

he's sitting,

and

he's not snorting

or

scoring,

and

it's not the club,

but it might as well be,

the way he's alone in a sea of people,

people who pretend real, real hard to be friends,

between those who will never, ever be,

or

would be anyway.

Red (and a first date)

He can't remember her name.

Honestly, the immigrant-hot, the way immigrants only always are, black haired *Pussycat Doll* (—not for real, but oughta/could be—) sitting across the table has a name that starts with 's,' ends with insignificant.

Watching her, watching him watching her, he's at least reasonably sure he won't have to say it again *anyway*, so he spends the majority of her touching story about her parent's struggles when they came here wondering what was in the water *there* that gave her that *ass*, the ass parked in the seat across from him on *this*, their romantic first date.

He brought her here, to the cheapest restaurant in the most expensive part of town because the patio is famous, and comfortable, for two things; the *Pussycat Doll*-ness of all the waitresses, and the two exits should the date go anywhere but his bedroom.

She looks good enough to eat, at least a lot better than the five dollar steak he ordered, so he overlooks her annoyances; the way she prods him for family history he doesn't have the heart to make up, the piss-poor makeup application immigrants always seem to sometimes do, the thing with not knowing her name.

She laughs at his jokes, and her jiggly bits jiggle the way that makes missing *LOST* for this somehow okay, so he offers her drinks at his place, and she accepts in that cute little accent immigrants always have, so tonight it's out the front door, a walk around the block at sunset before putting that ass in his car, parked conveniently in the no parking zone directly out the *back* door.

He knows her name will show up on his answering machine when she calls tomorrow to thank him for tonight, the best of her little immigrant life, begs him for the thrills he spent the next seven hours, (with one out for *LOST*--because if he leaves now, they can catch it--) sweating her makeup off in the sheets at his place.

Blue (and figuring it out)

The first time he saw her,

a little after she said

Hello

sweetly

the way she softly spoke

only when she was always shy,

he pulled the sun from the sky for her,

but it wouldn't sparkle enough

to match half the sparkle in her worst eye,

so he put it back in the sky, softly, only, said

Hello

back.

For every day with a number

and

a name after,

he followed her smile when she smiled at him,

spent every night with a number

and

a name

looking for her when she took her smile,

walked away.

Numbers

and

names

and

words

and

pages he spent since

trying to rid himself of it,

it

and

the rest of her,

her

and

the way she haunted him,

haunted him like she haunts him now,

as he writes, closing the book

—the latest in books worth of words

and

pages,

wondering if his ability as a writer will ever allow him

to write about anything with any passion

other than his inspiration for writing at all.

He breathes,

the way he's breathed since,

but it's lacking,

the way breaths since have,

and

he heads for the kitchen,

with it's clock on the wall already winding up,

a little concerned that the chapter he started

—the chapter about some other guy,

and

some other girl

ended up,

the way they always do,

less about some other guy,

really

none

about some other girl.

He thinks about Summer,

his favorite season,

as he reaches for the bread,

content to eat because he supposes he's supposed to,

the way he could tell her he's a writer

(—read words, too-)

words about pulling suns from skies

and

having to return them when their brilliance

can't match the brilliance in her worst eye,

not even the best sun on the best day in the season like her name, and

she would just shrug it off,

like the words,

from his lips,

lost the brilliance somewhere in his translation.

Maybe,

(the peanut butter spreading the way it spreads everyday,

reminding him it's far from the steak he could count on

sunny days in summer

when Summer made his home more *than*, cooked twice as often.)

she would shrug it off

because of the day she discovered the girl he pulled suns for

in the backyard,

and

more than

went back to being just his,

home;

words since, to her,

losing their flavor the way only the memory of another girl can make them,

his words withering,

steak to peanut butter.

So he's back on his couch,

peanut butter stirring slowly like the seconds on the clock that laughs at him,

alone

and

alone in front of a closed book,

a book that may as well stay closed,

the way the pages underneath don't have the words

to make the seconds stop laughing at him,

alone on his couch.

And

he knows why he *writes*,

strives to take the 's' off and add 'r,'

writer

the infinitely more significant consonant to make him like *them*,

all writers not great men,

left

and

leaving both grandeur

and

greatness to the characters they so desperately wish they had the courage to

really be.

Red (and the beginning of a bad, bad habit)

He's at this party and he's doing coke.

Off the top of the bathroom stall toilet paper dispenser with a rolled up twenty, and it's fucking brilliant, because he's a rockstar and he's in a tuxedo and the party, technically, is his buddy's wedding, (and his buddy would be disappointed, but he's partying down the hotel hall at the reception,) and he's here, doing rails with the best man.

Which, he supposes, would disappoint his buddy too, half the groom's side of the wedding party in the stall going

Sniff

while third uncles and grandparents give the stall, (the stall with the coke,) condescending looks in between washing and drying hands, but fuck, he's high, and there's girls here, girls in the kinds of dresses that scream

Do a line off my tits!

when they scream at him, which is often, and, he guesses, will be more often when he leaves the stall, the stall with the coke.

And the best man looks at him with his

We-should-be-doing-this-with-a-hundred-dollar-bill, we-look-so-good

look, and he fires up his

And-cutting-it-with-a-Platinum-Visa

look, wondering if they said that exchange, or just thought it and expressed it through the looks, and then he draws again, and he can't remember, and doesn't care.

It tastes like candy, there in the back of his throat and his brain, and it lingers, tasting like candy when he leaves the stall right behind the best man and gives third uncles and grandparents dirty looks at the sink and does up his unzipped fly for dramatic effect, (*just!*) and it still tastes like candy, to give the old fuckers something to think about.

The best man smiles, and it tastes like candy, and they pass the hand washing station and the third uncles and the grandparents, and they step back into the reception at the reception hall and the brunette with the peach (--or pink, *but definitely in the fuscia family--*) dress smiles, and it tastes like candy, and it makes her blonde, and he smiles, because she looks like she tastes like candy too.

He's halfway through asking her name and she's halfway through smiling and answering at the same time and he's halfway through not caring when some aunt from some side sits beside him and tells him

You look like the guy in that movie

and normally, that would be just the kind of thing he would love to hear and would earn even the fattest aunt, (and this one is,) his all and undivided attention, but he's high and something is to the left, to the left (like *Beyonce!*) and waiting for him to hit on her.

So he smiles and shrugs it off, but she's persistent, and asks something like

Fuck me with a Pez dispenser

or

How do you know the groom?

and he can't tell, because <u>he's high</u>, and he knows he doesn't want to deal with this pig, but is going to have to, even if *Irreplaceable* in the peach (-or pink *but definitely in the fuscia family)* has to be replaced.

So he's answering, and she's amused and he's amused, wondering if she'll come back with *Pitt* or *McConaughey* or *Beckham*, and she doesn't, and it's the ugly guy from *Memento*, and he's disgusted enough to leave the table and the some aunt and something, searching for the comforts of the best man and the bathroom stall.

. . .

Sniff

and it tastes like candy and he's back at it, back past third uncles and grandparents and past, way past tables with fat aunts and *Beyonce*, and he's dancing, suddenly, with some other girl, and *Beyonce* looks pissed and he doesn't care, and all he can think about is candy, and how much better the writing would be if he could write like and on this.

He's thinking about going home and writing and or going home and fucking this slut he's suddenly still dancing with, and she looks suddenly and surprisingly good, and then the *bride* says

Thanks for the dance

and walks back to her husband, his buddy, and he's losing chapters in his mind and not minding, on his way back to the best man and the bathroom stall.

Act 2

The Book of Doing Better
(By Doing Worse, First)

August

Red (and frustrated)

Fuck.

Fuck fuck fuck fuck fuck fuck fuck fuck fuck fuck fuck fuck fuck fuck fuck fuck fuck fuck fuck Fuck fuck fuck fuck fuck fuck fuck fuck fuck fuck fuck fuck fuck fuck fuck fuck fuck fuck Fuck fuck fuck fuck fuck fuck fuck fuck fuck fuck fuck fuck fuck fuck fuck fuck fuck fuck Fuck fuck fuck fuck fuck fuck fuck fuck fuck fuck fuck fuck fuck fuck fuck fuck fuck fuck fuck fuck fuck fuck fuck fuck fuck Fuck fuck fuck fuck fuck fuck fuck fuck fuck fuck fuck fuck fuck fuck fuck fuck fuck fuck fuck fuck fuck fuck fuck Fuck fuck fuck fuck fuck fuck fuck fuck fuck fuck fuck fuck fuck Fuck fuck fuck fuck fuck fuck fuck fuck fuck fuck fuck fuck fuck fuck fuck fuck fuck fuck fuck fuck fuck Fuck fuck fuck fuck fuck fuck fuck fuck fuck fuck fuck fuck fuck fuck fuck fuck fuck fuck fuck fuck fuck fuck fuck fuck fuck fuck fuck fuck Fuck fuck fuck fuck fuck fuck fuck fuck fuck fuck fuck fuck fuck fuck fuck fuck fuck fuck fuck fuck fuck Fuck fuck fuck fuck fuck fuck fuck fuck fuck fuck fuck fuck fuck fuck fuck fuck fuck Fuck fuck fuck fuck fuck fuck fuck fuck fuck fuck fuck fuck fuck fuck fuck fuck fuck fuck fuck Fuck fuck fuck fuck fuck fuck fuck fuck fuck fuck fuck fuck fuck fuck fuck fuck fuck fuck fuck fuck fuck fuck fuck Fuck fuck fuck fuck fuck fuck fuck fuck fuck fuck fuck fuck fuck fuck fuck fuck fuck fuck fuck fuck fuck Fuck fuck fuck fuck fuck fuck fuck fuck fuck fuck fuck fuck fuck fuck fuck fuck fuck fuck fuck fuck fuck fuck fuck fuck fuck fuck fuck Fuck fuck fuck fuck fuck fuck fuck fuck fuck fuck fuck fuck fuck fuck fuck fuck fuck fuck fuck fuck fuck fuck fuck Fuck fuck fuck fuck fuck fuck fuck fuck fuck fuck fuck fuck fuck fuck

I'm not famous.

Blue (and the end of summer, figuratively and maybe literally)

Summer, *season,*

is leaving him far faster than it should.

August *something,*

something with a *two* in front

the way two days ago was two, (*number,*) in front of May, (*month,*) blinked

and

gone,

and

he blinks, now,

knowing blinking

and

again

could turn August to September,

the way the days run the direction of the girls in his life;

and

he's not thinking about them tonight,

outside in August,

but the way the wind stings,

the feeling is about the *same.*

And

it's that longing, maybe,

that makes the wind cold

and

the sunset some duller than it should;

longing, maybe,

that makes him pull his bathrobe tighter,

sink further into the patio chair there/here

on the patio at his parents place.

His eyes fall

to the open

and

empty page right in front

and

miles away

of-from

him,

and

he wants to be able to express the longing, maybe,

in his head on it,

but his hand is too tired to travel the miles it would take

to reach the page,

so they rise, his eyes,

to settle on the sunset that seems to be settling

when it sets for him alone,

alone

because his parents are inside,

probably disappointed that he's *not*,

and

looking for jobs on the computer,

to them his eyes better suited for search engines than settling sunsets.

Dreaming was easier *before*,

as the sun hides behind a September-looking cloud,

before the sun hid from him

and

Bob the Editor took his manuscript

and

the results of his dreaming, (so his *dream*,)

with him

and

away

and

gone;

making dreaming,

and

working on his *second* manuscript,

the one miles away right in front of him

more miles away,

wondering what his editor is wondering

reading the words he's spent the past *forever*

pouring all

and

every inch of his soul into.

He's looking at the cover of the copy he kept for *himself*,

on top of

and

in front of the book he-writes-in-*when-he-writes*,

now,

and

then at the sunset somewhere behind September's cloud,

and

then at the cover again;

and

his fingers are *cold*, outside on the patio in August,

and

he's tracing the *Pining for*,

(in the prettiest font he could find)

lovingly

and

lovingly remembering how he felt when he typed it

for the last time,

lovingly remembering how it felt to finish *Pined For*, his first novel.

As he flips the first page

there on the patio at his parent's place,

he wonders if he has the strength to go back

and

revise it, should Bob the Editor deem it *unworthy*,

knowing he only has summer,

season,

before the deadline on his dream leaves him like they do too

in the season *after*,

far faster than it/they should.

Blue (and interrupted)

--*and then*—

The phone rings,

_____ his train of thought goes the way of Summer;

(gone,)

leaving him a half paragraph from a finished chapter

and

again;

because really, finished chapters are for authors

and

he's *not*,

and

not even a chapter closer when he ignores the writing he was writing

and

the phone call that made him—ignores both on his way somewhere decidedly

else

and

somewhere decidedly *alone*.

Red (and interrupted)

The phone rings and it's his big sister and *again*, and it's the fourth time this week and he entertains picking up the phone long enough to call her *Bitch*

under his breath and then hang up and keep doing whatever the fuck he was doing before she called; but it's less work than *not* picking up and doing whatever the fuck he was doing before she called, which is exactly what he does.

Blue (and watching the Girl on TV, and watching her *shoes*, and waiting)

She left her shoes by the door.

She didn't have a choice, really, Summer flooding the hallway by the door,
and
her shoes;

her jumping his patio fence,
running other than metaphorically
and
yet *still*,

away

 never bothering to call
or
return them,
and,
watching her on TV,
he's wondering why he never bothered to return *them*, either.

They're pretty,
her shoes

and

so was *she*,
so it's no surprise, watching *them*

and

then *her*

and

then *them*,

he's torturing himself the way he does Thursdays at seven-thirty,

when she's on TV,

and

her shoes are in the hall

and

by the door

and

he's remembering the Thursday he opened it

and

she bent over to take them off.

Lately he's been wondering if it was worth it,

the one and three-quarters beer they finished trying to finish catching up,

the *three years* without Summer his curiosity

and

longing

and

foolishness cost;

finishing never finished with seasons,

blowing through doors

and

chasing girls out of his life

and

onto TV,

leaving him

(and

two-quarters beer)

alone on Thursday, foreshadowing for Thursday,

tonight,

and

alone again.

Eight o' clock is cruel,

because she's run away again,

and

he can't help but feel that maybe she was never there at all,

and

he can remember Thursdays when Summer *was*,

and

he's missing her at least *half* as bad,

so when his pen finds the familiar grip in his left,

he's left

to trying to resolve his losses on paper that doesn't care.

He tells himself he *needs* this,

and

it keeps him

and

keeps him from calling Laura,

because Bob The Editor will maybe-but-probably-not be done editing his book soon,

and

he'll need new tragedies to fuel his hand

and

the fingers on it, fingers better suited writing words like

Alone

than pressing *seven-oh-nine*

and

the rest of the numbers that could maybe make writing words like

She

and

Left

in the past

and

gone,

like the girl on TV

and

summer outside.

Red (and the latest some-slut)

She says her name is Summer, like the season, and it's the stupidest name he's ever heard, but not the stupidest thing about her, and he's fucked up and she's fucked up.

So he keeps fucking her.

She came up to him tonight—and focusing between the

Fuck me harder (!)

and

Fuck me harder (!)

's is getting harder—but he remembers her coming up to him tonight, this pretty lost pretty little Polish girl, on the midnight of his night on the patio of at least the trendiest club in his city; coming up to him the way he watched her come up to at least ten guys before, ten guys who aren't, coincidentally, making her come now.

And she *is*, and it's more of the same incoherent babbling she babbled on the patio, thinking it's flirting and playing with his hair the way he watched her play with hair, at least ten and ten times before, his.

She's the last thing, really, pausing to aimlessly thumb at her asshole, he wanted to share his gram and his bed with, content to leave her with the next asshole, the next asshole's hair, because hers is blonde, and he'd like to think he's entering the brunette period in what will no doubt be looked back upon one day as the brunette period of his life.

But she babbled incoherently loud and long enough to scare away potentials of any pigment, and so, when the night ended faster than it had any right to, he stuffed her in a cab, and then pulled her out at his door, and then stuffed her in his bathroom and held her hair as she threw up and held her up as he cut and then held her hair as she *snorted*, at least twice enough to make carrying her upstairs and stuffing her in his bed and pulling off her pants *easier* than it should.

And she's stopped babbling long enough to start sobbing somewhere underneath him and he's knows he's fucked the *high* out of her, so when she sobs something about

Making a mistake

she makes the mistake of sniffing the line he sets out for her on the nightstand by his pillow, which she returns to, and, turning to turn away from Summer, there in his bed, he knows that if he wasn't the mistake tonight, someone *else* would have been.

Blue (and why they all don't matter half the way they want to)

One of the girls who didn't last

asked him what he wanted,

and

he didn't have the heart to tell her.

The heart

or

the lips,

or

the ability, really,

to vocalize with limited vowels

and

half-accurate consonants the feeling somewhere *deep*,

the stir

and

the shock

and

the numb

and

the awe of looking into eyes *other than*

and

realizing,

utterly

and

twice as instant,

you've found every damn thing you'll ever want-need

personified

and

pure

and

present,

and,

(maybe unmercifully,)

focusing those eyes

and

the recognition right back.

How do you say,

I want that girl

and

come home to her on some Wednesday to find she's curled her hair,

and

not be able to function for a week because of it.

That girl,

the one with the shape that fits seamlessly into yours when you lay contorted

the way you did

just after the Wednesdays in the world stopped being countable;

the girl that lying beside

or

behind

and

just sort of breathing on

or

watching breathe

makes not being as rich as you planned so hard to be,

(so 50 Cent)

or not as buff as,

(so 50 Cent again,)

or

not as handsome as,

so *Brad*

or

Beckham

or

whoever personifies the general aesthetic you find pleasing to the eye *okay*;

because when you open one of your

eyes—

(and

you can pick which—)

all you ever

or

ever will really want to see will still be there,

breathing slower than she breathed when she breathed the three words

(I love you)

before the light went out

and

another day passed

and

you didn't mind.

How do you push a feeling through lips

when words are always well shy,

knowing lips are better suited

saved for those attached to the rest of that one-whoever you can't wait to
explore

every other kissable—

(and

they all are—)

single part of, days like every

and

at least the forever you tell one another

(and

believe)

you'll be there for, ever

and

ever

and.

And

nights like that, when the eye closes and stays,

knowing you won't wake up president

or

ahead

or

anything else

and

who cares,

because presidents

and

somebody's can have every other thing but the right

(—because they don't—)

to lie beside

or

behind

her

and

listen to her slowest breath,

the breath she saved for the one attached to the three words

beside

and

before the flip of the switch

beside the bed *everysomebody* can't have;

and

fuck the weather when you wake,

because whether you're buying her the red pumps

or

the black pumps

(just because)

has taken over every other *whether-or* when you rest,

content

and

still restless to be in the weather

or

whatever

attached to your next day devoted to her.

Tell the girl *that*,

and

half-lie wishing the other half could make you whole

when you dream about *that* girl,

tell *this* one you'll call on Wednesday,

just the latest in a series *of*

better suited for searching for someone worth sharing shallow breaths with.

Red (and the new sex)

This…

He draws his writing hand back and it shakes a little, ready as the rest of him.

…*this* is the new sex.

It comes down again, resting crudely on his canvas, and he's *creating*, but it's not on paper and its *profound* and honestly maybe more fun.

Because he's *hitting*, (and some scumbag,) and he's crying, (the scumbag,) like he wasn't before he was getting hit; like he wasn't when *he* was hitting and *on* his latest some-slut, hence the hitting and the *creating*, new and exciting shapes and colors for his little scumbag face.

And it's the new sex for the way it *feels*, *dummy*, and *ing* might not be the proper English or even a word and he doesn't care, because right now he's a little *less* writer and a little *more* instrument of blind and monumental and righteous rage.

Really, it requires just as much focus *as*, writing or sex—he can't remember which he was tangenting about, the way creating blood-splatter patterns on cheekbones is distracting him—but the way the nerve he didn't know he had in his fist sends electric sex to his balls is at least a little better than the electric sex his latest some slut's mouth sends to his balls, *and it's open now, too* (—her mouth) but in defiance and not around his member, so his attention stays on *beating*.

He can't see the look on the rest of the face attached to her open mouth, but he can tell by the snarl in her scream that hitting (and *still*) this little scumbag is going to be satisfying and *more* than any other sex he's farther from, with every punch, anyway.

Red (and broken records, and such)

You're fucking insane

and coming from a woman like Psychic Beth, it *should* hurt, hurt but it doesn't because he's a rockstar and at least a *pagan*, probably a *demi*-god, and words like *insane* passed from lips *obviously* matter as much as what anyone else thinks and of him, *so not at all*.

Still, being called crazy by one so *most-definitely*, is worth noting and he does, leaving Psychic Beth's Psychic compound for the last time and mourning the pussy spoon-fed to him, words like 'Soul-mate' in the rearview like the rest of the chapter of his life he closes leaving her and her laneway behind him and *too*.

Red (and the importance of marketing)

He's *trying*, because these days he's told he needs to, but the whole marketing thing is beyond and above him and he's freezing his fucking balls off, and the water, below and around him, is at least half to blame.

The other half, Jen the photographer, the photographer who thought submerging him in some ice cold lake at six in the morning would make a hot photo for the title page of his website, is beyond and above him too, safely and warmly on a stepladder doing that thing photographers pretend people need *skill* to do, barking orders and pressing her pretty finger on the tiny black button before the *click* and before barking more orders.

She's barking *now*, now that the sun is coming up beyond and above him and she needs him to flex his washboard eights, but he can't feel at least half them *either*, and the handwritten pages he sacrificed for the art she said she would create when she lied to him are floating away, meaning the composition she intended--him half-naked (and her fully clothed) and him submerged (and her *not*) and him surrounded by soaked and ruined pages (and her safely and warmly on a ladder beyond and above him,) is going the way of the feeling in his fucking balls, so *gone*.

She's mad at the pages and the sun and at him, and for shaking uncontrollably in August and not, obviously, understanding the fucking cruelty of six in the morning, and she's about to, because she's two

to the left

to the lefts

from drinking the water and the paper, face first in the lake he's boiling freezing in.

And he's closer, slowly, to both her and the lake she's thirsting for, but between click *next* and *too-many* the tide picks up, and the composition is going the way of his handwritten pages, (so *gone,*) racing the horizon and the rising now risen sun somewhere where the day ahead is now; and as far removed as the last page he searches for, and misses, as she commands the composition returns and, a half breath after, declares the shoot is dead.

So he's carrying her and everything she brought to the lake, (which is too much,) and he's tired and the sand somewhere under the sea he's suddenly entirely too far in is shifting, shifting like Jen, and she's shaking like he's shaking and commanding he, (so the sand,) stop shifting, but only between breaths containing words like

Fantastic

and

Beautiful

describing her artistic genius in the art she captured, and she better have, because the beach somewhere on the horizon is losing its' magic, and he can't believe an hour ago he couldn't wait five minutes to fuck this girl.

He reaches the beach and the ladder across shoulder *left* is racing the photographer across shoulder *right* to the hot sand, and he's not far between, collapsing somewhere closer to Jen and closing

his eyes, wishing as she mentions the word

Payment

he'd fallen closer to the ladder.

She's up and off the beach far too fast, something about him needing to go to his car and grab his wallet as his left eye opens, eye closest to the ladder, and the right eye begs him to close it, eye closest to the beach she's already on her way back from.

By the time he opens *both*, sometime after rubbing the sand she's kicked at him from them, she's both blocking the sun and wearing more clothes, and she may be talking more too, but he can't tell, and the lake is in his ears and everywhere and his head is pounding and as he remembers he's her (long-long) ride home, he's hoping to hell these photographs turn out half as well as she screams, and, walking away in her *more* clothes, they're not the screams he was hoping for.

Red (and the tediousness of transcribing his writing)

Fuck, he hates computers.

The words come slow, and he's looking at his handwriting and wondering how so much can be lost on the screen screaming at him, typing words like

Fuck

and thinking he hates computers and that the emotion he pored into page *ninety-five* is dead and gone *here*, page *fifty-seven*, and the computer is killing his ego, eating pages of the manuscript he thought he was *far* in, the fucking word count feature telling him he's maybe *half*, but probably not, the writer he thought he was.

He swears and swears the font is too small but it's *not*, and he had two hundred pages of his new book finished, but the soulless machine will be lucky to give him *one-fifty*.

The words don't sing on the humming screen, and he reads them aloud and *back*, but it's not the aloud and back reading from his writing book, so he's close to giving up, but there's still *Kelly Ripa* to fuck, so he soldiers on, shoulders slumping and fingers breaking as backspace is the new *period*, more lost than gained.

There are things, he knows, he'd rather be doing, things with blonde hair and things underneath designer jeans, but these aren't the things that will guarantee his immortality, so they're gone, too, and he's typing the sentence about immortality and wondering why it doesn't look right in front of him. He reads it three times, and it's not coming, so he goes on, trusting his judgment and accepting he has two hundred more to transcribe before Bob The Editor hands him his manuscript back and he hands Bob The Editor *this*, his *new* guaranteed-to-get-published manuscript right back.

He can see the look on his little pig face now, even imagine the

I'm booked till never

retort he'll retort, but he's not the one hundred forty-five he was when he handed the last, and the sexy new vein in his forehead will pulse like it's pulsing now, *Enter* after a long and successful sentence, and Bob The Editor will see a thousand-thousand chin-ups in his eyes and that vein between, and he'll take his this, new manuscript, with a smile and a squeak and a

Thank You

and he'll get a

You're Welcome

and really, *fuck you*, because he deserves to be published and the things that come with it.

For now, sadly, there's the screen and the hum and the things it does to his eyes and the vein between, struggling with the software editor when it tells him

kinda

is not a real word, and he looks for the *Fuck Off* button.

Blue (and it's still Summer)

It's not that he's *jealous*,

not even like he would have any right to be—

it's just that he can't imagine anyone meeting her,

and

not falling completely in love.

So when she tells him about

Mike,

or

Trevor,

or

Steve,

or

any of the boys with the dull plain-sounding names,

he can't help but feel that *pull*,

like they're all trying to steal her away from him,

her phone calls

and

her erratic visits,

and

her push-pull that fools him into thinking she's anything but already

and

completely *gone*.

Really, though, how could Steve

(—and

he's the topic of conversation

as she speaks

softly

the way she only always speaks when she's scared—)

be anywhere near the kind of good enough

it takes to be with girls named for seasons?

She speaks of Steve

softly,

like she knows the sounds of syllables attached to penises other than his

send him the way they really do,

but her eyes aren't in it,

so when she speaks of Steve,

he knows she's just playing with him.

Still, she speaks of him often, often

and

between when he tells her things like

Bob the Editor hasn't called

(It's just that he makes me laugh, y'know?)

and Bob the Editor hasn't e-mailed, either

(And maybe that's what I need right now, somebody who can just, y'know)

and really, there hasn't been any contact with Bob—

(Who?)

--the Editor, remember?

(Oh, and he says he can get us into Pure, because he used to bounce there, which is kinda hot

But I'm kinda tired of big muscle guys, and the way—omigod, he's always looking at himself in the mirror)

And

he wants to lean over the coffeeshop table

and

taste her,

the honeysuckle

and

September

of her fat little lips,

honeysuckle

and

September

and

triple mocha latte,

like the one she *would* be drinking if stories about Steve

and

his muscles

and

his Mustang

weren't stealing it from her, her

and

those fat little lips.

Yeah, he wants to kiss her,

her

and

those fat little lips

right now,

because she can use them to mouth words

like Steve

and

Mustang

all night long,

but her eyes betray her, telling him in Technicolor blue

that Steve

and

Mustang

and

everything

 (in between sips of triple mocha latte)

is because he hurt her so *deeply*,

and

she doesn't know how hard she wants to hurt him back.

So it's not that he's jealous,

sitting across the coffeeshop table listening to stories about boys with dull

sounding names,

it's just that he imagines them having the courage to reach across the table

and

kiss her the way he only can't in the book he writes when he writes about her,

the latest girl worth writing books about,

and

the latest girl he loses

because he leaves his courage on the page,

half a line from a word that sounds out both his favorite name and time of

year.

September

Blue (and he's **DONE** writing--**forever**!)

He's *done* writing,

and

again,

and

sitting again

at the same coffee table

in the same corner

of the same coffee shop he's *been* coming to;

and,

again, he's reflecting

and

dwelling

on girls who *got* away

and

girls who just *went* that way.

And

he's not *over* them,

and

his motivation is gone,

and

he'll never be a writer

or

want to,

ever again,

the way *pining*

and

longing

fuel the writing

and

writing;

the way the *pining*

and

the *longing* are, now, far too exhausting to,

anymore

or

ever again.

And he swears

and

again

that he'll never fall for another girl the way he fell for Summer

or

the way he *really-really* fell for the Girl on TV

or

the ways he almost

and

kinda fell for Sabrina

and

Laura,

NEVER EVER AGAIN

EVER

and

then *This New One—*

a girl prettier than she has any right to be—

sits down

and

across from him

and

directly,

looks at him just as,

directly,

says

Hi

and

then

I'm <u>*This New One*</u>.

And

then he forgets all about the Girl on TV

and

Seasons

and

girls named for them

and

all the *every-other* girls,

and

he's sorry he wasted so much time/paper on them.

And

This New One

looks at him with eyes with colors *colors* don't have

and

HE'S A WRITER, AGAIN,

because even if he fucks up his

Hello

back,

she'll break his heart enough to fill *twenty* books.

Red (and the importance of eight)

Having an eight pack is the most important thing in the world.

More important than being published, almost—the kinds of magazines he plans on being on the covers of demand it, looking good and ripped and good and ripped under lines that scream

The New Face—And Eight Pack—Of Fiction!

and

Shakespeare's A Pussy!

and

The Face—and Eight Pack—That Will Make You Care About Reading Again (Seriously, Look At Those Abs!)

in photographs by Annie Liebovitz, showing off important new tattoos by *Cartoon,* headlining the important months, beside promising article captions like

You're A Fag If You Don't Wear This This Summer!

and

You Have To Buy This Now!   *Now!*

Yeah, the eight pack is paramount, eight because *six* says he's a pussy, and *ten*, no matter how many chemicals he fills himself with, just won't come.

The only good thing about being violently ill for three months—and he blesses himself for being an optimist—was the stunning emergence of his hip flexors, the extra crease along his rectus abdominus no amount of crunches could have created. He thanks Chron's disease or Ulcerative Colitis, or whatever the hell he had, and they couldn't diagnose, every time he takes off his shirt, admires the contours of his newest, prettiest (—or top three, anyway--) personal feature.

His fans—the ones who don't realize they're fans yet, (*but will have deliriously kinky stories to tell when they do*—) have appreciated the glory of his physique as well, their inept kissing and prodding and licking periodically interrupting his violent *fucking,* fucking and the time after, when they should be dressing.

His beauty—and there was *beauty* before the illness, but not like his beauty since—has invaded somewhat *welcomingly* every facet of post-illness life, time previously huddled over his writing book now at the mall, searching desperately for a shirt to accent the outright granite of him, and, increasingly, one he is not *allergic* to.

One to lie in a pile on the sand at the beach, or on the strange flooring tile of some pretty dirty pretty thing, or on the familiar carpet underneath his bed, next to an increasingly unfamiliar book, one periodically, and, lately, *seasonally,* filled with the words that will introduce the *whole world* to his beauty.

Red (and fucking David, the website guy)

David the website guy is David *his* website guy, and it's one of those good/bad things; good because David the website guy is good and cheap, bad because David the website guy is David the website *guy*, and about as far away from his other website contributor, *Jen the photographer*, as far away can go, like she is, after photoshopping his photos and surviving the dinner he took her to, the dinner she spent talking about how great her boyfriend is and the dinner he spent talking about how great her thighs are.

Looking at him, David the website guy, between explanations of and writing in the notepad he's writing notes for him in, notes about the website David the website guy is designing for him, he reminds him that it's okay that David the website guy looks like what he *figured* and *feared* the website guy would look like (—and David does—) all too tall and too pale with two-inch *only-a-website-guy-would-take-those-seriously* glasses and what has to be, pausing mid

This-needs-to-be-the-best-website-ever

in his notepad for measure (—*and it is*—) inch twenty-two of David the website guy's twenty-*four* inch forehead.

It's like he's trying to look like Bill Gates, so fucking *horrible*, and he reminds himself that if he ever writes a character based on David the website guy he'll need to work hard to make him less stereotypical, because if he wrote him *as is*, fucking nobody would believe him.

So he's back at his notepad, talking while writing and telling David the website guy just how he wants *his*, and when David asks why there needs to be so many shirtless photographs when the focus should be on the writing he stops writing to look up at him and his fucking forehead and it takes all the muscles (—*so a lot*—) in his left hand not to drop his pen and slap David the website guy across all twenty four inches of his forehead; because he's not *getting it*, his artistic vision, the way Jen the photographer didn't get it when she asked him why every photograph she took he had to be shirtless too, and she's lucky he kept his pants on and he's lucky the testosterone he took a half-hour before he showed up for *this*, (their first website design meeting,) isn't affecting his self-restraint the way it's clearly affecting his temper.

Which he tempers, offering some bullshit explanation of appealing to certain vaginally-inclined demographics when really he just wants shirtless pictures of himself, himself and his abs, on the internet. David the website guy offers his suggestions, and they're *bad*; shifting on the couch he swore when he bought would never suffer the indignation of corduroy against it's fine leather-*esque* surface, (and it is now, because David the website guy seriously showed up at his door in corduroy pants,) he smiles, watching him pull a pen from and offer, (like suggestions,) with a *twelve-incisor-too-many* smile, lips racing to disappear behind gums that would make Barbarro (—or whatever that fucking horse's—*the one with the gums*—name is—) fucking *super*-jealous; and he takes it and keeps writing, because his pen was dying.

And it's shit like this that will keep David *the* David *his* website guy; the way he just sort of looks born for the job and is willing to help him see his vision through, the way he knows he can dominate the conversation and the deal, bringing David down and then up enough to keep those lips racing and those gums exploding, taking over his features and his face when he smiles.

And they're threatening to absorb his beak nose, because it's located far too fucking close on his face, and the way those things suck attention, it won't be long, like the time David the website guy says it *won't* take for him to get his site up and running and up and running the way he wants it, and then David is too, something about getting home to the wife and kids he's amazed, frankly, to hear he has, (face like that) and looking at it one more time as it turns to smile horribly at him from the laneway, he's glad beautiful people don't need to be website guys.

Blue (and *This New One*)

He doesn't know what to say about her,

This New One,

save that watching the way the light through the blinds hits her body in angles

is at *least* the most important use of seven-something in the morning

he's ever-*ever* seen.

And

to him the worst thing in the world

would be to see an inch of her

marred by the *Maybelline*

and

MAC

and

makeup she insisted on

the night attached to *this*,

the morning the light is almost done kissing the lips

he spent the dark that *was* exploring.

So he decides he'd like to keep her,

and

here,

where the light that creeps up the side of her

is yearning to crawl back down,

down so the dark can give him reason to finish chewing on the quarter lip he

hasn't;

and

he agrees wholeheartedly when he draws the blinds,

stopping them from invading her eyes,

eyes better kept closed

until she flutters them to look on him again,

making,

in a flash of green,

the waiting worthwhile.

Red (and introducing, with fabulous-ferocity, Post Gay Bosco)

His best friend is violently homosexual.

That, and not liking it when priests touch little boys, is more than enough to convince him he is a *good* person; he reminds himself of this fact when he ignores his big sister's phone calls, *like he is*, and when he kicks girls out his door without the cab money he promised them last night, *like he just did*.

So *Ariana* or *Adrianna* can fuck off and his big sister can fuck off with her phone calls, because and really—ignoring the phone on the desk next to the front door *Ariana* or *Adrianna* will be knocking on when she realizes she forgot her panties—he's a *good* guy.

He met Post Gay Bosco at his very first writing seminar, realized he was gay and violently sometime before he shook his hand and sometime after he noticed how violently tweezed his violently tweezed eyebrows were.

They were friends anyways and after, and after a couple drinks after that seminar he realized Post Gay Bosco was just the same as him, only violently gay; he was a writer, too, and a womanizer—only the violently gay version—too, and an incredibly good time to be around, too.

They shared the same interests, or at least enough of them to warrant spending time together; they both loved his writing, they both loved violently abusing stimulants with depressants, and—(and this is the best part—) they both loved getting him laid.

He discovered early and much to his delight that women and *all* secretly desire to befriend and be friends with a violently gay man. And this—reflecting *now* on the parts of last night without *Ariana* or *Adrianna*, the parts with stimulants and depressants and bypassing the line at *at least the trendiest bar in his city* with his violently gay wingman—this is too easy.

See, Post Gay Bosco is a makeup artist when he's not writing or violently abusing stimulants with depressants, and the only thing women love more than *him* (a tortured writer with the body of at *least* a pagan God and a violently gay best friend) is getting makeup tips from a violently gay best friend looking to be *their* best friend, too.

So sometime between drink seven and seventeen last night at *at least the trendiest bar in his city* he chose *her*, and ten minutes and two drinks later Post Gay Bosco returned with her phone number and the rest of her and ten drinks after she said her name was *Ariana* or *Adrianna* he found himself the two drinks it takes from taking her home and taking her panties off, too.

Now, reflecting over a pair of perfectly pink panties, panties *Ariana* or *Adrianna* may or may not come back for, panties he may or may not return at all, he is and for the hundred-hundredth time thankful his best friend is violently gay, and thankful he's such a *good* guy.

Blue (and a Friday)

Friday,

and

his baby sister calls

and

he doesn't answer,

doesn't answer because he is with *This New One*,

and

he is happy.

Red (and a runway)

He's on coke and a runway, and the coke, really, is making the runway, required walking down, appear at least *infinitely* harder than it should be.

This, (taking a moment to reflect on the events and snow that led him here, to the modeling audition at the most prestigious and pretentious modeling agency in the city,) is part of (--like the photoshoot with Jen the photographer and the website with David the website guy--) part of Post-Gay Bosco's marketing strategy; model *slash* author at least a lot more appealing than nothing else, really, *slash* author.

And it appeals to his ego, standing here on the edge of the runway, waiting for the command from the nameless—*because-they're-busy*—husband/wife tag team running the audition/agency at the opposite end, the end he knows he's supposed to sort of saunter to, pop his *good* hip, (so *either*, really,) flash the wife of the husband/wife tag team his best *I-want-to-fuck-you* face because he's *supposed to* and *does*, the way she coldly commands the cattle cowering in chairs below and everywhere around him, some waiting their turn to stand where he stands now, some defeated, having failed already.

He knows he wants this, the attention from the blonde who came in here thinking she was walking out contracted and worshipped, only to discover the forehead she kinda thought was big in some photos *is*, and *more often*, her less fuckable brunette friend and her *not-the-five-nine-in-your-application* sister, and all, really, of the other cast offs and also-rans now intently watching his turn and the saunter and devastating criticism that follows, hushed and hungry and hunched in their chairs, waiting to picks the scraps of ego left after the husband/wife tag team tag team his flaws.

And there are none, and a look at Post Gay Bosco in the gallows to his left confirms it, so he puts *his* first, starts sauntering.

It's going well, the whole left-right-left thing, and he knows it's *this* easy, but the coke he's been railing since Friday is frying cells and synapses in his brain, and there's maybe a sliver of doubt where there was none before.

Doubt, because the week<u>day</u> *today* is about as far from Fri___ as it could be, and his nose feels like it's running and his lips are all Sahara and he thinks it would be cooler *there*, too, the lights trained on him like he wants and will be maybe a day *early*, as though fame and fortune and recognition and glory are better suited for *tomorrow*, the only day in September it *won't* snow.

He knows he's not fooling anyone, that being strung out isn't until year *two* of his five year plan, and, reminding himself there's nothing hotter, (*Sahara aside*,) than rehab, he makes the five left four rights it takes to reach the tag team end of the runway, pops his favorite hip, and smiles the smile of a man that knows the

rail waiting for him at the end of the audition will easily kiss away any criticism they won't-can't offer when he turns, saunters away again.

He'll be signed and *more*, and being appreciated for his pretty is pretty-much-if-not-more important than being appreciated for his talent, so the glamour of telling dirty- pretty-dirty girls in bars he's got a shoot tomorrow drives the smile the wife of the husband/wife tag team demands he smile when he completes the *prancing* portion of his show pony routine.

She'll ask him to read, he knows, and next, some text from a cue card he's watched seventeen cowering cattle fumble through, waiting his turn in the gallows beside Post Gay Bosco and trying to regain the feeling in his teeth instead of memorizing some writing decidedly *worse* than his *worst*, and when she does, he does, with the passion and precision of a writer reading their latest-best in a workshop like he *has*, and recently, and, apparently, more than enough practice to blow through the garbage on the cue card the way he *is*.

And the annunciation takes the hit, and a little, and only because he can't feel the lips he's pushing the air and the words that follow through, and he is too, before the cocaine in his brain will allow it to slow enough to worry about things like communication at all.

They nod, silently, and at one another and to him, and they might say something, but it's not bad and he can't hear it above the roar of applause in his head and the smattering of applause around and below him, and he's on his way off the stage and on the way to his seat to watch the rest of them, cattle parading on a runway to pass the time until they call him and sign him, not much time to pass before it's his turn, beautifully, on the runway again.

Red (and someone who may play the game a little bit better—or, Cousin Aimee)

She looks up at him from the mirror, there in the middle of Post Gay Bosco's apartment, and the look is different and it's *pure*, like the coke that was on the mirror and in her nose, now, and framing it is her *eyes*, and, looking up at him with them, they're the first and only he's ever seen that burn bluer, (so better,) than his.

And in the moment it takes him to say

I want to devour you

without saying anything at all, she's got

I could run circles around you

written in circles around the dilated pupils of her bluer eyes, and he realizes right there across the mirror that held his/her coke that she's him with a vagina, so *better* and by degrees, like the ones rising exquisitely to fill the space shrinking between the two of them.

And *one* would be better, inside her and tangled with her in sheets too weak to tangle between them when the devouring *he's dreaming about* struggles to confine the *one* of them they create to a bed; and bed only because conformity states coupling *start* there.

She showed up, before the mirror and the living room at Post Gay Bosco's, with her cousin, *her cousin-his-ex*, so she was hands off, and he was too, no doubt, for the duration of the plane ride they took here from Calgary, explaining in words too vulgar

for cousin Aimee's delicious ears that she, Denae, his ex and the one he *thought* he'd be fucking (and again and) tonight, was *his*, and she might have been, until cousin Aimee walked through the door six steps later.

And it's a hurdle, now, hours and the things hours on bring, but hurdles are for *fags* in short-shorts, so by the second time cousin Aimee said she doesn't do drugs and the first time Denae went to the bathroom and the first time she buried her face in his mirror, he knew all the

He's mine

on the three hour plane ride just made him *more* available, one of those *want-what-you-can't-have* joints.

And for the first time in a thousand-thousand girls and nights with girls in and out and in them, he's found his *equal*, and not like the sweetener he lied when he told Denae was spread in pretty little lines on his mirror.

He supposes it's the chemicals, and not the ones below and now in her, but the ones *in her in her*, mixing in the space between with the ones *in him in him*; that chemistry thing animals understand in the big bad *out there* when they saunter across their own, and then cousin Aimee does the mouth thing he does when he can't feel his face, but *better*, and between lips he wants to bite into until he-she-they feel it.

And he wants-to-is-about-to when Post Gay Bosco shoots his

bitch is rounding the corner! look, two seconds before he pulls away, maybe three before Denae rounds the corner, ruins his pre-post high.

Post Gay Bosco goes for the save, something about

Ooh, look at this, sweetie

but it's not sweet enough, apparently, to keep her from being all and at once between them; and the look cousin Aimee shoots him before turning to Denae and the rest of the night is

Your loss

and horribly and for the first time, it is.

A look at the clock tells him *six* is too close to *eight*, the *eight* they're leaving back to Calgary, so *six* sucks, the way *she* wants to but won't, and the fucking sun has a smile on it's fat face when it enters the apartment a half step after she leaves.

Red (and the morning after)

Post Gay Bosco is cooking eggs and theories, shooting him squinty Richard Gere *I'm-judging-you-right-now* looks, and he's trying to read/process him, but his read/process cells are frying in sync with the eggs on Post Gay Bosco's *stainless-steel-Rachel-Ray-2000-not-yet-Post-Gay-Edition* frying pan, so reading him is like anything other than *Perez Hilton.com*, so *impossible*.

And he tries to absorb the advice, because Post Gay Bosco is the ultimate accessory, the way the dirty-pretty-dirty girls worship him like new extensions, but he's particularly scathing this morning, and his dissertation on the inconsistencies of his game is probably better left for six in the mornings *without* heart palpitations.

The reason he's *Post* Gay, partly, (aside from avoiding the more socially awkward pseudo-stereotypical pitfalls *Pre*-Post Gays sometimes always seem to have,) is his decided and meticulously glossed inability to sympathize with the weaker of male emotions.

It's the best thing about him, every hour but *this* one, and most of the reasons he finds he has so much in common with someone he never imagined having anything in common with at all, and he loves it, the layers it adds to his already beautifully deep personality.

So he takes the eggs and they're over easy and he leaves the advice because it's neither, and, by the look of Post Gay Bosco's drug-accelerated lips, what he's serving (—other than that third egg
calling to him from the frying pan—) is far, far from the *over*, miles more from the *easy* of the two he's working on, thumbing aimlessly at things other than cousin Aimee, and half-listening to why he failed to have the opportunity.

The other half is healed again, half-half fighting the need to sleep, half-half searching his non-fried synapses for indicators in the ether and the hours before, reading wild in eyes undeniably wilder than his and wondering when and how he can see her again, devour things decidedly more delicious than the decidedly *less* delicious-*though-he-doesn't-have-the-heart-to-tell*, remains on the plate below him.

And all at once and before, cruelly, he can ask for that third, Post Gay Bosco mentions something in passing that does to his intestines what half-cooked eggs and a gram, easy, of beautiful--*but not as*-- cocaine has been trying to do in the hours with and minutes *since*—him with a vagina, but better, is coming back in *seventy-something*, for seven days, and his ex-girlfriend's sister's wedding.

And it's all he hears, tuning out the more and even ignoring the visual that accompanies, his third egg mysteriously missing from the *Rachel-Ray-two-thousand-not-yet* frying pan, the mouth that speaks speaking in mouthfuls and not even missing vowels in making fun of his shortcomings, because he knows he's *seventy-something* from some Saturday and some bridesmaid's dress on his floor, and Post Gay Bosco can have the fucking egg.

His tastes wait, like the rest of him, for something sweeter.

Blue (and more and not enough about *This New One*)

She's got the *prettiest* front door.

And

he doesn't know if it's white

or

beige

or

red

or

yellow

approaching the porch, because it always opens,

and

This New One

is waiting on the other side.

She's there

and

waiting

and

sometimes she's dressed down

and

sometimes she's dressed up

and

she's always dressed just a little better

than just right.

Sometimes she's in jeans,

sometimes

and

only after long days it's sweats

—he knows it's wrong when he climbs the steps

to hope/pray today she's wearing *neither*,

but the curves her legs take when she quivers slowly at the sight of him

make the effort of thumbing the button/pulling the drawstring

as unbearable as days without her, pants *or.*

And

tonight on the other side

she's done something with her hair,

something to make breathing harder than the bench presses he pressed

to puff his chest

and

impress her a half hour before

now

and

her front door.

She tastes like they all taste when he tastes her,

so *girl,*

but better,

like the flavor of ice cream they discontinued when he was five,

finding after missing it for twenty-one years

and

thirty-one flavors it's been hiding in the sweet that moisturizes her moisturized little lips.

Red (and really, this is no surprise)

So the *modeling thing* didn't work out; didn't work out because the *seriously-unafflicted-with-talent-or-the-appreciation-that-comes-with-recognizing-his-beauty* tandem of husband/wife agency-owners didn't understand that *no*, he doesn't need to audition for any modeling work; and *no*, modeling on weekends doesn't work for him, the way he no longer works for *them*.

Red (and a little on exactly what deadlines are)

Deadlines are *pumas*.

So beneath him, and under him, and pretty much *inconsequential*, because really, when the rest of him is *as*, the last thing anybody looks at are his ridiculously expensive hand-stitched shoes.

And he's fine with it and he's *used* to it—buying three-hundred dollar sneakers and having absolutely no one notice—*not* deadlines.

Deadlines, he muses, and muses when he should be attempting to make his—deadlines are for *poor people*.

He got the call three weeks ago, telling him what he *already* knew when he sent away his resume; that the job writing for the *fabulous-but-not-fabulous-enough* magazine was *his* and *all* and *only*; what he didn't know, more a testament to not caring, really, rather than reading the fine print (because really, fine print is for *poor people*) is that the *fabulous-but-not-fabulous-enough magazine* is a fucking *fabulous-but-not-fabulous-enough* Women's Magazine.

Yeah. So he sits at his office at the corner table at the corner coffee shop today, (Tuesday,) like he sat *yesterday*, (Monday,) like he'll likely and *more than* sit tomorrow, (Wednesday) and days after and until *after* the day of his deadline is that and *just*;

(dead and gone)

—sit at the coffee shop and just kind of *not* produce this next article, the one to serve as a springboard to superstardom as surely as the next some-slut serves his next but *not next to last today*—hot chocolate without sprinkles.

And *fuck them*, really, these women behind the article and the deadline and the Women's Magazine, entitled, appropriately and as creatively as only these women can be, Women's Magazine; *fuck them* for imposing and a deadline and imposing a deadline on someone as creatively sound as him.

They should be happy to *not* get this next article every single fucking day until the day they do—and that day they should be happy, *and more than*, too—*that* day is the day to make all the days they *did not* matter as much and too him as this waitresses' name on the name-tag attached to the shirt she *won't* be wearing in twenty minutes (for *at least* twenty minutes) if she smiles at him *one more time* the way she smiles at him on the way with his hot chocolate.

So *fuck* Stacey or Tracey or Mandy or Michelle—it doesn't matter—at least as much and maybe *less* than the deadline he says *fuck* to two minutes before he gets up from the table to, folow whatever-the-fuck-her-name-is on the way to the bathroom.

October

Red (and worse)

The cocaine is talking to him.

Humming, really, the latest and longest line in a line, *lately*, of *larger* lines, breaking into song as he inches his face closer to the mirror he cuts them on, and, catching his reflection split by the powder he's *seconds* from deliciously devouring, he maybe lies to himself when he recognizes the face staring back at him; nostrils primed and ready and two black holes *less* black only next to the black in the black holes on and in his eyes.

And they tell him, between dulling and devouring the blue surrounding them that used to burn brighter when he looked into mirrors without poison on them, that he needs the glamour

Create the image

Create the image

and the danger that comes with the drugs, being the bad boy he wants-needs to be worth the weekly trips to meet Spanish Jose, the seventy dollars and seventy dollars and seventy dollars the seven and seven and seven burns in his pocket before burning in his nostrils, and they're waiting, waiting for him to be the bad boy again.

He's closer but stops, now, and it's not self-restraint; the notebook that *used* to sit in *front* of him on the table and his mind has been set to the *side*, and he catches a corner on his way down,

the significance of the mirror and what's on it, and, looking down over it, what's *in* it, not lost on him as he draws, deeper than he should, because it tells him to, and tells him in song.

He used to tell himself, sitting at this table, that satisfaction was at the end of the next *line*; glancing at the empty mirror below and in front of him, he used to mean the words on the page, below and now *away* from him.

He meant to write tonight, because he *hasn't*, but he can feel the brain cell that had the next best-line-he-ever-wrote frying, and *poetry* is just another *p* word heading down the hall and out the door, and it can *stay* there because he's alone and alone with the only new thing that makes the *what-some-would-call-insecurity-but-he-wouldn't* stop bleeding, at least seven shades deeper than this milestone, his first nosebleed, staining the pretty snowflakes pink on the mirror below as it runs to run away from him, too.

Create the image

Create the image

and, tragically and beautifully he *has*, and he's the nothing he spent everything in increments of seventy trying to *pretend* to be, and pretend is following his favorite word that starts with *p* right out of his life; gone down the hall and out the door, saying something out of her lips, and not the ones that start with the *letter*, about him being a disaster comma beautiful, and it's perfect, the last and latest girl who came over this week and couldn't keep up—perfect because everyone knows that the bad boy doesn't keep the girl.

And it's hitting him, the cocaine, the way *she* did ten minutes ago, before the door and out of it, and he's remembering in fast forward the line he just snorted was the second in the time *since*, and the one he lined up for Amber, the girl who, ten minutes before, was the third one to come over this week and make the mistake of trying to keep up.

Now it's all falling apart, isn't it; but it's slow, like molasses in months after May, and it's sexy, and it dances with him like it should, a little less alone than the all alone he is, alone in his living room and realizing *this*, alone, is the very start of the slow, *molasses in*, sexy dance that will leave him ever and always alone, by, beautifully, never leaving him alone, not even a little at all, and there's solace in that, so *cocaine*, when he closes his eyes, lets it lead.

And they're open again and violently, because

Faster

Faster

the thoughts are leaving and his notebook is open for the first time in forever and his pen is hurting his hand and on the page it's all adverbs and adjectives and things he didn't pay attention to in English class, because the language and it's structure are beneath him and where there was plot and climax there's steroids and cocaine, and *climax*, because he's only writing with one hand and his mind is racing and his hand is racing and his hand is, now, racing, because the ideas that come *like he wants to* are all good ones, and *fuck* everybody and fuck everybody who reads this, his writing, and can't figure out what the fuck he's writing.

Red (and *yes*, a pattern is emerging)

So the whole writing for *Women's Magazine* thing—*like the whole writing-for-anyone-else-at-all thing*—didn't work out *either*; either as in just like *any/all* the other jobs he quits and *will* to pursue his destiny.

Red (and doing what only-every-music video ever told him is cool)

He knows its *wrong*, burning lights as red and raw as the bridges he burns when he burns them; burning lights in succession and speed so he can sell the kind of thing riding shotgun to make friends speed and leave as *fast*, the kind of thing he bought from the kind of not-friends who probably *carry* the nickname for the seat (--so 'shotgun') his coke is riding in.

It's enough, he knows, cocaine and a *quarter*, to put him away for maybe as long—his days of trafficking gram *singular* as far behind him as the latest red light he burned half a second ago; tonight his run is running to the same number, one customer and one sale for enough rock to kill at least as many people as he almost has burning lights on his bridges to sell.

He'll burn more of both before the sun forgives him for the sins the rest of tonight promises, because his buyer is one of his friends and few who stay despite his inflated prices.

Not that it isn't *good*, because it *is*, and *better* and by *far* than anything friends like few and tonight have ever abused—riding shotgun, the quarter is hard enough in it's little saran-wrap baggie to make him and *almost* and *too*; still there's the sale and *only*, so *sober* he stays, despite what the traffic behind the traffic lights he burns would say when he burns them.

And lately this is the only job he can seem to keep and lately it's the only job he wants to; so it's late, and he's alone, and he probably couldn't be happier.

If he had it in him, now might be the time to be scared, and at how decidedly *not* he is trafficking volume that weeks ago *seemed*, (scary) but scared would be *smart*, and he's playing the opposite and smiling as he makes the light at *insignificant*, the latest police-infested expressway on his way to becoming the kind of cool music videos promise he *can* be, with just a couple quarters *more*.

He'll get to the drop (--because one of the perks of dealing is the excuse to use words like *drop*, instead of *buddy's-parent's-garage-*) at the end of a half-dozen insignificant streets, feel something *south* of scared, twice as foreign as *bad* when he takes *eight* quarters *more* than the *sixteen* quarters his quarter is *worth*, looks his friend in the eye and assures him with a significant shake that he's saving a significant amount of the money he's *not* when he takes it in the hand *opposite*, not shaking or scared knowing it's *wrong* when he drives away significantly further ahead than he *would* be, had he spent the night writing and not burning lights as red and raw as the bridges he burns when he burns them.

Red (and the whole push-pull thing)

One, and he pushes, and it hurts sweetly like it's *supposed* to, hurts but not like the hurt of not having enough. The bar fights back, weights on either end pressing down when he does and pressing down when he doesn't, pressing the other way and getting to

Two,

two on the way, unfortunately, to *ten*, *eight* in between eight like last night, when he called Bob the Editor, got no answer, making *eight*, like *eight* in between, completely miserable.

Three,

and it's picking up and it's frantic, because yeah, he's a superbad saucy sex-champion with washboard eights and plump-like-the-cover-of-at-least-*Men's-Health*-on-the-way-to-*Flex* biceps and the features of a demi-god, (or at least the good-looking-no-horns demi-gods,) but he's twenty-six, and his initial goal of being published at twenty-three is three done, like the push at the bottom of the press, harder than it was *three* ago and away from where he wants to be.

Four,

and really, he's frustrated because Amber called the way they all do and *again*, *ten* away from *one hundred forty-five* pounds, called to tell him about her new man, some fuck who signed out west with the *NHL* and never played a *game* or a *period* or a *minute*, and maybe

a *practice*, but he's making money, and that's all she talks about and it's all the girls he talks to and about talk about, *so fuck each and every one of them*, Amber *and*, because from now on, money is all he cares about, too.

Five,

and it hurts, the way family dinners do, pain in his head and his balls hearing his big sister talk of *this* guy and how much he makes and *that* guy and what he drives. So he can be a superbad saucy sex-champion, *washboard eights and all*, and it doesn't matter, because the *zeroes* after the *eight* in his account don't add up, and the minus signs on the other side of where the zeroes are supposed to be aren't flattering either, so his manuscript is his ticket, money over art, and he can't wait

Six

for family dinners he drives away from in his Italian *something*, something stupid sounding and *hard to pronounce* and faster than *fuck*, fucking while and *faster* he leaves the laneway, sister's *that* guy and what he drives eating his earth killing exhaust, family dinner and some toes curling in and on his rearview.

Seven

and for a half second he hates it, and *Paris Hilton*, and how it's all about how much you have and how fabulous you are, having *less* and looking fabulous unfortunately *still* less, having over looking.

Eight

and he's over it and the endorphins are kicking and he knows two more reps and he's done, maybe two more years and he's published and more importantly rich, endorphins making him love optimism and *Paris Hilton*, excited

Nine

bringing the bar up and it hurts, but less, because *Paris Hilton* is on the cover of the new *GQ*, and his arms look more like *Flex* than *Men's Health*, which is new too, so

Ten

and the bar crashes before resting above him, above him for a moment and *only*, because he's reaching for his thin *(for-now)* wallet and his tight *(because-he-earned-it)* t-shirt, on the way to the mall and it's magazine store and then maybe his future, owed because of his talent and his work the zeroes *after* all everybody he talks to cares about.

He's on his way out the door and he's thinking, of what he wants and is *owed*, and he wants to be nervous at awards shows, maybe reading a line from his latest before some poptart hands him his statue, and maybe stumbling over the first *third* word before hitting it out of the fucking park and hearing their applause and the love and admiration and devotion in it, and thinking of the faces back home, here, now, and how they're gonna wish they held on to him when he's there, *gone*.

Which will happen, he promises and himself, *just* after he's stupidly rich, the kind of rich that makes putting a plasma under the pillow *rational*, sometime down the road from the day, *soon*, Bob
the Editor picks up the phone to tell him he's the greatest of *at least* his generation and he's called Tina the Agent, and she's Tina *his* Agent.

In the meantime and today, he's better suited for working out and the mall and magazines and waiting, waiting for real, real soon, the day he'll be nervous at awards shows.

Blue (and bad news, and Bob the Editor)

So to Bob the Editor,

the words are *just*,

words

like

dream

and

publish

and

write,

strung together in sentences telling stories,

but really

and

to him

the words are much

and

more,

each

and

every

with all

and

everything

in the space between, at least as desperate as the *last*.

He tries to convey what he can't,

somewhere between his head

and

hand the soul intended for the page loses just enough,

enough to keep Bob the Editor from blown away

and

to keep him from calling Tina the Agent

and

to keep the phone call to the publisher

from Tina the Agent

from happening anywhere but in his *always* dream.

So the look on Bob the Editor's face

when he hands him back his dreams

and

his future

and

his everything, three-hundred eighty-nine pages of everything he had

and

has

and

at least half he *doesn't*,

the look on his face isn't the one he spent the last six hundred meals waiting

for.

For the look of him, Bob the Editor hasn't missed meal *one*,

looking fat

and

fed

and

smug;

the kind of fat

and

fed

and

smug

just fat

and

fed

and

smug enough to be comfortable killing dreams.

He hasn't said word *one*,

but the knife is clear through his chest cavity

and

twisting

and

he's well on his way to dying the death he maybe started dying six years

and

all those words ago when one pretty girl walked the *other* way,

introduced the knife

and

his chest cavity, started twisting.

Maybe he knows he's going to have to let that go,

and

maybe he knows Bob the Editor handing back his manuscript,

anything other than sold,

is the first and painful,

(like a knife through his chest cavity,)

step, like the *other*-other way,

away from where she walked

and

was.

He reaches the left to take it,

and

back,

but it shakes, because taking it,

and

back

is failing, from word one

(You)

to word seventy-seven thousand something,

(You,)

every word in between at least everything he had,

and,

apparently, nowhere near enough.

Bob the Editor is smiling,

and

he's trying, but the sides of his face,

especially the *good* one,

hurt worse than the time his sister threw the ball,

and

off his face,

some sunny day when she could still count on him being around to *catch* it,

and

he could still dream, like he can't, ever again,

when his hand closes around paper colder than he remembers.

So go on, Bob the Editor,

and

he's *waiting*,

waiting

to hear that his plot structure

is weak

and

his characters lack color

and

his dialogue doesn't sing,

and

so he won't be published.

Say something, Bob the Editor,

about the hours, spent alone

and

open

and

vulnerable

and

raw

and

hunched over some table in poor lighting while the world

and

years

around him,

hours left,

spent at the beach

or

the bar

or

somewhere *better,*

wasting away hours

and

being better for it,

the hours slaving

and

pouring on paper not worth a goddamn thing,

and

certainly not bringing the girl worth the writing back

and

costing him the girl who loved him

and

now,

apparently,

the pounds of paper the garbage he printed on,

words worth *less* than the ink of the pens he wasted too.

Tell him, in your most profound voice,

because he's waiting

like he's *been* waiting,

how six hundred dollars, dollars better spent on the *trivial* things,

mortgage

and

bills

and

food,

qualified you to deduce, in your infinite wisdom,

that the sum of the hours

and

the hurt

and

the sacrifice

and

everything else,

the everything else he put into,

Pining For Someone who May or May Not Know They're Being Pined For

that even the title is *wrong,*

first words *wrong,*

seventy-seven thousand something after little,

if any,

better.

He's waiting to hear that maybe he has potential, that *this*—

(and there are simply no more words he can fathom for the source

and

sum of his sharpest pain,

now perhaps and probably the greatest failure in a life *full of)*

—*this*

just isn't the manuscript,

that maybe years

and

more

of the absolutely nothing left will

be almost everything he needs to develop into a potentially publishable, (because he might as well make up words,

for all the sense the words strung together in *not*-sentences made in his novel,)

potential author.

He's still smiling,

Bob the Editor,

fat

and

fed

and

smug,

and

though

and

because he's thinking secretly fulfilling black thoughts at him,

he still can't smile back,

muscles in the sides of his face,

especially the *good* one,

not strong enough

or

maybe too devastated to *pretend*,

six-hundred-something on,

that anything Bob the Editor is about to say will be worth

six-hundred-something

and

six years,

some two thousand one hundred ninety days

and

fifty two thousand five hundred sixty hours,

hours he wasted

believing

that the words about to come out of Bob,

the Editor's,

mouth would be anything other than _____ ,

any word he chooses simply not enough.

Because to Bob the Editor, words are *just*.

Red (and Bob the Editor has bad news)

Bob the Editor looks like he tastes like licorice, and not in that good, *I-like-licorice* kind of way, no, looks like the texture more than the taste, like he wants to sink his teeth into the meat of him, bite down hard, and draw pieces of the sweetness into his mouth.

Yeah, licorice like *that*.

See, Bob the Editor needs to choose his next words carefully, at least a lot more than his last, because the man whose life he holds at the end of his lips is at least a lot of pounds *better* than the one hundred forty-five of their last sit-down.

Better, and because of steroids and testosterone, and the kinds of things that make saying, like he said

I've finished editing your manuscript, and I feel you need to make some changes

downright and damn sure counterproductive to Bob the Editor's future plans, and, really, omit the *plans*.

When Bob the Editor walked into the public library meeting room he walked out of three months ago, with his manuscript, his manuscript and his blank cheque, he was damn sure that the next time he saw him, four hundred-seventy-seven dollars lighter, the next words out of his mouth would be

Congratulations, this is the greatest thing I've ever fucking read I've already given Tina the Agent a copy and she's already read it and agrees you're the greatest writer of our generation

or something very, very close to that.

So when it is not, as he feels his face going the color of the licorice Bob the Editor looks like he tastes like, he can't-won't blame himself for the words, next, and because he's very good with them, he throws his way.

Red (and there's a revelation here, so stay with it)

She calls him a *tragedy in training* on her way out the door, and it lingers, longer than her name and the shade of cinnamon on her gloss and all the other insignificant details of tonight's otherwise *insignificant* girl, not worth remembering save for the panties on the guest bedroom floor and the surprisingly articulate assessment from someone who, two turns and *at least as many lines ago*, couldn't vocalize the vowels in the moans she managed around the same panties previously taking space between her tongue and the other mysteries muscling her half-screams.

Still, it's maybe more powerful than the tequila he chases the memory of her and how she sees him away with, stumbling naked in Post Gay Bosco's living room looking for the only thing, lately, that makes the word before *room* worth anything at all.

And it's there on the pedestal posing as the minibar, and it's precious and it's waiting and *not for long*, and as he's cutting he's looking out the window and the sign on the side of the convenience store through the window is *buzzing* and talking to him and him alone, *Enjoy Coke* in pretty big white letters, letters made up of pretty white lines, so *Enjoy Coke* and not the Coke the fat bastard coming out of the convenience store twists a cap to pour down his fat bastard throat.

So they enjoy coke together, him in the dark and alone in Post Gay Bosco's living room, alone and beautifully because Post Gay Bosco is at a Post Gay bathhouse, and he's not judging, doing

what Post Gay's *do*, and alone because the insignificant girl and her vowels and *not* her panties are gone too, and *not*, because the fat bastard out the window and across the street is indulging too, right along with him.

So it helps, and he spends the stumbling down darkened hallways trying not to analyze her analytical little observation, but it's creeping in at the corners like the spider making him less alone on the wall beside the switch in the bathroom he throws after and like her panties in the garbage by the sink he stares in.

Tragedy in training

And he doesn't know if the dick in his hand he pulled out to piss in is half-hard from the phrase or the mouth that both surrounded and surmised him, and hell, it could be the coke that caused all *three*, but goddamn if he isn't feeling a *tingle*, like the one about to hit the toilet, and a touch of excitement, like he's achieved something to be insulted so…

beautifully

or

…accurately.

And the scariest thing about such scathing self-realization, catching his cold cocaine eyes in the mirror, is how not scary and soothing, (*like the piss,*) her words and the vowels missing make him feel.

Post Gay Bosco's toilet water is blue, and no matter how hard he pisses and how often, (and it is,) he flushes, it won't fade; sparkling clean and blue and screaming

Fuck You

when he pisses and flushes, because at home the same cleaning agent, with blue, runs like the insignificant girl the first time he whips out his cock.

So,

tragedy in training

and *fuck her*, because the abs she was kissing-licking and losing coke, (so *money,*) in the recesses between an hour ago took *much more than* to sculpt, and she has no idea.

Presentation is everything and *obviously*, so the indulgences he sacrificed beside and between the time and the pressure and the *pulling*, keeping and counting calories and repetitions in repetition and then sacrificing the only thing that could overlook the number of crevices on his stomach, his *eight times ten* every week so insignificant girls can numb their lips with the pretty snow he blows, (so blow,) his paycheck on.

And it's still

Tragedy in training

when he flips the switch beside the spider in Post Gay Bosco's Post Gay bathroom, and the electricity goes but *stays*, hardwired from sex and stimulants, so sex *and*, and he's alone and on fire, and the alone is not as beautiful as before, making the fire uncomfortable for the first time, stumbling back down hallways headed for bedrooms with *straight*, so sanctuary, scrawled in neon lights, but only and burning in his head, because neon signs above bedrooms are about as real and there as *anyone*, save spiders.

So maybe he can see the

tragedy

in between the neon signs and rainbows and disco parties and the thousand-thousand things in high-definition and at once he sees because of what inspired the saying strangely taking precedent in what would otherwise and should be *Wednesday*.

And it's got to be the coke, because the feeling he's feeling in the parts of him that *still*, (feel) would be what he would describe in and if he was a *character* in his novel as *out of*.

He pulls the post gay sheet with it's *higher-than-any-self-respecting-straight-man-would-buy* thread count around where, *if he could feel*, his ears would be, and the fucking fabric is at least as alien as this fabric, and

in training

is going beautifully.

It's like the girl, the insignificant one with her now monumentally *not* insignificant insight is gone, but the things he's

done to himself to earn this insignificant evening have manifested themselves, a pair of arms made from steroids and magazine covers and rap videos and cocaine wrapping themselves around him, warm and making the alien post gay thread count sheets a little more comfortable when they press into the parts of him that still *feel*.

And for the first time and for *once*, maybe and maybe because he's trying not to admit it to himself, he's sick of running the race he's been running in fifth gear since before he was sick, and even that couldn't stop him and maybe that's why he stayed, the word after *was*.

And these fucking alien arms are holding him and encouraging him, telling him in warm-*if-warm-was-a-language* that *this*, alone in really, fucking *fabulous*, bed sheets that it's *okay* to *not* be at least everything (—and it would take pages if not hours—) to not be all the things he tells himself he *has* to be, every second of every hour of every day of his life, other, than, apparently, as the tears come—this second, right now.

He calls himself the names he needs to—and none of them are good, and some of them are really rather inspired—to stop these…things…coming from his eyeballs, because be knows he's so coked out that liquid of any kind should be hours--*and he'll be up for all of them*—away, but the metaphorical—*and fuck he hates that he's a writer and understands metaphors at all*—arms tell him to cry like the pussy he apparently *is*.

So he's a little boy and only and again, and in the time it takes the tears to stain the post gay thread count sheets, his sister can have the fabulous life to herself and all the other motivations he won't admit to anyone and especially himself bleed *like he thinks he wants his nose to* somewhere below him, leaving like the insignificant girl, (so *everyone,*) who couldn't-wouldn't see the rockstar writer for the little boy curled in cocaine clutches somewhere decidedly *north* of where he dreams, if he *could* tonight, he *should* be.

The arms are connected to a girl, and her name is *doubt*, and he feels she feels closer to him than any of the others and even Cousin Aimee; and maybe just for tonight she can hold him the way, if she were any other, *even,* he would hold her and *down.*

Blue (and everyone's girl)

He doesn't want *everyone's girl*.

It's not ideal, really;

sharing *some*one should mean with *no-one*

and

else,

not *every-some-other-body* who desires her the way they *do,*

when they call her

or

text her

or

hug her hello,

hoping her *hello* <u>back</u> is the ticket to bending *hers;*

over

and

in sheets better suited for swimming with *just* him,

bed-if-it-was-water like a pool for *just*

and

just big enough for two.

So he holds her *tighter* than he should, away

and

the other direction,

treading water decidedly deep

and

leaving ends *shallow* for bars

and

boys in bars who *would*

and

want her,

so *every* boy in *every* bar.

Because really, she's *one-in-a*

and

pick a number,

as <u>long</u> as it *is*,

like lashes sometimes covered in *MAC*

but always connected to eyes with colors *colors* don't have.

And

she's got *that* ass,

so color somewhere *else* too;

some family member some families *north*

—no girl ninety-nine percent like *Ivory* is blessed

with the jiggle she leaves in jeans.

So *Pure*,

the soap,

is what he wants

—*<u>everyone's girl</u>* can stay *where*,

the word attached to <u>*one*</u>, else;

all he needs is the number,

and

This New One has his.

Blue (and absence=absinth)

Time apart is *teeth*,
and
pulling,
(so *bad*)

—she's saying gone is *days*
and
a *couple*;

he's hearing *long*
and
too.

 And
details are daggers
and
too many *too*;
she's running out of sides to stab,
mouthing words in sentences,
sentences with words like Wednesday, the day *before* the next he'll hold her.

So he does
and
tight,
busying her lips with his,
resting

and

pressing his upper against her upper

and

lower

and

upper, again,

and

again-again

and

anything to keep hers from mouthing words

and

throwing daggers.

She pulls away, *This New One,*

and

first

and

because she *has* to

—he would hold

and

still for time

and

past,

and

past the time attached to the cab she called,

the cab to take her away,

for time *far*

and

long

and

too.

So when she separates, his mouth moves

and

away from hers,

and

it hurts, too,

but he mouths words,

attempting

and

failing, miserably, to attach them to feelings

and

about her leaving.

He's trying, he knows she knows,

telling by the quiver in his upper lip,

to articulate that the quiver is because of the *cold*,

on his lips, both upper

and

everywhere

—the cold he feels away

and

attached

and

not

to hers

—but she's wearing *those* jeans, the ones that make

articulate *arithmetic*,

so pretty much impossible.

Which means in between fumbling words with lips,

upper

and

lower,

better suited for pressing on

and

against hers,

he's standing away

and

far

and

too in shoes

and

on knees shaking

because her shoes are boots with fur,

and

he remembers fucking her in them

and

wants to *now*,

wondering what's kissing the parts of her he wants to

underneath *those* jeans.

If he was clever, he'd fight with her

and

horribly,

and

horribly enough to make her stay

—but clever comes late,

time

and

too late

 after the cab she called to take her away from him.

So horrible *stays*,

the feeling he feels as she pulls away,

away from the words seconds south he could-would-should have thrown, like

daggers,

to keep her tangled in the sheets

and

sweat attached to the sex they'd call *make-up*,

smearing hers in between kissing

and

thrusting

and

away the feelings she'd feel

because of the horrible things he'd say

to keep him from feeling horrible the way he *does*,

watching her pull, like *teeth*, away

and

far

and

for *far too long*.

Blue (and two weeks in which absolutely nothing can/will be accomplished)

So she's gone for two weeks,

and

it hurts like fractures.

Fourteen days,

and

everyone like the time after *nine*,

summer spent in a cast, hell after the hell of freshman year.

Its *work*, she says,

and

it's important

and

he's new

and

new enough to *not matter*,

not matter until she swears he matters,

swears between lips *Baskin*

and

his buddy *Robbins*

made millions on.

So he goes about his days without her in them as best he can;

but

days without her in them

are really days with *only* her in them,

the way she steps through his thoughts

maybe more assuredly

than the steps he tells himself he takes without her.

And

he tries to keep her name from his every other thought

because maybe he's tired of her face filling the ones *between,*

but it's as useless

as trying to get his heart to stop jumping

when she pushes her tongue against her teeth

the way she pushes her tongue against her teeth

when she smiles,

only in his every-other thought.

Red (and a Saturday)

Saturday, and his big sister calls and he doesn't answer, doesn't answer because he is fucking, and doesn't answer because he is fucking high.

November

Red (and a minor setback)

He tears his manuscript in half.

His bitch sister calls, halfway through ripping up the second half, because and to Bob The Editor, his second half is *garbage*, and because his big sister is a bitch, he ignores her call when she calls and when she calls back, he continues ripping.

He's got a *second* second act somewhere, and if Bob The Editor thought his original masterpiece was anything other than and *absolutely*, then he'll spoon-feed him the 'sensitivity' he claims his vision lacked.

See, he was a pussy sometime ago, sometime *before* convenience stores and Omar and realizing how *just plain better* he is than everyone else; and when he was vaginally-inclined he liked to write the kinds of things that would and could, if any ever read it, make girls *weep*.

So it makes sense somehow that if Bob The Editor wants him to Sally-up his vision, he do it with words *already* written; he needs to be a star and today and *now* and *right*—and, since his genius doesn't recognize time, words *then* are just as perfect and perfectly-fitting as words *now*.

So when the ripping is done, there will be changes and *few*, names of characters from novels past changed and altered, along with the odd sentence or situation, to accommodate and serve his story and his dream and his destiny; serve, like Bob The Editor will, when he reads *this*, his next and *greater*, (impossibly,) book, and does what he is compelled to: namely get him fucking published.

Blue (and a major setback)

He tears his manuscript in half.

His baby sister calls,

halfway through ripping up the first half,

because

and

to Bob The Editor,

his first half is garbage,

and

because he has work to do,

he ignores her call

and

when she calls back, he continues ripping.

He's got a first half somewhere,

a first half he prays *ups* the aggression Bob The Editor so wisely ascertained

as missing from his first draft;

a first draft he knows he can mold to fit the tone

and

vision he envisioned for his breakthrough manuscript.

See, he was *angry* sometime ago,

sometime before the clarity that comes with dreams

and

relentlessly pursuing them;

angry enough to write words that reflected the pseudo-darkness

he pretended to have inside of him,

words that would

and

could, if any ever read them, make girls weep.

And

he supposes it makes sense somehow

that if Bob The Editor wants him to *Norris*-up his vision,

he do it with words *already written*;

he needs to save his life

and

now—

and

since he's running out of time,

words *then* are just as perfect

and

perfectly-fitting

as words *now*.

So when the ripping is done, there will be changes

and

many,

names of situations from novel *past*

changed

and

altered,

along with the odd character

and

plot detail,

to accommodate

and

serve his story

and

his dream

and

his urgency; urgency he prays Bob The Editor *will* appreciate,

when he reads *this*,

his next

and

greater, (hopefully,)

book,

and

does what he so desperately needs him to—namely get him published.

Blue (and the first of a few that are little *less* about writing, and a little *more* about being in love)

She says she only wants one thing for her birthday,
This New One,
and
it's the one thing he
can't
won't
give her.

And
she says she doesn't want the *substitutes,*
the pretty-shiny-pretty things he would happily
and
rather
spend half the money he *doesn't* have to see her smile.

Smile
and
the way she *wasn't* last night,
night attached to the morning
and
the memory
of the look in her eyes,
eyes with colors *colors* don't have
filling with the things he swore he would die before seeing
eyes with colors *colors* don't have
filling with.

So today the look in her eyes is on him like his first tattoo,

and

it hurts maybe *more*,

promises to stay with him just as long

when he picks up the pen,

the pen to say *sorry*,

let her read his writing.

The thought of it is *snakes*,

(so scary,)

still not as,

scary as the look on *last* night,

so he starts,

the first of a thousand-thousand pages crumbled

and

beside him

so she can be *too*

and

again

and

finally.

To make up for their first fight, she wants to read his writing,

writing he wrote before he met her

and

when he thought writing *mattered*;

mattered the way it *hasn't*—

(and

just like he hasn't written—)

since the day at the coffeeshop she interrupted his writing maybe *forever.*

It should be a *relief,* her birthday gift,

because he's poor

and

a writer

and

she swears softly without swearing

it's all

and

everything she wants;

but he's a poor writer,

and

the writing he writes when he writes about her can't compare.

So how does he tell her that he would need a thousand-thousand

pages

in a thousand-thousand books

to describe just the first of her thousand-thousand curls,

curls he wishes the thousand-thousand he curled today

regretting last night

could impress her the ways he needs these words to.

If he were a better writer,

he could tell her she makes him wish he could throw like Brady on Sunday

and

only,

Sunday

so Monday

and

Tuesday

and

he could spend shopping for the kinds of things he wants to;

the kinds of things he needs Superbowl rings to afford to buy her.

Maybe he could *articulate,*

adjectives

and

metaphors

to share the secret of the times she turned her back

and

he tried to give her the moon;

tried

but came two inches too short

everytime he reached to take it.

He could spend vowels describing-denying-defending those on her tongue

when she called him an asshole

for the trying-teasing to touch *hers*;

but last night is pushing the pen

and

away from last night,

and

he needs something *too*

and

*to*night,

something to make seeing

and

anything other than her saddest smile slightly *less* heartbreaking

than the day attached to every night he dreams about losing her.

It will be his fault *then*,

he knows,

like it was *last*,

so half of what he writes and crumbles is

Sorry

and

for being crude

and

not half the man she's fooled he is

when she looks into his eyes with eyes with colors *colors* don't have

and

Sorry

for the *last* thing

and

the *next* thing,

sentences on pages she'll never read

about how really, the only thing scarier, (like snakes,)

than losing her is falling,

(like he is,)

in love with her before a decent interval

and

Sorry

that the only sheet he'll hand her tonight will have the words,

and

just,

the words to describe *how*

and

much

and

really

when he looks into eyes with colors *colors* don't have,

colors that fall to read the page in her hands,

and

Sorry.

Blue (and the quiet reflection that comes early and much more often, *now*)

It's been moons

and

many since the *full*,

moon

(in memory,)

moon on the Saturday he met T*his New One*;

now,

on this new one

and

under the first moon,

full

 or,

alone since he met her,

he has the time away to realize time away is terrible.

And

it's crazy maybe

and

makes him *more,*

that despite moons numbering many,

every one spent under

and

with

feels as *new* as her middle-name,

a name it's taken this many moons to realize she's *still,*

appreciate the way he realized many ago he could change to *only*

and

feel as satisfied.

And

he doesn't miss the clubs

and

drinks inside them

he surrendered to surround her on nights like *Satur,*

tequila straight-up can't tickle his tummy like she can,

the peach in schnapps is half the taste

and

fun

of tasting *hers,* too.

Too,

like the number

and

more, if he's good,

times he can make *her*

before *he*

comes,

over like she looks forward to him coming,

every single Saturday night he's not out,

so every single Saturday night.

Those times *every* time

are ten times

the thrill of the shot

or

the girl that gives him the eye to make him think he *has* one;

because blonde hair

or

brown hair

or somewhere-between hair

can't curl like her hair

and

toes

under

or

over him when he pulls on number any of her ten thousand curls.

Blue (and of pedestals and placings)

He is careful placing her on her pedestal.

His arms shake;
he's scared the harder he holds her,
the faster she slips between his fingers.

She's precious,
after all,
and
perfect,
(still,)
and
though she's spent nights
and
the fights in them away,
This One stays *New*, so her pedestal stays home.

And
he's not to blame,
and
none could blame him,
because her upper lip is *fatter* than it should be
and
he should be *too*;
nothing tasting half the sweet of her kiss comes with calories under *tons*.

She's as bad for him

(the way she holds his heart in the way she words the *his* name attached)

as cholesterol,

but there's none in her hips,

hips he holds

and

up

and

on a pedestal.

So back she goes,

and

he holds harder on her way up.

His arm shakes, she slips a little; but back she goes.

Maybe *hers* curves his way a little on the way,

curves

and

the way that makes *more* than his arms shake,

and

in anticipation of making legs

and

between hers shake too.

And

then

and

only he *won't* be careful;

anything *but* in the way

and

parts

he'll play with

and

between,

but right after,

moment

and

no more,

back she goes

 and

back she stays.

And

for as long as she will,

her home will be here

and

higher,

and

he'll be below

and

admiring,

always,

and

wondering, sometimes more

and

times between too,

what he did to deserve day comma *any* with her

and

her lips,

lips with the calories

and

only he knows he'll never count or care to.

December

Blue (and the end of the year)

So he's *here*,
and
the year is gone,
 (the year he told himself he'd publish his book)
and
save his dream
and
his life,

and
he's *nowhere*, step shy
and
none closer than he was when he told himself;
and
now,
day-the-last
and
year *later*, he can't breathe.

He realized it when he got out of bed,
and
the weight of the world on his shoulders hurt somewhere in his chest
—he tried to breathe through his nose when he brushed his teeth but the
breath wouldn't come

and

his shoulders wouldn't shrug

and

his heart hurt

and

maybe *stopped*,

maybe just for a moment,

maybe debating whether living *this*,

the rest of his life,

having failed so brilliantly,

is worth living at *all*.

And

sure,

being in love *helps*,

dulling the pain that follows,

and

only momentarily;

the realization this morning that this morning *is*,

in fact,

the first of the *every* mornings

he'll wake up

and

beside *This New One*

and

realize his failure is complete.

It beat again, his heart,

and

still,

now four hours on from capping the toothpaste

and

realizing (with that last twist of the cap)

that he's not published

so *he's not a writer*

and

the things it *cost*

--seasons

and

other women

and

--aren't worth the thing he *gave them up for,*

and

he's mad at Thursday

and

the Girl on TV for walking away,

and

he's mad at himself for picking up his pen

and

trying to do something about it.

If he could have just settled, *then,*

realized that the girl

and

the career

and

the dream weren't his to hold,

then maybe, at least on sunny days,

he could have told himself he was *happy*,

living in the mediocrity his father so smartly realized

and

recognized

and

assigned him to

years ago,

when he *began*

to not amount to *half.*

Red (and a perfectly legitimate question with a perfectly illegitimate answer)

Where do you go

he asks somewhat *violently*; and for the life of him he can't think of the most appropriate way to tell him to fuck off and mind his business, so he goes with

Fuck off

and

Mind your business.

But delicately, and because Post Gay Bosco *is*, concerned as he is about something obviously inconsequential and insignificant because he is *here*; here like he always is and getting ready for tonight and tonight's debauchery, so questions like

Where do you go

can go and to wherever Post Gay Bosco, in his stimulant and depressant-enhanced delusion, foolishly opened his mouth to ask him at all.

So he turns, and to the kitchen table with the stimulants and depressants, content that

Fuck off

and

Mind your business

succinctly and accurately detail his position on said subject, but Post Gay Bosco violently, (or at least as violently as a Post Gay man can,) grabs his stimulant and depressant grabbing arm, turns him around, asking mind-turn with the reckless abandon only stimulants (and too much) and depressants (and too much) can;

Where do you go

and *often* and *always* and at least *half* the time.

And it must be the stimulants and the depressants making his eyes the crazy they are when he asks him, because and honestly and for the life of him, he doesn't go anywhere; anywhere at all.

There's home, sure, and in the morning attached to the nights like *tonight* he'll spend abusing stimulants and depressants and the women Post Gay Bosco invited to tonight's party—home and the occasional *her place*, if the latest some-skank has one without a man or with a man who's away for the night it takes him to turn her inside out—but and for the most part and honestly, *away* isn't *far* or *often*.

Enough, and to warrant violent, (or at least as violently as a Post Gay man can,) arm pulling and the kind of persistent and violent nagging only women and Post Gay men can, and *more than* when he opens his mouth and again to ask

Where do you go

again, too; and he knows that Callie or Michelle or Shauna or whoever the fuck shows up tonight is going to get it *extra* hard, the way he feels the familiar anger rising inside of him, inside of him and knowing the only cure is to put it inside of *her*, instead.

Blue (and a perfectly legitimate question with a perfectly illegitimate answer)

Where do you go

she says,

saying softly

and

asking *more*,

softly asking

and

deserving *much*

and

and

for questions she asks as to where he spends at least *half* his time.

Time without her

and

away,

from *This New One,*

and

answers

for

he just doesn't have when she looks at him,

eyes with colors

and

all that,

and

he can't bring himself to speak, because he honestly doesn't *know.*

He supposes his world just kind of *swallows* him,

time lost to his living room

and

the clock on his living room wall,

pretending furiously that any second

of any minute

of any hour

will be *the,*

second Bob The Editor calls to tell him he loves his revisions,

calls to tell him he's saved his life.

So he looks at her,

This New One,

and

into eyes with colors *colors* don't have,

and

it breaks the piece of his heart this December hasn't already broken,

and

maybe his failure as a man is complete,

because an *answer*

is just one more thing he can't give her.

She says she misses him,

misses him when he goes the way

and

the where

he doesn't

and

can't know;

and

he's not lying when he says he misses her too, knowing he must,

and

that time apart is *still* teeth

and

pulling,

but

and

for the life of him

—the one he knows he wants to spend the rest of with her

—he doesn't know what she means when she says he goes,

away

and

at all.

And

why would he go anywhere, really,

and

where would he go,

when looking at her

and

into, *eyes with colors*

and

all that, is *enough*

and

much much more *than*

to make Summer a season

and

just,

and

the Girl on TV just lower case

and

a,

another pretty girl on TV that matters as much

and

less

as all of the *every-other ones* before *her,*

the ones with the time he wasted pining

and

wishing

and

wanting for

wasted

and

as,

the time she tells him he spends anywhere but beside her.

So,

Where do you go

softly

and

again,

and

again he doesn't have the heart or breath to tell her he does not know.

Red (and the inevitable unavoidable return of cousin Aimee…and the inevitable unavoidable beginning of the realization he has a problem)

Cousin Aimee is back and looking at him desperately with eyes that say she desperately wants the coke he desperately wants to do *with-off* her.

And it's been months and minutes since he's seen her and minutes and less since he's waited-wanted to; so when he says the first of five things he'll say to offend her, maybe the time makes the offensive *less*, because her fight back has more *fuck* than fight back in it.

So he's at this bar, now, and she's at this bar, and somewhere decidedly else at this bar his ex-girlfriend (and cousin Aimee's cousin) is searching the *other* somewhere else's at this bar for the both of them.

And he doesn't care and he's sure she doesn't care and he doesn't care because she's black and blue like his ego; so *bruised* when he looks at her black-black hair and thinks of *pulling* it, sore when her blue-blue eyes tell him without telling him she's at least *twice* and maybe *more* the pretty he possesses.

She's down for a week and her-cousin's-his-ex's-sister's wedding she says, says without saying she's down for doing the line down his pants off what's inside them/beside it.

And he knows she knows they're in trouble and *hunted*, taking off after taking shots to the patio of the bar his ex, her cousin

picked for the wedding party, but goddamn if the party isn't *here* for now— the patio before the *anywhere else* he would rip the clothes unmercifully smothering the kind of curves he's waited months and minutes to and from her.

So there'll be dancing, (with the hiding,) and on the way to and *before* the anywhere they'll end up and together; dancing and grinding and touching and the other things that make the *other* things, things worth waiting for *worth waiting for*.

She'll be better at them, naturally and *un*, the kind of beautiful shots of liquid cocaine and lines of *not* liquid cocaine can't mar the way he'll try to when he's pulling on or biting through the prettiest of her thousand-thousand pretty parts.

But that's later, and *ideally*, and no matter how hard he wishes she's still a Vanilla-tipped cigarette away from him on the patio of some place they're in and in trouble and hunted.

So for the *all-you-can-do-is-wait* portion of the night, in between studying the way vowels form between the cotton-candy lip-glossed cotton-candy of her lips, he watches the way she's silently screaming when she whispers; screaming she wants him and still not screaming half as loud as he screams when he whispers he wants her *more*.

And in between drags of Vanilla with cotton-candy chasers she asks if he's *holding* and for once and sobering he's *not*, and it hits him harder than the sight of her and *first*, so he half-prays Spanish Jose is awake when he flips his phone, a half-second *after* she grabs his hand to head for anywhere else.

Unfortunately and not, there's dancing and drinks he spent cigarettes anticipating on the way; and when the pressing against on the floor can't equal the pressing against on the bed, the drinks he drinks to make the clock move forward maybe move faster.

And when the two of them fall into the cab he spent the escape from the bar *yearning* to, it's going anywhere but straight; is or *isn't, and his head is spinning too fast to tell* and *her head is spinning* and the cruelest part of it all, really, is all at once *he's not in a cab at all* and *he's in Post Gay Bosco's apartment alone*, alone because she's gone, and all he has to hold are a flipped cell phone with *no-way-Jose* and a side of his face strangely stinging and the promise she promised him when she promised she'd fuck him at the wedding, a week away and not *now*.

There's coke somewhere in him and below him, and he's reasonably sure he-she-they were having a good time; before the blackout and before the slap she must have given him and before she left.

And before he knows it, he's reaching for his keys, thinking the hell with promising Bosco he wouldn't drive (the way he knows he promised him before they hopped a cab to meet Cousin Aimee somewhere downtown, earlier tonight and *ages* ago) on his way out the door and to drive after her.

Red (and this a big one, but bear with it, it's pivotal)

He's *awake* and *now* and maybe he wishes he *wasn't*; because awake and now is *driving* and at least fifty miles *north* of what is legally acceptable, north on a road he can't remember running north without traffic and the kind that doesn't really care for fifty over *at all* on.

Still, a frantic-still-sluggish look at the rearview mirror all at once and now tells him he's *alone*; a frantic-less-sluggish look at the digital clock on the dashboard he can't remember dashing behind tells him he's alone because it's *fucking four o'clock in the morning.*

Which morning he can't-tell-doesn't-care, but the cocaine he's sure he's strung out on is wrestling the insomnia somewhere behind the *more* tired of his tired eyes, twisting to tell him how he ended up *now* and fifty north northbound on some road not particularly worth running north *or* on.

So he's *driving*, he knows, and fast, and it's late and he was sleeping or at least *almost*—a frantic and not-sluggish-at-all gnashing of tongue against teeth tells him the numb is Novocain, as in *cut-with*, and, as far as shitty-stepped-on blow goes, he must have done a *ski-slope* to make this seemingly totally irrational series of events seem anything *other than.*

The memories come, as memories do, in clouds and flashes of light underneath and around them; the feeling is always *first*, and the static of tonight's tells him a storm is coming and he listens and

he stays on the accelerator before he remembers why he *wants to*, lets the lightning hit in between peering periodically and nowhere near frantically enough at deserted boats and empty warehouses presenting themselves out his right side window and infinitely more concretely than clouds with memories inside them.

By the time the light burns read at *Parliament,* he guesses and with confidence the overwhelming anger he's *seething* through is directly related to a *female,* the burning in his jeans as he dives under the bridge at *Cherry* lets him know it's directly related to a female he's not directly related to.

So his sister and her bullshit, bullshit from the four o'clock *without* black are out the window like the black and that incinerator, the cloud with the memory of the afternoon phone call ignored and *gone* and *he is too* from under the bridge and too fast and the incinerator can stand stoically judging him from it's perch on the waterfront from it's *new* perch in his rearview.

So it's a fight and a girl and not his sister that's got him driving like a Rockstar *because-he-is* at four in the morning north on *Lakeshore* and north to nowhere apparently and *particular,* he's scanning clouds from under overpasses for fights and yesterday and it's coming like morning and *down,* horribly, and the light at *Logan Ave,* and as fast and as hard as he presses the right *in-more-ways-than* pedal, he can't stop morning and sketching and *Amber,* not the girl, but the *light* at Logan, the light he can't-won't stop for, the light as far away as his reasoning for this drug-induced suicide run.

It hits him sometime *after* the light he needs to be *green* goes *red,* right around the time the Novocain gives enough to tell him he's smiling as some fuck in a *Focus* has the nerve to lay on the horn with his brakes.

Yeah, it hits like the *Focus* tries to; he's still smiling as near-death-experience number two brings the *namesake* without trading paint, and it's a girl and his fault, and *why the fuck not.*

Knowing why he's devastated and suicidal makes being devastated and suicidal the kind of fun it *should* be, so he's on the gas harder than the second time he's just remembered *her* hitting him, the girl worth speeding and suicide.

The memory stings as fresh as her manicured little hand, and he's tasting all five fingers and admiring her inability to ball a fist as *Carlon Ave* leaves like *Logan* and apparently Cousin Aimee, Cousin Aimee he remembers leaving *north* of slap seven.

And the whole *self-hate-doubt-loathing* thing is probably chemically-induced and *for sure* out of character, but this new *pussy* in him shoots to his balls like lightning and out his window, and it's suddenly raining and it's just as well because it kinda makes the fact that he's suddenly crying okay and *easier* and he's the *opposite* in his pants and he doesn't care why.

This new spectrum of human emotions he's been running like out from the overpass and along the motor slab prison that houses the city's hydro is decidedly poor form; for being someone who prides himself on lacking the *female* of feelings, so compassion and—

--and some asshole in a semi turns onto the expressway ten paces too close and ruins his train of thought and a new one rolls out of the station and tells-asks him wouldn't it be fun to slam into the back of him and

--he figures the coke wears off, because he's sleeping again.

Red (and what he's dreaming about, asleep at the wheel)

And it starts sweet, all *Mr. Smith-on-the-i-Pod-because-it's-the-greatest-Uncle-L-ever-did-and-Doin'-It-is-about-to-come-on-and-he's-pretty-sure-he's-about-to-and-to-and-too* and Cousin Aimee is on the couch beside him wearing the kind of thing that would make the *Cousin* part, even *his*, matter as much as the rain outside, *so not at all.*

And the shit he doesn't know will drive him crazy *literally* four hours from two minutes from the minute it'll take him to cut-snort is driving *him-them* crazy *figuratively* and it's making *figuring* his favorite-*favorite* word, watching her figure and figuring how many minutes it'll take to free her from the clothes *oppressing-repressing* it.

And she's saying something as the cutting starts, all left hand and *VISA* card, and the countdown starts, and in memory this would be called foreshadowing and it will be four hours from now, but he's not listening because *not* now…

…

…*now* the latest in a series *of* is ready for consumption and though *he's pretty sure he's sick of this shit* he's pretty sure she's pretty fucking pretty and pretty fucking sure he's pretty much ready to fuck her so *fuck it*, and
Snort
she follows faster than she should.

What happens next *happens* and he's sure of it, but somewhere between chewing on the taste and tip of her tongue and thumbing the thread of her thong he says in between chews something that makes her take *her* hand away from said thong and apply it somewhere *less* and somehow *still* provocative, (so his *face*,) and it's the first of four and in a hurry and he is too and to stop her from hurriedly striking him again.

It's more for the *principle*, the way the numb in his mouth numbed the five manicured little fingers across it; the numb helps *there*, yeah, but betrays the reasoning *north* of his mouth when he watches her mouth the kinds of things that *kill* the kinds of things he'd intended for her and this evening and right *now*, really, before the assault *verbal* and unfolding unexpectedly and less welcome *below* him.

And he tries to stop *hers* from spitting and venom with the pressing and caress of *his*; unfortunately the fucking coke has made his *lips* as useful or less than what he knows he was seconds from using on *her*, his problem-solver now more the *problem*; shifting lifelessly and listlessly *under* the *wear* he's waited months to *not* for her.

And she's out the door and *angry*; and his face stings, *alone in the living room at Post Gay Bosco's*, and her promise to fuck him at the wedding a week away and *not* now isn't good enough, so he's searching for his keys and out the door to the parking lot below—*the parking lot and the car he promised Post Gay Bosco would stay parked before this evening got fucked the way he hasn't and deserves to...* ...deserves to so he's driving, and *to* her.

(Making his dream more *a memory*, even more *a reminder*, a reminder to WAKE THE FUCK UP, because he's asleep at the wheel.)

Red (and waking at the most opportune time, really)

And he sees headlights he *swore* were her eyes, *the way they shine so fucking magnificently on him*; and he's awake and *enough* to swerve *hard* into the lane he *should* have been in all along, leaving the honking-skidding pickup truck in the oncoming and, now, *behind him* lane.

And all at once he's happy to be *alive* and *awake* and then all at once he's *angry*—angry that his coke and his high have gone the way of the girl he's relentlessly pursuing—knowing that knocking on the door of *her-cousin-his-ex's-parent's-house*—the house housing her and *her-cousin-his-ex*—may not go over so well, coming down and five in the morning.

Still, these are the circumstances, *and all that*, so he takes three left turns to make it to *her-cousin-his-ex's-parent's-house*, two left turns away, kills the ignition before his ascent on the stairs, harder than it should be, and his *knocking-rapping-pounding* on the front door, harder than it should be, as well.

And there's an answer and *angrily* and *eventually*, and it angers him that it's *her-cousin-his-ex's* father answering the door; and, from the looks of *her-cousin-his-ex's*   father,   the   feeling   is   *mutual.*

He's mentioning something *aggressively*, *her-cousin-his-ex's* father, something about *five in the morning* and something about *smelling alcohol on his breath* and something about *parking on the front lawn* and something, supposedly, about *never-being-welcome-here-again*, after what he did to *her-cousin-his-ex* way back *when*; but his words

are wasted when he sees his *ex*, (and more importantly,) Cousin Aimee, wiping tired eyes and peering over over-protective shoulders to catch a glimpse of the delightful commotion he's causing.

And just the *sight* of her, looking at him with her blue-blue eyes, eyes telling him to *ignore what comes next* and eyes telling him she *appreciates* the effort and the chance he took and *would again* to be here and *now* and mouthing things like

You're fucking insane

making her *words* every bit as enticing as the *rest of her.*

He knows she forgives him for *whatever-the-fuck-he-did* to make her leave and make him *chase* her, and all at once *each-and-every* of *all* the lives he endangered were worth it and *again*, when she moves *closer* and to move words to *move* him.

And she's passing *more* through the vanilla-chased cotton-candy lip-glossed cotton-candy of her lips; and it's all for *show* when she tells him to *leave* and not come again, and all at once he *isn't* having the cops called on him and the evening is *settling* again; after angry fathers and confused ex-girlfriends shamble off back to *wherever-the-fuck-they-woke-from*, Cousin Aimee gives him a kiss on the side of his face she *stung* with her manicured little hands, whispers words *even more sweetly* when she whispers

Fuck you at the wedding

before licking his lips.

And before he can catch her tongue in between the lips she licks, she's turned and halfway up the stairs, leaving him to wonder how he'll survive the week without her and thanking the drunk *he is* for making her sexy little saunter a sexy little saunter in slow motion.

Blue (and every Starbucks in the world, probably)

He can be mad about it,

and

he *is*,

but the city is fucking dirtier than it was yesterday

and

though he failed to meet his goal,

he knows he has to keep *fighting*.

Well, knows *now*,

and

it took the French guy selling coke at the Starbucks on the corner,

next to the table with the little girl

with the curly hair

to realize that

yeah,

a year has passed

and

he's not published,

and

Bob the Editor might not have loved

Pining For Someone who May or May Not Know They're Being Pined For

as much as he did,

but if he was strong enough to bare his soul once,

maybe putting aside his second manuscript to rework his *first* isn't so bad.

Like opening an old cut, sure,

and

as he grabs the *triple-mocha-something* from the counter,

gives the drug dealer a dirty look on his way out the door,

out the door

and

on his way to both *This New One*

<u>and</u>

his writing,

balancing both so his future can be better than what he leaves behind him.

Red (and though the year is over anyways, one last shot)

Bob the Editor's got *that* look on his face, and he's about to get punched in the mouth for it.

And his is moving *too* and *again* and mouthing something that sounds like an answer he doesn't care to hear, an answer to a question he's asked before and with less urgency, and a question he's answered 'yes' to before too, 'yes' the answer he really needs to hear *now*.

He says something, Bob the Editor, about having someone *else's* manuscript to edit and just not having the time to edit *this*, his new and improved (—if perfection is in fact capable of improvement—) perfect manuscript, but he isn't hearing it, words from the mouth mouthing them, because all he can picture is *punching* the mouth mouthing them.

So he gives him his best *do-what-the-fuck-I-want-you-to* look, the one he's grown fond of throwing right before his favorite follow up, *I-just-punched-you-in-the-mouth*, but for all his menace, pounds now *north* of 145 and the last time he sat sick in this seat, Bob the Editor just isn't having it.

Blue (and though his failure is pretty much complete, one last shot at it anyways)

Bob the Editor has *that* look on his face,
and
he's only got five minutes

—five minutes for his dream
and
his life
and
the whole rest of it
—to change it.

So he sets in, mouth mouthing words about dreams
and
failings
and
falling,
falling
and
picking himself up,
picking himself up by tearing up half his dream
and
his manuscript
and
replacing it with *this*,
his new
and

last dream he holds in hands shaking,

and

hands, hands still shaking, to Bob the Editor,

mouth mouthing *please* for the fifth time in five minutes.

He says something back, Bob the Editor,

trying to hand his new

and

last dream back too,

something about having someone *else's* manuscript to edit,

but maybe he reads **<u>DESPERATION</u>** written in bold

and

capital underlined letters

somewhere in his desperate eyes,

because he hesitates handing his new

and

last dream back halfway, says something *else* instead.

Something about appreciating the *way* he asked

and

the work he put in on it,

this new

and

last dream halfway in his still shaking hands

and

something he swears sounds a lot like acceptance

and

salvation

and

hope

and

one last shot in the sound he makes with his mouth when he mouths

Okay.

Red (and a Sunday)

Sunday, and the hospital calls, twice, and he doesn't answer either, doesn't answer because he isn't sick anymore.

Red (and one week—so one thousand—later)

Cousin Aimee is back, back because she never really went anywhere other than *away*, away and for the *week-that's-felt-like-five* the way he's been waiting, waiting for here and *now* and her and this wedding.

And the invitation he leaves on the table below says it's for someone *else*, something about her-cousin-his-ex's sister and something about this being *her* big day, but the fucking invitation *lied*.

Lied and *a lot*, because looking at Cousin Aimee wearing the dress she's barely wearing and yet wearing oh-so-well, this wedding and this day and this moment are all and *only*—the way they have been since his eyes met her eyes and his eyes said

I want to devour you

and her eyes said

I could run circles around you

--all and only about *her*.

And he supposes it's the chemicals, again, and not the ones below and beside the invitation he plans to snort them off of on the table below him, but he ones *in her in her*, mixing in the space between the ones *in him in him*, that chemical thing animals understand when she forms vowels between the cotton-candy lip-glossed cotton-candy of her lips, tells him

It's time.

Time, so he moves closer and towards her, thanking *the-God-there-isn't* for making her and thanking Spanish Jose for making that run, and the closer he gets to her and the cotton-candy lip-glossed cotton-candy of her lips, the more he forgets about the *details*, the details and the danger in them.

Details he knows he *shouldn't*, forgetting the maneuvers he maneuvered moments and moments *without* her ago in order to maneuver her and moments *with* her; and away from the watchful eyes of her-cousin-his-ex and the rest of the bridal party watching and for him outside *here*, the room adjacent to the reception hall in the bottom of the church he can't wait to *sin* in.

And for a moment he thinks of Post Gay Bosco running interference for him somewhere upstairs; lying in church and telling the rest of the bridal party they look *half* the gorgeous Cousin Aimee does across from him and *closer*; a moment, and then she's *too, close to think about anything other than her* and her eyes and looking into them and then looking *away*, away because her eyes burn bluer, *so better*, than his.

And he knows he's a moment, (so eternity,) from tasting her and the cotton-candy lip-glossed cotton-candy of her lips, and in that moment there is a part of him that tells him he *shouldn't*, shouldn't tear into her dress and the package containing the coke he can't wait even a moment to do with/off her, but it is a part of him he ignores.

Ignores, because he's

Red

and a rockstar and because there are no consequences in *this*, the world he'll own and is *owed*, so he takes the last step to her and the tearing of her dress, reaches to tear it.

Reaches, and with the reaching there's thinking and about the *taste* he's about to, right after the tearing and off of her *Oh-my-the-God-there-isn't* purple *Prada* or *Chanel* or *something-equally-insignificant* dress, tasting the cotton-candy lip-glossed cotton-candy of her lips, each and every *all* of them.

So he's reaching, and for her and with both hands, and he's not thinking about the coke he's leaving beside the invitation on the table below him because and *really*, the coke is not the star tonight, not even really riding shotgun, and he's sure her *dress* will be when they break out of here, shotgun because he can't picture her anywhere but *on* him and his lap and she reaches to touch it, *his lap*, and then a shotgun goes off somewhere behind and at once all around him.

And it's not a shotgun at all, but it might as well be, because it's a slamming door and the hand moving away from the doorknob after slamming it is her-cousin-his-ex, her-cousin-his-ex and the rest of the bridal party.

Her-cousin-his-ex and the rest of the bridal party, and, somewhere in the ether and insignificant, the fuck, Post Gay Bosco, giving him his best *I'm-an-insignificant-fuck* look.

And what happens next happens fast and too, and far too fast to hold and onto, *her* like he wants to, because she's moving and the other way, so *away*, away like *too many* have moved.

Somewhere in the ether and insignificant, her-cousin-his-ex is screaming and at him and at her and at *them*, and she's crying and it doesn't matter, because across from him and away, Cousin Aimee is crying and all at once, and all at once it might be the saddest thing he's ever seen, seeing eyes *bluer*, (so just plain better,) shine bluer still framed by the tears he all at once knows he's caused.

It kind of *stops* him, her tears and watching her eyes cry them, and all at once all of the every-other things that occupy the seconds he spends hours watching her eyes cry them don't matter near as much as each and every tear does; not the punches his face takes, not the words his ears take, not the promises to kill him his heart takes.

She turns, Cousin Aimee does, crying and sometime between a scratch-to and a shout-in his ear, turns crying and leaves him to a closed door and an enraged her-cousin-his-ex and a gang beating from an army of purple hued bridesmaids and an insignificant, the fuck, Post Gay Bosco, who may be crying too, shrieking something insignificant about the violence, and it's all insignificant, because she's gone.

The way they go, women and the ones who matter, so *away*.

And he's angry and he knows why, knowing that all the

Red

and all the cocaine and all the muscles and all the pretty he possesses still wasn't enough to possess *her*, and the feeling stays, feeling angry and insignificant long after everyone *not* has left him too, alone and with his drugs and his violently insignificant best

friend, in the room adjacent to the reception hall in the bottom of the church he wasn't even man enough to *sin* in.

Blue (and a pretty-fucking-big plot twist)

I'm pregnant.
Yeah.

And
with two words,
two words screaming in stereo even when spoken softly
and
with the volume way down,

every other word he'd been keeping
or
saving
or
planning to say, *to*day
or
one day,
matter as much as one days before *today*
because *today*
and
with two little words,
those two little words mean *day* with *every* after
are going to be far too different.

And
not in a good way
and
not *now*,

not that

with the lips

and

tongue attached to vowels

and

consonants wouldn't be *the one he would want to*

and

with

and

one day;

one day better *some*day

and

other

and

not *to*day,

like the one yesterday probably tomorrow he knows he *won't* be the kind of
man it would take to be enough for *This New One*

let alone this *next* one.

Maybe it settles him,

somewhere *south* of the eyes he looks into,

eyes with colors *colors* don't have;

settles him to picture

looking south

of eyes with colors *colors* don't have

into arms holding

something with eyes with colors <u>half</u> his colors have,

(have because *half* of *him* stares back at him,)

something he made with someone worth *making* with.

Settles him for a *second,*

until the world creeps in at the corners,

the world with utility bills

and

hospital bills

and

post-secondary bills,

bills

and

bills that cost the *other* kind,

the bills he needs more *todays* than *today* to save

for the day he's prepared for her to walk up to him,

look into his eyes with eyes with colors *colors* don't have,

and

not be able to look *south* to the lips that move to *move* him

when they move to say

I'm pregnant.

And with two words,

This New One makes every word he wasted

wording *ways he would protect her*

matter as much as whatever he was doing before she spoke them;

so *not at all*

when she takes his breath in a different way than the way she still takes his

breath

every time she words any-*every* other words.

He wants to look *north,*

to the first of her thousand-thousand curls,

the first of each/every curl worth the first of the thousand-thousand kisses

she *deserves*, but

she holds him with her eyes,

eyes with colors *colors* don't have

and

tears, too,

and

too many to catch

and

stop,

like he realizes, sadly, *he has to,*

promising *anything* after *this.*

Somewhere south the first of them explodes in a miniscule puddle,

a pin drop on the floor beside the stain his soul can't leave

when it crashes in stereo at her feet.

I'm pregnant.

Two words,

words that make the three he spoke when he said

I'll never hurt

as much a lie as *everyone* before

You

the one *after* the *three-hundred thousand six-hundred seventy-four*

it took to love her enough to look into her eyes,

eyes with colors *colors* don't have,

and

believe in the soul he *used to have* he would never,

could never,

hurt her the way she just spent two words telling him he *has*.

So he's failed,

and

again,

and

he can add *parent* to *protector* to *writer* to *son*,

latest in a list he could write,

and,

for once, *believably*,

maybe the first chapter in a book about a boy who might be *better off*...

The thought is the latest thing he fails to finish,

fails like he fails to finish his book,

like he fails to stop her tears,

tears he promised himself

words before he promised her she would never shed,

and

he knows

she knows

he's failed to protect her from the kind of hurt *they both knew* he was capable

of.

Blue (and rationalizing, maybe)

It's not that he couldn't see it,

<u>life</u>

with the little thing trying to come to

and

inside his favorite-*favorite* place;

it's just that he knows <u>what's left of his</u> isn't enough for *This New One,*

(let alone this *Really New One,*)

and,

selfish or not,

inside of her

and

his favorite-*favorite* place

is the *last* place he's willing to share.

Not with the black boys,

black like their intentions for her when they come around her little store in

the mall, offering little gifts this holiday season,

praying that

preying

on her naïveté will get them to the place he shares with six-week four-day old

semen.

And

it's more than that

and

he knows it,

but it's easier

and

by far

to keep every shade of grey running through his mind color blind

like it *could* be,

(the way it runs on his father's side,)

father suddenly the *second* scariest word in the words he knows,

second to

mother

and

unplanned,

so,

hurt

because of what they've agreed to do,

and

worse either way,

the word he swore to her he *couldn't.*

He wants her to know that if he *could,*

resources, responsibilities

and

other important *r* words north of what they *aren't* this winter,

it *would*

and

for the first time

in too-many-years

and

more girls be *conceivable*

and

her;

the first

and

only with eyes

and

hair

and

shape

at *least* as attractive

and

therefore *logical,*

(as though that word enters an equation conceived with wine

and

too much

and

a lack of

and

much *too much more.*)

He wants her to know it would be *hard,*

latest

and

next

in a line of words lacking too,

to find one to *call* something born of something as beautiful as her,

something to call a little boy

or

little girl born with both colors *colors* don't have

and

colors *nowhere good enough*

in eyes that would open months

and

seasons from a night with too much wine

and

opposite logic

to look upon the eyes that combined to make them.

Because really, *Billy* sucks

and

Suzie is plain,

and

names like seasons are *last,*

and

last season he couldn't dream of dreaming of names like *Chance*

or

Sawyer

or

Sunny,

names of his heroes, heroes with names TV told him were name heroes have,

and

he has neither the name

nor the hero

in

or

around him,

to be for *Abby*

or

Jessica

or

any of the names that fail *like he would* to be good enough for their little boy or girl.

And

he knows instead of mouthing vowels to choose names with,

he'll stick to consonants, mostly,

and

sorry for doing this to her and at Christmas,

Day

knowing any-*every* surprise she unwraps can't compare in her mind

or

<u>belly</u>

to the surprise *he's given her <u>there</u>*

and

early;

and

though he'll ensure the baubles he buys shine brighter than the baubles he would have had *not*,

the unwrapping,

(to put a pretty name on an *anything but* procedure,)

will weigh on her mind *heavier* than some bauble he's paid more to weigh her wrist

and

almost,

so *nowhere near* enough.

Blue (and some more bad news, so *just in time for Christmas!*)

So she's looking at him

and

alone

and

finally,

in the living room

and

safe

and

away from the holidays

and

the *everyone else* they shared them with.

She's looking at him with eyes with *colors,*

and

all that;

and

she's *sad,*

because what he gave her for Christmas can't compare to what he gave her

before

Christmas.

And

a book of every word he ever wrote about

and

for her,

so a book of *apologies,*

handwritten

and

presented *earlier,*

(*because really*

and

to the world outside the living room it still is,

<u>*Christmas*</u>

can't save <u>hers,</u>)

and

the smile she smiled when he gave it to her

faded

hours before *now*

and

the living room they're alone in

and

sharing with the elephant *inside*

and

all around her.

So the holidays are her eyes,

so *sad,*

like the thought that makes his stomach turn the way

and

nothing at all

like the way her stomach turns when he thinks of spending their first New

Year's Eve in some hospital room clinic

instead of the *anywhere else* they should be,

wishing the *everybody else* they were with

would go *somewhere else*

too.

She's been *May-weather*

and

all winter,

punching like *Floyd*

in the fights they fight,

somehow as pretty as *Pretty-Boy Floyd*

when she hooks him harder

and

enough

to make the elephant *move*,

alone in the living room again

and

fighting

and

again

too,

and

this time

like last

and

most times

about something he can't remember being worth getting into the ring over.

So it's sad

and

add an *m* before,

and

he hates to see her *either*

and

anything but

smile

the way she *used* to,

before holidays

and

elephants

and

boxing rings

and

reasons for *both* giving reason to take it out on seasons.

She's still

This New One,

so he can't find the fight to fight back,

fighting back frustration

and

something more *foreign,*

something that fights on the other side of the eyes

he watches her fight with,

something wet

and

weak

and

willing,

should he blink hard

and

long enough to allow it,

to show her just *how* this situation is making him, too.

He'll stand,

he knows,

in the living room

and

Christmas,

and

not,

fake the strength

and

hide the shake in his knee

and

the shiver in his voice when she falls into him,

and

her fight is lost

and

her fear pours through sad eyes

and

he holds her

and

lies a little when he tells her he knows everything will be okay.

Blue (and not being there)

Today
is the day
This New One
had her *abortion,*
and
today
is the coldest day of the year,
and
today is another day
he *wasn't there*
and
wasn't there for her.

Red (and the veil begins to lift, maybe just a little)

Cousin Aimee is *not* here; anymore and it makes him angry, angry she goes the way they all go in the end, so *away*, away and before he could do the kinds of things he's waited for and been promised to do, do and to the body he's dreamed of doing them to, every *other* night since *last*, the night she went away.

And he's angry, *sure*, and sad, *maybe and though he would never admit it*, this feeling rising inside of him he simply labels anger *lite*, thinking and often of black-black hair blacker than his heart and blue-blue eyes bluer than they have any *right* to be, and hating that and for the *first* time, the anger he labels *lite* and anything other than *sad* weighs and on him more than the anger that *is* and *only*.

And maybe someone rational would call it *progress*, days removed from a breakdown in a church basement; he calls it like it *is*, so *cracking at the corners*, and he knows it's going to take stimulants, (and many more,) and depressants, (and many more,) and fucking the latest some-skanks, (and many, many more,) to regain his *alpha* and his center and to center himself, center himself so he never *fails* and never *feels* again.

Still, this one is a *loss* and it bothers him, the whole *not having his way thing*, and between Bob the Editor not calling back about his revision and Cousin Aimee not calling back and saying her flight to Calgary was cancelled and then hanging up and calling back to say she's on her way over to devour him, him and the stimulants and depressants he's going to need to get over the fact
that she's not going to call and then hang up and then call back—the end of this year isn't *half* the promising the beginning promised to be.

So he's angry, *yes*, and lonely, *maybe and for the first time*, and then and *not* for the first time, his phone rings.

And for the second it takes him to reach and for it, it's Cousin Aimee and for him.

And then the second after he flips the receiver and puts his mouth to the mouthpiece to mouth

Hello

his big sister says

Hello

back the way she's been *trying* to, and the

Hello

she says back is not half the

Hello

it should be.

Blue (and **finally** getting through)

I'm sick
she says,
before
and
around
other things, things that matter *now* as much
and
much less
as whatever he was doing before he flipped his cell phone to hear her say it.

He ignored his baby sister's calls
for months
and
many,

and

it's weighing on him like
and
the way

her words are,

words like
been trying
and
to tell you

and

keep for testing

before

Inoperable,

the last word he hears

before the *weight* of words,

carried in the dump truck that's doubling as her voice

topple him

the way they've been waiting to

for months

and

many.

And

there's a word for her condition

and

it starts with '*c*,'

and

he's *known* for months

and

many

and

ignored her for all of them

because he was afraid to face it,

and

now,

of all the weighted words

it's the one he's

waiting

to hear;

the one to make the tears come

the way they want to

and

the weight of being

worthless

and

helpless

meet up with his favorite new adjective:

Hopeless.

But it doesn't come,

doesn't

or

does

but he doesn't hear it,

and

it may be because she's too scared to mouth it

or it may be because he's too scared to hear it,

but it lingers,

over

and

all around him,

sitting on his living room floor

while the clock on the wall draws breath to laugh at him

and

again.

And

she says

Say something

softly,

and

he can't even manage to, any other words than

I'm sorry

seeming worthless

and

hollow

and

entirely

nowhere

near

enough;

and

even to hear himself mouth them,

in the wake of winters

and

unborn babies

and

decisions against them

seems a slight to her the way it was to *her*

This New One

not even

and

less than a month since tragedy *last*.

And

she's on her way over,

This New One,

and

suddenly the part of him that planned sharing his latest finished chapter is dead,

(too,)

and

replaced by the part that plans sharing this *latest* bad news,

and

if he had any left,

he'd

hope

that *more* bad news isn't more than enough to make her leave him like his baby sister *just promised to*.

And
on the other end of the phone,
she's wanting more time,
and
it's *literally*
and
figuratively
and

tragic

either way he looks at it,
and
it's just the latest in a line of things he can't/couldn't give her when he hangs up the phone,
promising to call her back
and
reminding himself to do so before the tomorrow she might not have.

Blue (and the fucking hospital)

He has to find her.

He's getting frantic,
and
whoever designed the hospital should be fucking *shot*,
because
Section C, they said,

room *three eleven*,

and
it all sounded wonderful over the phone.

In the skyway, three rights, up two flights—
but the rights aren't rights,
they're
kinda
rights,
kinda *not*,
so the guess work is turning what should be
five
into
thirty -something,
and,
despite all of the beautiful girls
who only

always

seem to work in places like this,
he just wants to find his baby sister.

He got the phone call
then,
but
the date
and
time
of Mom's message weren't nearly as important
as the words in it,
so trying to remember
when
is about as necessary,
and
twice as useful,
as the *Information*
and
Reception
kiosks scattered here,

with no information
or
receptionists

in the section he's lost in,
the section decidedly not *C.*

Her lung collapsed—

her *good* lung—

for the second time just over a year,

so she's spent the time *since*

here,

breathing through tubes

and

waiting for foreign doctors to cut into her

with foreign objects,

cut

and

hack

and

slice

and

tear

through skin

and

tissue

and

muscle

and

bone,

skin

and

everything else *far too precious* to be subject to such intrusion,

to patch

and

stitch her, leaving, hopefully, something *not*

less complete

than what they started with,

something with a smile

and

a shape

and

a spirit he's spent his whole life counting on being around his whole life.

Yeah, he'd very much appreciate it if they would leave her *whole*,

her

and

the memories of her,

the memories that anchor him in the

now,

the memories of the smile

and

the shape

and

the spirit worth searching halls decidedly not *C* for.

Blue (and visiting baby sister)

She says she doesn't feel good,

reaches for the button at the side of her bed,

the one to call the people who are *supposed* to make her feel better,

supposed to,

but

can't.

When he doesn't feel good,

it's a headache;

when she doesn't feel good,

its cells dying

and

blood where it shouldn't be

and

coughing that won't stop,

even for buttons by beds,

and

the light green pajamas that follow.

They'll come now,

silent in their pajamas,

tell him decidedly *louder* that he has to leave,

her

and

the blood,

for another day,

until they decide *hours* are *visitable* again.

He'll go home

and

try to write,

write the words that will take him away from all this,

try to make him *magic*

like *Johnson,*

the kind of name that has the power to make the sickness not stay.

He'll go home,

and

the words won't come,

and

Bob the Editor won't call,

won't like he hasn't,

two months on now,

months she has spent *in*

and

mercifully *out*

and

unmercifully *in*

that bed

in

that place,

a place he's spent too much time in,

wondering how anywhere with people walking around in pajamas can be so

crushingly *sad.*

He'll go home,

and

turn the key,

and

the darkness will be waiting to swallow him,

warm

and

silent

and

away

from fluorescent lights

and

the hum of machines that hum, but look like they don't need to.

The clock on his kitchen wall might give him another break tonight,

the hum from machines that look like they don't need to

staying in his ears as he climbs in his car,

wondering if it will outlast *Timbaland*

and

the music he tries to cheer himself up with again tonight,

and

well into the pressing his head against his pillow

he calls sleep.

The book he-writes-in-when-he-writes

is closed on the seat beside him,

and

it might as well *stay* that way,

the avenues on the way to the darkness filled with *Timbaland,*

(not so much,)

and

humming,

(maybe *more,*)

and

memories of his sister's face

then

in memory replaced by the mask of her face

now,

the most,

more important than the colors on the streetlamps that separate him from the

kind of loneliness he's accustomed to,

the kind that awaits

eagerly

his return.

Red (and dreaming and again, and dreaming again of Cousin Aimee)

Cousin Aimee is back and she's *sad* and he's sad because Cousin Aimee is back and only *here* in his dream.

And she's looking at him, Cousin Aimee is, with eyes *sadder* than he remembers when he remembers looking at her *looking at him* and up from a table with cocaine on it; so about the only place he remembers her looking at him from at *all*.

And this is where the dream straddles that *nightmare* line, the way she usually and only straddles him in the kind of dreams he has *not often enough* and about her—because this is where she straddles her straw between fingers and drawing lines that *won't end*, won't end because this is, *from appearances*, a dream, a dream *or that other thing* because the lines won't *stop* and she won't stop drawing them.

And the blood that begins to run away from her nose caresses and coats her lips *comma* both; and for the first time since gazing on them grazing on them is oddly nowhere *near* the appealing it should be.

She looks *worse* now, and scared, drawing lines he reads between in eyes just plain *better* than his; eyes that scream
I'm scared
before she parts the blood marring the place he's wanted to call home,
I'm scared
whispered between lips he's wasted time and dreams on waiting to *own*, lips looking *now* and *only* completely *unlivable*.
I don't want to
she says, spitting blood, and before
anymore

and the saddest thing is that before the blood that is supposed to be tears starts running away from eyes that scream

stop

she draws again, because she *can't*.

And then he wakes up, <u>mercifully</u>, and Cousin Aimee is gone, un_____, and because it was a dream and *only*.

He *tells* himself, rolling over and choosing to ignore the spot of blood staining and sharing his pillow.

Blue (and the fucking hospital, again)

The little girl has no hair.

She might be

fourteen,

she might be

twelve

—the point is, he's sitting in this room hoping medical science can keep his
baby sister from looking like *that*,
because they found something that *shouldn't be there*
when they x-rayed her collapsed lung,
(like a collapsed lung *should* be there;)
looking like little *Stacey*
or
Kimberly
or
whatever it is,

because looking like *that*,

whatever it is,
isn't as important as looking at what's *not* on top of her head.

Like it makes her *less* somehow.

She looks at him,

right now,

kinda smiles,

smiles like she's got hair on the top of her head,

and

it kinda breaks his heart.

Kinda,

like *does*,

because the nurse with the truckload of mascara is talking

to her *Baby Phat*-wearing *not*-Mom

about a birthday party,

and

it's fucking *epic*,

because the little girl is looking

through him

with eyes that should be experimenting with truckloads of mascara,

and

instead of birthday parties,

she's looking at him

like she wants him to save her life.

So maybe birthday parties can be relevant again.

Or maybe he's exaggerating

—maybe the chemo

or

the chemicals

or

whatever the fuck she's on to make her hair fall out

is working,

and

she's fine,

and

she's gonna *be* fine,

and

the birthday party is for her,

just the next birthday party before the next

next

one.

Either way,

the chapter he was working on,

(the one where the hero

and

his girl live happily,

and

ever

after,)

the one he started five minutes before *Baby Phat*

and

the little girl with no hair sat down across from him in the hospital emergency

room, is pretty much *shot.*

He knows he could start a new one,

maybe one about a pretty sad pretty little girl with no hair,

but writing about real life is *almost* as depressing *as*,

and

less rewarding than,

real life.

(And

this from a guy with all of his hair.)

So he just sighs,

closes his notebook,

and

reminds himself that when he finds the balls to open it again,

there'll be at least three paragraphs describing how *pretty* his heroine's hair is.

Blue (and beside his baby sister when his year dies, and maybe she does too)

He has a tiny blue vein

that sticks out on his forehead

when he's scared,

and

it's sticking out now,

the way it hasn't

since.

He tells her,

quietly

and

quietly in the way

he only

always

talks

when he's scared,

that if she would please *stay*,

he'd move the heaviest thing he *couldn't* move,

move it

and

move it

and

more,

move it until moving it *more*

is like moving it *at all.*

For one more day

or

hour

or

minute

or

second

or

smile;

(however many seconds said smile takes,)

he'd *move* it,

the heaviest thing he couldn't move,

move it for a second

or

minute

or

hour

or

day,

or

however long said smile could stay.

She just kind of *breathes* there,

her

or

the machine that breathes when she breathes;

so *the machine* just kind of breathes there,

and suddenly every Monday

or

Tuesday

or

Wednesday

or

Thursday

or

Friday

or

Saturday

or

Sunday

he didn't answer

her call

is running like the tear that runs down the cheek of her good side.

Next January

Blue (and his sister, and going the way his dream goes, so <u>away</u>)

She smiles at him

and

it's prettier than she should.

Then,

she was *always* the prettier of the two,

younger by just *one*,

prettier

and

smarter

and

stronger

and

better

than him,

her failed

and

failing big brother.

It was,

is,

would be

his job to protect her,

the way big brothers do.

She is still prettier.

Prettier,

but the tube in her mouth hides his favorite dimple

and

the paper cap shines under the fluorescent lights

where her hair *should* be,

shining the way it *did*,

and

brighter,

under the fluorescent lights,

lights here,

in hospital,

washing her skin,

skin once tanned

and

dark,

now ivory at least,

lights stealing memories of summer as they hum violently overhead

and

everywhere

around him

here,

the hospital room chair beside her hospital bed.

And

still,

she smiles at him,

and

it is far

far

softer than she should.

It's okay.

His stomach rumbles by the time she hits the *apostrophe,*

the period

making the failure from escaping his throat

impossible

when she speaks the way,

now,

she speaks.

This room,

these lights,

that bed

have taken

and

changed

and

returned,

(but less,)

her voice, too.

His job was, is,

and

would be

to protect her.

It's—

Her voice cracks

and

he tries not to scream.

She closes her

dark,

dark,

dark eyes,

the circles underneath threatening to swallow them,

all of them,

whole.

She can still hear him,

the Doctor said,

or might have,

the fever on the way in making it hard to tell,

it's just that she's not strong enough to hold them open anymore.

Still, she

was

is

and

would be

stronger,

far,

far,

stronger

than him.

--okay.

Her eyes close,

and

there is nothing on television tonight to make it okay.

Blue and Red (and the meeting, profoundly)

His hand is shaking as he reaches for the bathroom door, there in the hospital, twenty-something doors from the door his baby sister hides behind, disappearing even now as he hurries to the washroom to vomit, vomit so he can return to her.

It comes, and goes, hunched over in some stall, and the pain isn't bad, not bad like her pain, and he would give any-everything to take it from her, even if taking it from her meant holding it, the pain, like he can't hold her, too weak to move and even almost speak, and she may only have moments, moments he's wasting washing his hand, and—

Hey

he jumps a little, thinking he was alone here in the hospital bathroom, and, eyes racing to the mirror, fall from his face to the face of some asshole with a smug look on his face, bathed in the unmerciful light from fluorescent tubes, twenty doors south-something of where he *should* be.

(Hello)

What're you in for?

He didn't even get the '*o*' out before the grinning fool spoke again, now reaching to rinse his hands and studying him in the mirror and the unmerciful light, so he studies him too, too afraid to turn to look, so looking through the mirror, gathering all he needs to know in the moments, wasted, it takes the tap to turn *off* from *on*.

He's dressed for a club, this prick, and a club's muted light, the orange of his cheap spray-tan *twenty-something shades too ridiculous*, and he should be twenty-something doors down, with her *until*, but he speaks

You look like you're gonna get an enema

again, and he's unbelievable, like the white lasered on his teeth, and instead of answering, he gives him his back, and it's not enough to keep him from pressing

Ha, I knew it—

(I'm not here for an enema)

and he hates himself for responding, and for looking at him over his shoulder, but the hand dryer is twenty-something feet the other way, and the silence of the first ten feet was too uncomfortable, ten feet thinking of *her,* so—

I know, buddy, but the look on your face—

(I've got family in here)

--so *sad.*

And he can't tell if this asshole is condescending by nature, or if it's just the cut of his cheekbones, the presentation of his jaw giving him unwarranted arrogance. He can't tell, and doesn't *care,* reaching for the dryer, and for the button, the button to drown him out and—

Yeah, family is the most important thing, you know

He sighs, because maybe there's an air of *vulnerability* in his voice and even though he resented guys like this growing up, with their good looks and their easy charm and their perfect hair (*and his*

is, damn him, like coming to the hospital for *anything* warrants that much time in front of a mirror) the fact is that he's in front of a mirror too, and, after six hours of talking to someone who can't talk back, maybe a minute talking to some-anyone but himself won't be so bad.

What's your name?

And it's like he read his thoughts, looking at him through the mirror while he turns to dry his hands in the hand dryer opposite.

(Blue--)

(--and yours?)

My name's--

--Red.

(nice to meet you, Red,)

finding it perfectly arrogant and wildly appropriate that he would introduce himself by his last name and last name *only*, as if by introduction implying that he's a part of some fraternity or collective, some group of similarly absent-minded thugs far too uncivilized and far too cliché to address one another by *given* names.

Watching him watching him in the mirror, and still too afraid to face him, he bets *Red* has at *least* one buddy named *Moose* or *Ballsy* or *Tits*. *Yeah—*

he chokes,

--nice to meet you, too--

--so it's not an enema?

His persistence at making the failed joke work, combined and oddly accented by those horrible and horribly white teeth forces a smile, and a smile he quickly closes, afraid *Red* will catch the image of his teeth in the mirror and find them lacking as well.

(No, it's not an enema.)

That's good—

His teeth threaten to swallow his face.

--take it from me, those aren't fun.

He nods at him, and *Red* nods back, and he's reaching for his pocket to signal this aggressive bastard that their time together is ending, if not *ed.*

Then, what is it?

Or not.

(My sister's sick.)

Aww, that's it—

(Pardon me?)

His temperature is rising, the *knew-it* look on his pretty little know-it-all face. He would leave, but *Red*'s hands are dry, curiously, and he's still at the hand dryer, and—

--that's why you look like shit.

(Wha—)

I'm joking man, I'm joking—

And it's not funny and he thinks, for a moment and seriously, about hitting him square in the nose and watching the ugly red of blood spill from the pretty orange of his pretty orange skin, but he's fumbling around with the hair dryer and he's curious

about what the hell he's doing.

Ask me what I'm doing.

He smiles wider, impossibly, and there is a parade of mischief parading across the glint in his blue, blue eyes.

Here, ask me what I'm doing—

And he *would*, if he could get a moment, but there is something so overwhelming and oddly engrossing about this fool, watching him trying to dominate the conversation through the mirror while he fumbles with the hand-dryer there with him in the hospital bathroom.

(What are you—)

Coke, Blue.

I'm doing coke.

And he is, and he does, right there across from him from the top of the hand-dryer in the hospital bathroom.

He's shocked, really, that this prick would be arrogant enough to take a rail so carelessly, knowing that the guy in there with him is *in there with him*, at a hospital, and knowing his sister is sick and still acting like he's dressed, at some club in some club bathroom, and all at once he's disgusted and repulsed at everything *Red* is, and yet he can't turn to leave because *Red* is asking

Do you want another?

and he can't figure out why he would word it like that

and he turns to leave but *doesn't*, because he turns to face *Red* and realizes, horribly,

that he's alone, there in the hospital bathroom,

and he's looking directly in the mirror

and *Red* is looking back at him

and smiling that fucking smile.

. . .

Red and *Blue* (and the big part)

And it is as crushingly heartbreaking as he imagined/feared it would be, so when the vacuum from the hole in the world sucks every inch of the reasoning and struggling and humanity he's spent days with endings analyzing and resisting, he *accepts* this one, *maybe the only day really, really, really worth fighting the end of,* with the arrival of the tear he'd been waiting to cry since the Tuesday she was diagnosed, and the real world became justified in *running away from*; the day the fragile in him broke, and the named the fantasy he started living *Red, Red,* and for really no other reason than it was the color, splattering silently on the devastatingly red tablecloth (*he remembers white because he's a writer and it's more devastating to picture it that way,*) drop of blood that preceded the diagnosis and the reality of it.

Red because it reminds him every time he thinks and *becomes* it, why reality is worth running as *fast* and as *hard* and as *forever* and ever, *world on his shoulders or not, away* from.

Red, and it explains his writing and why it runs on and on and on, because *fuck* reality and the rules and the structure of it, because he is the one *exception* to it, the one who doesn't have to lose or *anyone,* the one who shows *everyone else.*

And TV told him it would be this way, that destiny would kind of karmically spread her legs for him, that he would have some great purpose or at least audience to justify said rules fantastically *not* applying.

So sitting there, watching his *Blue*/little sister *Red*/big sister **still not breathe**, he's going through at least every scenario he's ever seen, and as each option doesn't work, and flying around the world fast enough to turn back time like Superman seems *less* an option, reality is creeping in the corners he kept at bay with lines and lines, and it's the saddest…*second* saddest thing.

So everyone who reads a passage that isn't spoon-fed like *she* had to be, too many Tuesdays since the Tuesday they told him, *can go fuck themselves*, because he fought harder than anyone, *Superman included*, to reason on paper why something so unreasonable had to happen to someone as special as *him*; still only half as special as the soulless slab already reduced to memories and decaying and killing *fantasies*, so *Red*, right in front of him.

And maybe for once *Blue* is sitting there smug and satisfied, because he finally has something sad to write about.

And maybe more tragic, though probably and totally *not*, is how at this moment and here, watching something that *just memories ago* sprang form the mud and the poverty of the old farmhouse *beside* him, he doesn't know or care if he will ever have the strength to pick up a pen and fight through the halves of himself, halves somehow not equal a w<u>hole</u>, it takes to put any word other than

sad

on some recycled tree his writing is not worthy of anyway.

At once he is grateful the fucking cocaine is keeping him from the numb his *less*, now, family feels when the nurses and doctors and whoever else may be in the room with him fail to keep them from *exploding*.

Grateful the cocaine keeps the coffee mother spills on the side of him (—the coffee she figured five minutes and her soul worth the cost when she left to find it, two after he left for self-realization in the men's room—) from scalding him when it *does*, and it doesn't matter and mother's wailing and father's, for the first time in the forever he can remember, wailing, because he might be as *gone as what-used-to-be-his-sister is*, and staring at the body she borrowed when she was *here*, he can't reason how to bring her *back*.

Every time he was mean to her, the time he slapped her and the times between, are marching alongside every name he called her, every name other than beautiful and precious and *better*, through the hole in the center of him, and their marching call is fucking with his mind and it's thoughts and his thoughts or how to write this and right this and *make it go away*.

Someone made the mistake of telling him, months north of *seven* and *comprehension*, that everyone he loved would die one day, and if he could reason enough to remember anything *now*, he might remember reasoning, aloud and louder, deeply and to himself alone, that everyone *else* could die, *except* for everyone he loved.

Looking at his sister's corpse, he is nowhere near rational enough to attribute the crushingly heartbreaking sense of failure to the promise he's broken to the seven year old boy he's become too

ugly to have any right to have been.

And the numb in his mouth is nowhere near the numb in the area his soul used to rent, and he knows *Red* would smile if he could feel his face, because being a fucking rockstar and dying young, despite his best efforts, *is just one more thing his bigger-better sister did first.*

Red and Blue (and the '*worse*' part of '*things get worse before they get better*')

After awhile, you run out of things to hit.

He *heard*, anyways, but faces of sisters the *opposite* of alive, now, have him aiming anyway and *too*; aiming for patches of drywall without knuckle marks or the blood stains that stain walls when knuckles *aren't strong enough* to leave any other marks, anymore.

And it's at least the least of his concerns, his hand, because he can tell himself it's shaking *here*, in the bathroom of the hospital his big/baby sister just died in, because of broken knuckles and *not* dead sisters, and it's just the latest lie and a *baby*—*like his sister*—lie compared to the *big*—*like his sister*—lie he learned he'd been lying to himself the last time he was in this very bathroom.

And it's probably got an important-sounding name, like *Split Personality Disorder* or *Paranoid Delusional Schizophrenia* and he probably has *Body Dimorphic Disease* too and *Narcissistic tendencies* coupled with rampant *Social Anxiety* and an *addictive personality*, which explains the steroids and the cocaine addiction and the *coming down*; and suddenly doing another *bump*—what with dead sisters and *realizations that the past year has been spent under the belief he was* <u>*two different people*</u>—is about as appealing as *not* hitting the hospital bathroom wall again.

So he does, and again, and only after reaching into his

Red

pocket with his

Blue

hand, and dumping the last of his *eight* down the hospital sink drain; and his hand is shaking and he tells it to *stop*, stop because and really, only *half* of him is a drug addict, so really and only he's only *half* missing it.

Besides and again, there's hospital walls and *again* to hit, and he does, praying that some orderly or some substantially-sized and significantly-upset male nurse will come in alarmed and angry at the mess he's making, because he's got at least a knuckle on his

Red

(with blood) hand to break and *open* like the rest and his heart, and he wants *whoever* to hurt like he hurts too.

He knows *This New One* and his family are waiting down some depressingly bright and brightly-lit hospital corridor to grieve with him, and for a second the logistics of wondering whether they and more importantly *she* know that he's *high* and *has been*, or of the part of him that *fucks* and violently and *other* girls, and the idea that he's gotten away with it for this long both placates and baffles him.

And *how* is a mystery for another moment, realizing somewhere between punch twenty-seven and punch forty-fucking-two that he's at least *twice* the writer he thought he was; taking the depression that comes knowing that even with twice the chances, twice the effort and twice the paper, he's still and tragically <u>unpublish</u>ed and _____able.

And it's a whole *other* kind of hurt and he files it away, because a memory of his *Red*/big sister *Blue*/baby sister plays across a blood-stained projector screen strangely made out of hospital bathroom brick, and priority states he *punch it away*.

Red and Blue (and, understandably, not quite ready to take another phone call)

So the phone's ringing and *again* and it's the same generic ringtone and the same ringing and ringing and ringing and ringing; the same ringing and ringing *and* he used to ignore when his Red/big Blue/baby sister *used* to call when she wasn't *dead* and it's the same ringing and ringing and he used to ignore when she was just calling to tell him she was dying.

So it's *important*, this ringing, or it could be, so he reaches for the phone, there in the hospital bathroom just down some brightly lit hall from where his Red/big Blue/baby sister *just died*, reaches for it with what is left of his

Blue

hand, the better of the two and

Red

and covered in blood and broken and gnarled knuckles and what looks like hospital bathroom wall plaster.

Yeah, he reaches for it, and is *still*, and is becoming at least exponentially more desperate with each passing

Ring,

his dementia telling him that maybe it's his Red/big Blue/baby dead sister on the other end, calling impossibly from across time and space to tell him

Its okay

and that she *forgives* him, and for not answering phone calls *just like this one*, and that she loves him, even though she *can't* anymore; can't anymore because she's dead.

So he partly knows, in the rational, so

Blue

part of his brain that it's not his baby sister, and that he's just setting himself up for more disappointment when he flips the receiver and whispers *Hello*

into the tiny mouthpiece, whispers because he knows he hasn't the voice/soul left in him for anything more.

His hand is shaking and only in part because it's all fucked up the way the rest of him is too, and the *Red*

in him encourages him to hurry the fuck up because it could be his big sister calling to say goodbye and *better* and without fucking tubes in her mouth.

Still, he's *miles* from reaching it and he might be crying and he might be screaming and he can't tell, the way his tear ducts and his vocal cords gave out sometime before his *tenth* knuckle, and every inch of every mile is a memory of her face before she got sick and a memory of her face *after* she got sick, and he would *too*, but there is simply nothing left in the stomach he stretches across the hospital bathroom floor to give up, *like he won't*, stretching and reaching for the phone.

And there's more miles and each has a toll to pay, reaching with swollen fingers across floors, literally, and memories, existentially, flashes of living a life wrong, so memories of Erin and Nicole and Val and Amber and Denae and Krista and Candice and Crompton and Blair and Krista, again, and Iwona, and Summer and *the one-who-looked-kinda-like-Mariah-Carey*; (so the first of those with names he can't remember) and Laura and Christie and Lindsey with an e and Keri Lynn and Sabrina and the latest-some-slut and the next-to-latest, and Cousin Aimee, twice, and Lana and Lara and Callie and Rhonda and Jenn the photographer and he's *close* now, *thank-God-if-there-is-one-and-if-there-is-one-he-can-pretty-much-fuck-off*, and he can almost reach it and over every granule of every gram of every brick he ever put up his nose and through every river of every whatever-chemical he ever put in his arm and the Girl on TV and *This New One* and *fuck me, she's here* and there's a light around her and it's

Red

because she's an angel *sent by a God he doesn't believe in*, and

Blue

because the light from the brightly-lit hospital hallway is shining around her, standing in the doorway of the door she just opened to find him, reaching for a phone that has stopped ringing on a bloody and broken hospital bathroom floor.

And all he has left in him to think, before the darkness takes him too, is *thank the God there isn't* for voicemail.

Red and Blue (and more from the manual of dealing with shit like this)

So here's what you do, given enough time, and here's what he does. He's sitting on some floor somewhere, and *where* matters about as much as it *ever* has, to him and his stream of consciousness and his writing; *so not at all.*

He's sitting on some floor and he's staring at it and he's wondering, watching fresh memories scatter on the tile or vinyl or wood or concrete in front and around him, what memories to label

Blue

and what memories to label

Red.

See, given enough time, time removed from tragedies like dead sisters and alive ex-girlfriends and treating them as though they're anything *but* and because of drugs and, strangely, aversions and addictions to them *at the same time* and at the same time as living—*if one could call it living*—two different and yet somehow the *same* lives, one can begin the painful process of piecing them together.

The problem is in the fitting, the way the edges of memory

Blue

overlap the edges of memory

Red

making the piecing together—memories like days, and words said to *one* now, in the context of another life—at least and every bit as hard as it *should* be.

Red vs. Blue (and a long overdue conversation)

Put it down

because she's gone, and there's no need to pretend anymore.

Pick it up

because she's gone, and you wanted to escape and you want to escape and you deserve to escape.

Put it down

Blue says, *Blue* or the half or the part of him that is;

Put it down

it, the straw slightly shaking in his slightly shaking *Blue* hand, it and the mirror with the fucking *last* of his coke, coke waiting for him at home, home from the hospital, not shaking one goddamn bit in his *Red* hand.

So,

Put it down,

and he knows that *half* or *part* of him wants to and *really*—the *Red* half, the half connected to the hand not shaking, really, really *does not*.

And its

Fuck you

out loud and to himself and no one else, no one else because he is both and alone, horribly, and it's

Fuck you

because *Red*—so at least half and part of him—is angry and all the time and a drug addict at least half that.

Fuck you

and the straw goes up and the mirror follows, his slightly shaking *Blue* hand still bloodied and red and still slightly shaking but doing what the fuck it's been told, because *Red* is *alpha* and *still*, too.

Put it down

before he can draw, because at least *half* or at least a *part* of him doesn't want to be a drug addict anymore; doesn't and doesn't want to live in denial that half or at least part of him *is* and *has been* for far too long.

And it's funny   *And it's tragic*

isn't it   *isn't it*

that the reasons for putting the straw in his *Blue* hand and the mirror with the fucking cocaine on it in his *Red* hand *down* are the *every-all-exactly the same* reasons for picking up the straw in his *Blue* hand and the mirror with the fucking cocaine on it in his *Red* hand *up*.

Put it down

because his baby sister is dead and

Put it down

because *This New One* has been pregnant and with his child and he's only been there, apparently, *half* as much as he should have; *half* meaning he missed days around the pregnancy and the procedure she had on the day *he wasn't there* to make her *not* pregnant with his child anymore and

Put it down

because he's twenty-*late* and unpublished and unsuccessful and he's starting to think he never will be, and

Put it down

because this sure as hell isn't going to help.

Pick it up

because his bigger, better sister is dead.

Pick it up

because she was never his bigger, better sister at all, just bigger, better in the sense that she experienced everything first.

Pick it up

because he has a *girlfriend* he didn't know he had and he's been fucking every-other some-slut every other day and behind her back and behind her back while she laid on *hers* pregnant with the kinds of things that happen when he does the kinds of things he loves to do to girls *like* her.

Pick it up

because he's twenty-*late* and unpublished and unsuccessful and he's starting to think he never will be. And, really,

Pick it up

because she's gone, and you wanted to escape and you want to escape and you deserve to escape.

And the *Red* in him is winning and *why not*; finding out he's half-heartbroken and *often* and over a variety of otherwise-unworthy *some-skanks* is about as depressing as realizing the people who walked away and out of his life—BamBam and Psychic Beth and a hundred-hundred girls were more than half-right to and when they called him *crazy*.

Spanish Jose stuck around, though, and because he's a *real* friend, and proof is not shaking one goddamned bit in his *Red* hand.

On the *other*, *Blue* still red with raw knuckles and dried blood, there's the *nowhere* a year spent in *half* has him; burning bridges and holes in his nose and knowing neither, neither nor the holes in his arm or the anger that comes, months on steroids more than *half* the time, and all of a sudden the *everyone* who walked away no longer has the question *why* attached, like his *Blue* fingers to his shaking straw.

Fingers better suited for pens, and

Fuck

meeting Bob the Editor *twice* as often as he thought he did means he's done at least twice the writing and had twice the chances, too; if he can be sick for three months and *only one and a half*, really, then he can put the fucking drugs away long enough to focus on his dream before it goes the way of baby sisters and just about everybody else.

Baby sisters, and

Blue misses her

and *Red* misses her

and *he* misses her,

so

Pick it up

Put it down

Pick it up

Put it down

Pick it up

        Put it down

and do it

NOW

       NOW

because you need to escape

because you need to face this

and you need to get away

and you can't run away

anymore

SO DO IT NOW

      SO DON'T DO IT

NOW

NOW

NOW

Pick it up

and then he remembers her

smile

and he picks up the fucking straw and rams it in his fucking nose

and

then he remembers her

die

and he remembers being too high to stop it.

Pick it up

and then he throws the cocaine and the mirror it sat on into the fucking toilet and leaves the bathroom, turning off the light on his way into his living room with his *Blue* hand, and it does not shake, not one goddamned bit.

He does not miss it.

Blue & Red (and picking up the pen again and for the first time *since*, and kind of, really, for the first time at all)

Pick up the pen with the hand that shakes and is shaking because the voice tells you to.

And right after you do and it does, the voice says

You're a loser

so you write

I'm a loser

and the voice tells you you're a drug addict and you write

I'm a loser and I'm a drug addict

and the clock on the wall is laughing at you and you write

The clock on the wall is laughing at me

but no one would believe you,

because you're not that good a writer.

Yeah it hurts, but not the way the thing that killed *you* when it killed *her* did, so you listen to the voice when it says

It hurts

and you write

It hurts

knowing two or two hundred words wouldn't-won't-aren't enough to relate *how*, so you leave it *at*, nowhere near enough.

Maybe you're self important enough to believe, in your delusion, that you'll be able to describe something *indescribable*; something that hundreds *better* spent hundreds *pick* picking and failing at.

Yeah, it's the new *acne*, isn't it, something to claw-scratch-maim-*obsess* over, something you can blame both failures and defeat on.

You'll probably call it *love*, you selfish-sad fuck, the yearning or pining you've wasted pages and pens and time, (unmercifully,) on—at least the last better spent *anywhere* but where you spend it, everytime and only in the presence and company of your closest companion, an inanimate iron account of what you're wasting laughing its' batteries out at you.

So please, write

I'm a loser

at least one more time, and rest assured that you're latest self-assessment is at least *extremely* more accurate than the last thousand-thousand delusions you've bled black and *blue* and maybe even *red* on.

Hell, you could probably call it *progress*.

So cap off tonight's *inspired* session with a turn of the light, right there next to your only friend the fucking wall clock, and breathe deeply there in the dark, satisfied and alone and a loser and a drug addict, because *hell*,

congratulations!

you're *one* night down to your *last* one.

And maybe then, because loathing and *self* is more fun than living and *for*, pick up the cell phone beside you and check the message you've been too weak/afraid too since it's last ringing and on bathroom floors *time* and *alive sisters* ago.

Red and *Blue* (and *half* of the last person in the world who deserves this)

Hi,

You've reached _____

(Red)

(Blue;)

I'm not around (conscious) *to take your call, but if you* (save my life) *leave me your name and number after the tone, I'll get back to you as soon as I* (heal) *can.*

Hi _____, this is Tina Tsallas from the Creative International Agency. I was given a copy of your manuscript, _____, from Bob the Editor, and if you could give me a call back at 555-*I-JUST-SAVED-YOUR-LIFE*, I'd like to talk to you about representation.

Again, it's Tina (might-as-well-be-God-motherfucker) at *555-I-JUST-SAVED-YOUR-LIFE*.

Thanks, _____, talk to you soon.

He gets the message when he wakes up and *when he can*, so four and a half days later, and in the middle of Stage One of the Five Stages of Grieving, so sometime around the *funeral*.

He handles it the way one would imagine he would.

Act 3

The Book of Resolution, Absolutions, and Shit Like That

Blue and *Red* (and the whole point.)

It's sitting in front of him—right there in front of him—and it is *at least and everything* he's ever dreamed of.

It is all and everything that is *good* and *pure* and *true* in him, and it makes all of the other things that are *not*, abortions and abusings and of women and stimulants and depressants and clocks on walls and hospital halls and bathroom stalls and month long illnesses and terminal ones *too* not *not* matter but somehow *okay*, because what is right there in front of him is enough to make him *whole*.

And sitting there, right there in front of it, *both parts of him* smile, smile like he hasn't and for the first time in months.

He takes a breath and to *clarify*, forcing air through deviated septum and blackened lung and closes his eyes and opens his eyes and the fact that it is still there—*still sitting right in front of him*—is enough to force his eyes closed again, for fear the tears that come will make him less a man, witnessed by everyone witnessing his moment, here in this *his* agent's office.

So he picks up his pen with his hand that shakes and it is shaking now, but *healing*, and the broken knuckle he opens by gripping tightly and *too* doesn't mind and the blood that drips on its surface, *right there in front of him*, is heavy-handed *maybe* and symbolic and *entirely appropriate* and more than happy to join the tiny stain his tear splash made, right there beside _____, the blank line he fills with his name.

And the publishing contract reads <u>*Red and Blue*</u> like he *dreamed* it would, and even when his dreams became less *like* and started starring *Cousins*, and even when dreams couldn't come because of cocaine, and even when dreams were withheld in favor of tossing and turning and thinking of quitting he did not, and entirely because of this—and maybe a little because of his way with words—his dreams—

--both of them--

just came true.

And the parents he never thinks about or writes about are here and for him the way they have and *have always* been, encouraging him to dream and supporting him and really, probably, really glad he did not take the jobs attached to the job interviews his father sent him on.

And Post Gay Bosco is here and he's violently crying because he's violently gay, and he's violently holding onto *This New One*, who, and although she may resent him for the half-life he *enabled* and *endorsed* and *helped keep from her*, is crying not so violently and violently holding him back.

Bob The Editor is sitting decidedly non-violently, but through and between tears he swears the big bastard is grinning and maybe even the smallest bit proud, paid as he is and responsible for finally coming to his senses and handing the draft he did—two halves of very separate books with very separate perspectives, meshed together to form something *Red* would deem masterful and *Blue* would deem printable—to Tina the *his* agent, who sits, paid as she is, smiling and too.

And he knows his bigger-better baby sister is smiling too and somewhere, and he promises to dedicate the book that's coming and *finally* to her, her and all of the beautiful and beautifully broken girls it took to break him in two, two so he could come together to write *one*, the name beside his and the dotted line, the name of his book to be published.

Red & Blue (and a Monday)

Monday, and he calls his bigger-better baby sister and she doesn't answer, doesn't answer because she's dead, doesn't answer but her voicemail *does*, so he calls just to hear her voice.

Red & Blue (and for the hell of it…two perspectives on the dream he dreams in color and that night; or *the first of the dreams he dreams without nightmares*)

Getting your picture taken *rocks*.

Times *eight*, like the abs looking like they were sewn, under a photographer's flash, under, really, the tightest of his *ever-tight* tummy, flexed and oiled and mugging like the rest of him here, now and the moment and *in it*—really, really in it—in the months since the moment months ago he *made* it.

So *signed*, like he waited moments and moments in and around months and months that matter now—*signed*, and moments ever after—about as much as the clothes he's wearing for *this*, the first publicity photo shoot *since*—so not much at all.

Standing there, he's sweating *not*, basking in watts comma many and taking orders many more, smiling at *least* inside and taking it at least as easy as it *is*.

Because he told himself for moments and moments in and around months and months that he was moments comma *any* from *this* and his dream and everything else he's been entitled to since he wrote *One* after *Chapter* many-many months ago.

Uwe the *fantastically-somehow-appropriately*-named-director screams something in lieu of a *pivot* and requesting it; by the time he finishes the (half-German-half-whatever-the-fuck-he-mentioned-in-passing-and-every-time-in-cursing-and-*that*-dialect-*since*) half-command, he's halfway through performing said pivot already; already relishing the next of *every* moment he'll spend under these quite literal spotlights.

And the literal to accompany these already-masterfully-executed masterpiece photos is for a newsletter from his new parent publishing company, and that's all well and good, not *as*, the article he's writing in his head *for* the writer writing it in the *Someday Soon* issue of GQ; the cover and feature piece some two-hundred *and-most-of-them-ads* pages behind a picture of his features taken at a photo shoot *just like this one.*

Yeah, it'll be a page turner too, entitled boldly and in font *just as*

The First Real-and-Really-Talented Rockstar Writer

over or under the *next* masterpiece photo of him doing something *quirky* or *provocative* and *probably both*, as evocative as evocative can be, a summation of some *less-talented-but-cute-in-a-snide-way* writer's detail of his meteoric ascension to Godhood.

. . .

Getting your picture taken is agony.

There's *hives* again—well, maybe *hives* is an exaggeration, but, taking a moment to glance down at what is visible of his all-at-once-nowhere-near-chiseled-enough-chest, the splashes of vibrant red spreading like Nazis over the Eastern-Europe-*because-it's-that-pale* map of his anatomy is entirely disconcerting; the way the newly-red continent of *pec left* has eyes on conquering the suddenly-smaller mound of *not*-muscle he calls *pec right* has at *least* all of his attention.

Were he able of focusing any of it elsewhere he might surmise it has at least *most* of his photographer's attention as well. The otherwise-otherworldly Ukrainian man re-appears and *violently* from behind the lens of his incredibly expensive-looking equipment, shouting something in Ukrainian to an army of assistants, Ukrainian and Scandinavian *and not*, and not any of them can move fast enough to find the once-inhabitant of the empty seat branded 'Makeup Artist.'

So it's to be more waiting and agony as the otherwise otherworldly Ukrainian man orders his shoot paused, paused until the waiting and agony are ended by the re-emergence of a vacant makeup woman, waiting and agony replaced by mountains of skin concealer and agony, all in the name of *more* photography and agony, much more and *too*.

It *matters*, this photo shoot; this photo shoot and this article, to be published *like he will be* in his new publisher's semi-annual newsletter—it matters and because and not only because each flash
(if it is to ever flash again today, *fucking hives*) signifies making it *like he has*.

And it doesn't *feel* real and *why would it*, really, years in living rooms under lights decidedly *less*; flashes coming and *only-ever-so-often* as inspiration and motivation and in his mind and *only* and never in front of him the way they are now and *again* and *finally*, as finally in front of him the otherwise-otherworldly Ukrainian man resumes with the *more*, photography and agony, too.

Red and Blue (and from the book of Resolutions—the Girl on TV.)

He ran into the Girl on TV.

Where and when *matter* as much as he might, in his doubts and his fears and his head, to her now, and years removed.

So many years.

This is what happened. And really. <u>And what he wrote about.</u>

Hi.

(Hi.)

How have you been?

(Good—

--I've been good.)

<u>I thought of you everyday.</u>

<u>Everyday.</u>

(--You?)

Busy, but good. What've you been doing?

(--Working.)

(Writing.)

(Working.)

<u>Writing and about you and for you and to tell you I'm sorry I didn't tell you I</u> <u>love you any of the everydays I spent with you; writing and about you and to</u> <u>get over the nights attached to the everydays you crossed my mind.</u>

(You?)

Same.

(Good! Well, I gotta run…)

Yeah.

<u>So, I want you to know I'm sorry—</u>

(I'll see you)

<u>*I'm sorry.*</u>

(See ya.)

And then she goes the way she *always* goes, *away*, and for the first time since she fractured him, the parts of him that remain *don't miss her* and don't mind.

Red & Blue (and a Tuesday)

Tuesday, and he calls his bigger-better baby sister and she doesn't answer, doesn't answer because she's dead, doesn't answer but her voicemail *does*, so he calls just to hear her voice.

Red and Blue (and from the Book of Resolutions--------Summer)

Summer is here, Summer in summer, sitting in season and dressed for it, across the table at the restaurant he asked her to and to resolve things he-she-they deemed utterly irresolvable, seasons and hotel rooms ago.

And it feels *good*, as resolutions go, and she looks better and as though seasons called winter left winter weight and the weight that comes with issues and *comma many* and *unresolved* in seasons better suited, so *any* save the summer he sits in and across from.

Summer says she's for bars and the boys and tables in them, dancing on them and away and removed from winter words like *resolution* and responsibility; but there's a hole in Summer's smile that says her days, days without clouds or the thought of them may not be as far removed or gone as summer's sun fools him into thinking.

Summer sits with him, across the table and under summer sun, and says slowly, in the way things in summer seem to come, that she *knows* she settled for second, from the second he told her she came first.

And he says

Sorry

and it feels good, and _____ for dreams and maybe crushing hers when she chased the girl of *his* right over the back fence, the back fence connected to the house she couldn't quite call home anymore.

And he says

Sorry

and it feels good, and _____ for Happy New Year—happy, until he went for the belt of the pants he passed out in, and he follows it with

Sorry

and it feels good too; _____ said with *more than just eyes* this time and for sevens in February he forgot to say it and for Saturday's skirt and maybe for the Saturdays, everyone, since.

In short, like Summer's Saturday skirt, he says _____ for all of his-her-their grievances, airing them in the open air above the restaurant he spends with Summer in.

And she smiles sadly and it's *sad*, because Summer is leaving for her job on a cruise ship and *again*, better to stay somewhere where summer was better suited.

This summer is different and he can see it in Summer's smile; it's sadder still when she says

Goodbye
and
 Good Luck
(I Love You)

(I always will)

and gets up slowly, like Summer should, to leave him to a season never the same when she walks the way she always walks
away
and, for once,
forever.

Red and Blue (and from the Book of Resolutions…Psychic Beth)

Psychic Beth is sitting across the table from him silently, silently reading his mind.

And the *Red* in him doesn't believe in psychics and the *Blue* in him doesn't believe in psychics, so the whole of him really, *really* doesn't believe in psychics; and when she opens her mouth to break the silence and mouth

It's nice to meet both of you

he tells her that it's nice to see her again, again and for the first time and months and many, and the many months it's been since she last opened her mouth to mouth

You're fucking insane

many months and fractured personalities ago.

Reading his mind—his mind, and more likely the expression on his face, she relaxes with the psychic shit, mouths of

Thanks

and for inviting her *here*, to *at least the trendiest restaurant in his city*, and of <u>healing</u> and the _____ they'll do over at least the most expensive dinner in his city, the way he continues to do with the people in his life he's wronged; the people in his life he's wronged who will pick up the phone long enough to learn it's him and long enough to stay on the line longer than it takes to tell him

You're fucking insane

or call him a

Tragedy in training

the way they tend to even *now*, months north of drug addictions and struggling with the *writer* part of struggling writer.

I sense you're happy

she says, breaking the silence again, and again with a psychic observation so profound, it couldn't possibly come from observing the grin on his face before and when he answers

Yes

and

Thank you,

the latter words, judging by the look on Psychic Beth's *never-been-surprised-because-she's-psychic* face, he's guessing she's never heard/imagined him saying before.

And she follows with

I sense you're at peace

which pretty much means they're having a conversation, now, and he ignores her psychic follow-up about having two fractured personalities *then* and pretty much one singular personality *now*, answering her politely and engaging in polite conversation <u>back</u>, the _____ of his mind dismissing the itch somewhere north wondering how the hell she knows about *Red* and knows about *Blue*, and the *Red* in him is laughing inside and thinking she's fucking insane and the *Blue* in him is scared Psychic Beth *might really be.*

And she winks now, reading his mind the way he can't believe she can, and it's the first of three winks she'll wink his way between now and the wink she'll wink his way, picking up the tab, here at *at least the trendiest restaurant in his city,* and telling him

You're going to be famous

on her way out the door.

Red and Blue (and from the Book of Resolutions, Cousin Aimee)

Everybody has dreams

she says, and draws deeply from the cigarette attached decidedly *phallically* to her lips, draws deeply and exhales *just as* from the cancer-inducing stick undoubtedly contributing to killing *hers*.

And the rest of her, too, sitting across from him on the patio of *at-least- the -trendiest* bar in his city, trying to look the anything but happy for him she *isn't*, studying him studying her studying him, asking with eyes simply still *better* if he's happy

Yes

and with *Her*

Yes

Her

being *This New One*, and not *her*

Cousin Aimee

and, being Cousin Aimee, if he misses *it*

No

the thing between them *then* that turned out to be the only thing between them (—*fractured personalities and These New Ones aside*—) from being any-everything other than *everything everywhere else* other than between (—so beside, and probably *for*—) each other and *only*.

But that's what other lives and whimsy are for, and as a person paid, now, to write stories with possibilities and plenty of *both*, he leaves this possibility for some page someday when Cousin Aimee ashes her cigarette on the table mercifully between them, says between lips still somehow phallic

Congratulations

on being a writer and

Congratulations

on finding someone (else)

and the lies between lips sound almost as sweet as he remembers/imagines hers tasting when she says she's happy for him.

She knows he knows she's lying, so it's

Everybody has dreams

again, taking the conversation back to the point before it became awkward, (if having any conversation other than

Draw this

or

Fuck this

with Cousin Aimee has ever been anything *other than*.)

Awkward.

She *almost* says, almost breaking the ice and steering the conversation back to the familiar, but when the familiar is

Draw this

or

Fuck this,

he's glad she restrains herself, starts telling him about her dreams—the ones that don't include him, anyway—instead.

And it's silently heartbreaking, kinda, listening to her talk of his success and how she's happy for him and then talk of the success she knows is around the corner for her, knowing she knows he knows she's *lying*, and looking, not around corners but through eyes that say silently and desperately

I Love You

and, sitting there, knowing that collecting the love of beautiful and beautifully broken women does little in the way of saving them the way he *wants to.*

So he sighs, *not silently*, sits silently, silently listening to a twenty-something dream vocally the way a six-year old would, dream of being a lawyer (and not a drug addict) and a mother (and not a girl who's lost) and a volunteer (and not the kind who volunteers far, far more than she should/has.)

And she's not six, and the cocaine and the nights with the bars and boys in them *and the alleys they left her in after* promise she never will be again; still, watching her dream and knowing she's feeding off the realized dream he dreamed, he'd never be cruel enough to let her believe anything otherwise.

Red & Blue (and a Wednesday)

Wednesday, and he calls his bigger-better baby sister and she doesn't answer, doesn't answer because she's dead, doesn't answer but her voicemail *does*, so he calls just to hear her voice.

And he cries, there on his couch in his living room, and his clock doesn't have the heart (so batteries) to laugh at him.

Roommate Cheque holds him, because he somewhat miraculously stayed and weathered his storm—stayed here on his couch—and he's all at once reminded of a Wednesday night in May, when, after chasing Sabrina away, he fed him hot soup in hopes of healing him; healing him the way the soup simmering on his stove promises to.

Blue and Red (and from the Book of Resolutions...*This New One*)

So he's sitting across the table from *This New One* and he's looking into her eyes, eyes with colors *colors* don't have, and he's trying to keep the tears in *his* from catching *hers*.

And he shifts a <u>little</u>, more than a _____ uncomfortable across from her *here*, at at least the trendiest restaurant in his city, draws breath and to say *Sorry*.

Draws and stops, like the tears in his *won't*, eyes unable to hold her as he escapes to the menu below him.

Sorry,

the writer in him knows, nowhere near eloquent enough to save her and to save him and to save the relationship she assures him he doesn't *have to*, only half-knowing the sins he's committed in *color* and *lately*.

And the tears *Red* cries and in front of her and the tears *Blue* cries and in front of her and the tears *he* cries and in front of her are for the each and every transgression he committed while

Red

and away

and for each and every horror he subjected her to while

Blue

and beside her

and for each and every, all and only the hurt he put her through, being both *not there*, unmercifully, and *there*, maybe unmercifully *more*.

And it makes the sense to *him*, he knows, eyes rising uncontrollably to meet and fail to meet hers, it won't make *or make better explained* to *her*, so he doesn't open his mouth to explain at all.

So it's

Sorry

softly, and nowhere near enough for dead babies, and *being there*, and for *not being there*, and the drugs, and Cousin Aimee, and the drugs with Cousin Aimee, Cousin Aimee and each of the every-other insignificant *some-skanks* he spent time comma *any* away and from her, her and those eyes, eyes with colors *colors* don't have.

Sorry

in place of explaining lessons learned, time taken from sisters the *opposite* of alive teaching him time *is*—despite a year's efforts to the contrary— *not his to take* and for granted the way he's taken *her*; maybe the one with reasons to leave *most*, now the one and only across the table from him, now and *not* away, the way, mercifully, she chooses to stay.

Like she tells him she *will*, tells him without telling him and with eyes with *water* colors, crying *now* and with him the way she *is* and still; and the sinner in the whole of him knows he doesn't deserve her, *but in lieu of dreams and living his*, he'll take her, *thank-you-very-much*, too.

She tells him she loves him over calamari, and the *Red* in him rests, knowing she's not leaving the way they *all* do; not leaving and making the ones who *do*, The Girl on TV and Summer and sisters—so the ones that fractured him—right down to Amber and Keri Lynn and Laura and Sabrina—the ones he abandoned *chapters* ago—*okay* and *history* and nowhere near worth splitting personalities for.

Red and Blue (and, finally, from the book of Resolutions…his bigger-better-baby sister)

Thursday is a holy day because Thursday is the day he stopped being _____ and he started being

Red

and he started being

Blue.

And now that he's *both Red* and *Blue* and now that he's _____, again, it doesn't matter; kinda like now that his bigger better baby sister is dead, Thursday is just another day that doesn't really matter any more *either;* Thursday just the day the Girl on TV went the *other* way, and Thursday just the day sister promised to *follow.*

He remembers sitting across the table from her,

Thursday

laughing about some joke that didn't matter then like it doesn't matter now,

Thursday

and the first of *every* without her or her phone calls, ever again.

And he was laughing and she was laughing, and for a moment he wasn't scared about her lung collapsing the way it had just

the

Thursday

before, and she wasn't scared about her lung collapsing *either;* and maybe for just a moment they were **two children playing in a sandbox** the way they always used to.

Yeah, a moment, and everything was okay,

Thursday

passed, the way moments and days *do*, and in the very next, she started bleeding from her nose.

He closes his eyes *now*, the way he couldn't *then*, watching her laughing and bleeding and lost in the moment before; the moment she didn't know she was sick and *very* and dying and *slowly* and he thanks *the God-there-isn't* she had one more moment before the blood stained the white tablecloth between them and she looked down and realized, like he had a moment before, that real life is worth running *away* from.

He knew he would lose her, lose her like the Girl on TV and Summer, and in the forever it took him to find her eyes, he could not lift his from the

Red

staining the tablecloth and the

Thursday

and the memories he had and knew he wouldn't get to have between them.

So he was out the door behind her and he left her there and he's *sorry*, sorry for the year he was in denial and scared and too and to pick up her calls when she called him; refusing to hear her say

I'm okay

or

I'm not okay,

and always

It's okay

knowing, somewhere deep down, that she *wasn't* and that *it's really, really not* and not having the strength to face it.

So,

Sorry

and one more time and at her grave, *now*, facing what's left of her and what's left of his life knowing he's going to live his dream *without* her; wondering why it hurts and *worse* than all the every-girls he wasted so much time on and, tragically, promising that his next book will be *all* and *only* about *her*, and just really, really wishing she stayed long enough to read it.

Red and Blue (and one last love note, for saving a soul)

I love you.

I miss you.

I always will.

Next-Next January

Red and Blue

Fuck.

I'm famous.

www.ingramcontent.com/pod-product-compliance
Lightning Source LLC
Chambersburg PA
CBHW032004110726
47901CB00004B/967